No Bed for Bacon

Also Available in
Common Reader Editions

The Complete Henry Root Letters
The Diaries of Auberon Waugh
The Marsh Marlowe Letters
The Last Cuckoo
(The very best letters to The Times *since 1900)*

No Bed for Bacon

Caryl Brahms and S. J. Simon

Introduction by Ned Sherrin

A COMMON READER EDITION
THE AKADINE PRESS

No Bed For Bacon

A Common Reader Edition published 2000
by The Akadine Press, Inc., by arrangement with Ned Sherrin.

A Common Reader Edition and fountain colophon are trademarks of
The Akadine Press, Inc.

ISBN 1-58579-015-X

25   10 9 8 7 6 5 4 3 2 1

To our parents

INTRODUCTION

Caryl Brahms and S. J. Simon would have relished the fuss which attended the opening of *Shakespeare in Love*, a film which brilliantly used many of the characters and situations with which they had delighted their readers in *No Bed for Bacon* back in 1941.

Lady Viola, from the court of Queen Elizabeth I, is enchanted by Shakespeare's theatre, dresses up as a boy player, is taken on and falls in love with Shakespeare, who is inspired by her to write a play.

In *Shakespeare in Love* they are rehearsing *Romeo and Juliet*, the poet's inspiration will lead to *Twelfth Night*. In *No Bed for Bacon*, *Twelfth Night* is the current play. At the end of Shakespeare's love affair with the Lady Viola he is moved to start work on 'a play that needs a woman and cannot be acted by some prancing boy . . . It will be tragical. It will be about the most fascinating woman who ever lived. It will be about Cleopatra.'

It is not surprising that three of the greatest humorists of the century, Tom Stoppard, Caryl Brahms and S. J. Simon, if confronted by Shakespeare, Burbage and a young noblewoman (or the daughter of a *nouveau riche* in *Shakespeare in Love*) should come up with similar stories.

Tom Stoppard borrowed a copy of *No Bed for Bacon* from me before he started work on Mark Norman's original screenplay in order to avoid duplicating the jokes in the classic novel. No-one has ever questioned Sir Tom's wit and only one moment in the film pays direct homage to the novel – Shakespeare practising various ways of writing his name, 'Shaksper, Shakespere, Shekepar . . .'

Ironically some little time ago Fidelis Morgan, an established screenwriter, submitted a screenplay of *No Bed for Bacon* to David Parfitt, the producer of *Shakespeare in Love*. Parfitt returned it telling her that he didn't think a film about Shakespeare would be good box-office.

Whether Mark Norman had access to this script I do not know. He has been quoted as saying he got the idea from his son. Judging by his contributions to the disastrous *Waterworld* it would seem that Tom Stoppard's work on the final draft was critical. Apparently the original heroine of the movie was to be called Belinda until Stoppard pointed out to his collaborators that the name was an eighteenth century invention.

As the battle for the Oscars hotted up the American author of some Elizabethan bodice ripper sought to bring a suit for plagiarism. No more has been heard of that case.

I was amazed at the number of letters and phone calls I got from Brahms and Simon fans from all over the country when news stories of the alleged plagiarism of *No Bed for Bacon* broke. Clearly their affection for the book had remained strong over the decades.

Who were these two writers who together invented a form of anachronistic historical humour which would lead eventually to the television series *Blackadder* and *Shakespeare in Love*?

A White Russian Ashkenazy Jew from Harbin, Manchuria, and his Sephardic collaborator whose forebears two generations earlier had been firmly ensconced in Constantinople were not perhaps the obvious pair of writers to celebrate with wit, warmth and the occasional custard pie the genius of England's most famous playwright.

S. J. Simon, an inspired bridge player and writer, and Caryl Brahms, ballet specialist and theatre journalist, teamed up in the 1930s to caption David Low's 'Musso – the Home Page Dog' cartoons in London's *Evening Standard.* They had met when both had rooms in a lodging house in Hampstead owned by one of Caryl Brahms's mother's friends. At the time she was finishing her education at the Royal Academy of Music and he was studying agriculture and working part-time at a bridge club. Both adopted pen names, Simon abbreviating Seca Jascha Skidelsky and Brahms abandoning Doris Caroline Abrahams, so that her parents would not know that she had embarked on an independent writing career, and choosing Caryl as a conveniently ambivalent first name in an era when it was considered a disadvantage to be a woman critic.

Their first extended collaboration was the classic ballet murder mystery *A Bullet in the Ballet* (1937), quickly followed by *Casino for Sale* and *The Elephant is White*, another comedy set among expatriate White Russians. With the outbreak of war in 1939 they embarked on *Envoy on Excursion*, their least successful book, blemished by their hectic efforts to make their readers laugh in what they considered their 'war-work'.

Out of their disappointment with *Envoy* was born the first of their historical novels *Don't, Mr Disraeli!*, 'not a novel set in the Victorian age: but a novel set in its literature'. They and their reviewers found it hard to define the literary form that they had invented. 'Lampoon? Farce? Pantomime? Crazy Revue? Extravaganza?' asked the *Evening Standard*, deciding in the end that it was a 'masterpiece of wit'. In the *Observer*, Frank Swinnerton settled for 'phantasmagoria'. Whatever it was, their new form earned them the happy title 'Lunatics of Genius'.

9

However, in 1940 they were faced with the problem of equalling their achievement; for their publisher, Michael Joseph, wanted them to write another novel, 'exactly like *Don't, Mr Disraeli!*'. To repeat their effects was anathema to them anyway, but it was the time of the Blitz, in which they were both employed as air-raid wardens. A diary which Caryl Brahms kept during 1940–41 (and from which I have quoted extensively in a memoir, *Too Dirty for the Windmill*), emphasises the affection the collaborators felt for the City of London and its traditions.

I went to see the City on the Sunday after the fire . . . through St Paul's Churchyard past the stone that commemorated the last time the City was burnt out in 1666, and along devastated Watling Street, fantastically void, where Pepys had seen the Lord Mayor of London running without his wig, and been sent by him to the King at Whitehall to tell him that the fire burnt so swiftly that they could not pull down the houses in time to stem it . . . The City had been burnt out again. I was upheld by a sense of the continuity of history.

(Pepys and *The Diary of a Nobody* were her favourite bedside books.)

It was this love of the City's past which inspired, not the equal of *Don't, Mr Disraeli!*, but, instead, a novel which surpassed it: a warmer, richer book which in its playful rearrangement of history revealed higher truths of character and timeless jokes. This was their first shot at a book which dealt with the British in farcical predicaments. Hitherto, Brahms and Simon had enjoyed creating a gallery of 'funny foreigners': now, albeit in an historical context, they were examining the English and bringing them to life with the same affectionate mockery in the same deft and stylish prose.

No Bed for Bacon, if it has a theme, imagines that Sir Francis Bacon wishes to acquire a bed that Queen Elizabeth has slept on to leave to his children's children's children as a gilt-edged investment. Lady Viola Compton, a young girl from the Queen's Court, visits the theatre and is so infatuated by Shakespeare and his plays that she disguises herself as a boy player and inspires *Twelfth Night* and the playwright's affection. Before they embarked on the project Caryl Brahms wrote to an academic friend in Cambridge to see 'if there would be any serious objection from Cambridge if we were to write a fun book about Shakespeare', and to get a suitable list of books on which to base her research. Brahms-Simon research had a quality all its own. 'While initially innocent of the fact that Burghley was Lord Chancellor of England,' wrote Brahms, 'I read in Nicoll's *Progresses* that Lady Burghley had given Gloriana twenty-three silver buttons, one broken. Hey Presto! Burghley, clearly, was a mean man.' She stored her information in headings on a series of index cards. Simon's approach was more wayward. According to his collaborator it consisted of 'carrying around Black's *History of the Elizabeth Age*', which she vowed he never opened.

They were soon in despair about the novel. 'There is so much we cannot capture. So much that lies outside the scope of a comic book,' Caryl Brahms told her diary on 30 May 1940. Two days later she and Simon spent the afternoon 'naming the Globe Theatre'. That evening, Crete fell to the enemy. On 4 June, 'Will Shakespeare chose a boy player . . . and took Master Bacon down a peg or two. He was a nasty piece of work, but, by God, a stylist!' The same day the Kaiser, to Caryl the 'poor pathetic villain of my youth', her only reference in her memoirs to the First World War, died at Doorn.

So the events of the war jostled with the daily business of Elizabethan English show business. Their publisher demanded 75,000 words by the second week in August, only just over two months away. They attacked the page and 'Bacon gave Shakespeare a few lessons in stage-craft'. They had worked out that to meet their deadline they had to write 7,000 words a week and, with Simon on full air-raid warden duty, they could often only snatch an hour a day together. When their fire-watching shifts failed to coincide they left notes for one another in the log-book, to the bafflement of the District Warden. 'Glib, Glab, Glob' ran one from Simon. To Brahms 'it was clear that Skid was making suggestions for the naming of the Theatre to be called the Globe'.

Throughout early June they felt the pressure. 'A hard ungrateful session. Six hundred words. But we've finished building the Globe Theatre and got an Elizabethan audience into it. Tomorrow we burn it down. The fun writers have!' By 13 June they were rowing. 'Couldn't have hated Skid more. I mean to have a contract drawn up by my own solicitor the moment *No Bed for Bacon* is finished, to restrain us from doing another book for three years – Skid says five. It is to feature heavy penalties for infringement.' However, a couple of days later they were 'having a lovely time with the poets in the Mermaid Tavern . . . another good work session . . . Shakespeare coming upon Ben Jonson writing his epitaph. Shakespeare read it, "Good," he said, "but untimely." I wish one of us could do heroines.'

Brahms solicited an extra week from their publisher but did not tell Simon. By 25 June they were approaching the halfway mark, 34,800 words. 'First potato ceremonially tasted by Gloriana in today's work session.' The next day they gave Burbage a father, 'of whom we are inordinately fond. On the morrow Shakespeare had a row with Bacon over *Twelfth Night*. "Mister Bacon," Shakespeare demanded, "did I write this play or did you?" Bacon look at him. He shrugged.'

On 1 July, 'we sent Elizabeth on a progress to

Greenwich in today's work session. The book is going to be too short and too slow. In spite of Elizabethan England, two fires and Shakespeare at work in his theatre, it contrives to be about absolutely nothing at all. Why did we ever start it? Why did we ever suppose we were the people to do it? Why didn't our agent stop us?'

They were arguing again on 4 July. 'A shattering row. I cried but managed not to hiccough.' Then, working on a scene in which Shakespeare coached Viola in the Willow Cabin speech from *Twelfth Night*, Simon looked up as he typed out the blank verse with a look of awe on his face. 'You know, Caryl, this palooka can write.' (*Palooka* – from a Russian source – was the favourite Brahms-Simon word for an enthusiastic amateur.) On 13 July, 'worked like two furies'. They wrote 3,000 words. 'A lot came from contemporary sources,' she admits, but 'Shakespeare's clowns worked out the business for throwing the first custard pie in *The Taming of the Shrew*.' The next Sunday they 'polished off the Armada' (something of an afterthought) and Caryl took time off to go to a Prom at the Albert Hall with her fiancé who was on leave: 'The echo beat the drummer to it every time.' The pace on the book had quickened. 'We expect to finish by today week, with two weeks in hand for cutting and tightening and the week's grace of which I have kept poor Skid in complete ignorance.'

Essex's rebellion took up the remaining days of July and on the 31st they embarked on the Court performance of *Twelfth Night* given at the Temple Hall – which, in their contemporary England, had just been destroyed by the Blitz.

1 August – Small work session. Shame on my head, for Skid was, for once, not entirely unwilling. But I was slow and submerged. We did the puddle and Sir Walter Raleigh's new cloak. It was raining. 'Elizabeth of England looked at him. A gleam came into her eyes. She beckoned . . .'

The next day the book was finished, and Caryl Brahms, with absurd pessimism, wrote: 'While it is unlikely to be as bad as I think it is, there is a strong possibility that this time it may be even worse. The final stages were marked by my picking up an ashtray and emptying it over the wretched Simon. I have been wanting to do this for years. The relief was exquisite.' They celebrated at *L'Ecu de France*.

Were they premature? On 26 August their publisher warned them that the printers had made a mistake in their calculations and that *No Bed for Bacon* was only seventy-four out of the stipulated seventy-five thousand words. 'You can't publish at eight and six if you're under seventy-five thousand. So we're all in favour of cheating our public.' Instead, they embellished the Armada, and began to complain of Michael Joseph, 'who hopes to get to heaven by virtue of the humility he brings to advertising the latest Brahms-Simon'.

The design for the wrapper arrived on 10 September. 'Have written . . . to point out that I have a prejudice for having my name spelt correctly on my own wrappers . . .' The amended design was still controversial. 'Elizabeth of England, still in pink but this time back to front – Better!'

The proofs arrived on 25 September:

Sentences we never specially thought about leap out and make us laugh. Sentences we sweated blood over ride the page with ease. Sentences we thought so good die on their commas. And most satisfactory of all, there's still a chance to put things right. We have a new printer, for our old one was blitzed at Plymouth . . . If they had to be blitzed I'm glad it was in Drake's town. Skid looked up from his proof copy. 'Remarkably correct,' he said, impressed.

'How far have you got?'

'Two pages.'

The review copies were sent out on 27 October, and the collaborators kidnapped a copy and 'rushed madly to de Bry's where we read it aloud to one another over toast and caviare, gloating over the cover, giggling at the refeened maize-coloured binding with our names in purple on the back, and we bellowed at our own jokes – and even at one another's'. Friends with access to review copies telephoned their enthusiasm. 'Queer, but infinitely comforting.' The first review in the *Daily Sketch*, six days before publication, was 'Civil!' The official launch was on 9 November. They went to Bumpus's bookshop. 'Greeted by Mr Wilson . . . with a whoop that brought book-loving heads up from quiet browsing with a click.' 11 November was the anniversary of Bacon's birthday. Their publisher wrote, 'This is Bacon's Birthday – may he furnish all your dreams of luxury. Not Skid's – we don't want him turning up at the office with a string of expensive greyhounds . . .' Caryl's diary goes on, 'Our special book assistant at Selfridge's spoke warmly of *No Bed for Bacon*. Celebration lunch of oysters with Skid.'

Two days later the novel was reprinting. 'Before the end of its first week . . . Elizabeth in pink looks awfully good in the middle of Selfridge's Oxford Street windows.' She continued to monitor the reviews:

A sober and good notice in the *Manchester Guardian*. I would rather be praised in sober manner by the M. G. than by any other paper in sight. And the book has been called by a Birmingham paper, 'A merry vindication of Shakespeare' – after all the great tomes that have been written to prove that Bacon wrote the plays and then considerably left masses of clues in them so that we should know it. So much simpler I suppose than signing his name. Oysters with Skid to celebrate our second imprint.

It was the end of celebration for a time. Caryl Brahms's fiancé, an RAF ferry pilot, was killed delivering a plane and she retreated to the Cotswolds. As she got over her grief, more good notices began to arrive – particularly one from Clifford Bax, 'who declares stoutly that we are not "fundamentally unsound", as we have blithely admitted on our title page. Fundamentally, he insists, we are sound, and it is only superficially that we are absurd. Couldn't like this more.'

With the perspective of time, Caryl's doubts about the quality of *No Bed for Bacon* faded. She was encouraged when Ealing and Alec Guinness nearly – but not quite – filmed it; and delighted when Nevill Coghill told her that he was seriously thinking of recommending it as required reading for the English Schools at Oxford. Together Brahms and Simon have made such warm and credible figures out of Shakespeare, Queen Elizabeth and a whole gallery of Elizabethans, real and imagined, that the reader never needs a refresher course in sixteenth-century history or Shakespearean commentaries. Those who snap up the lightly scattered allusions collect a valuable bonus; those who miss them will never feel that they have been excluded from a private joke. The beautiful crafting of the sentences, the nimble triggering of the smiles, the unsentimental treatment of the romantic incidents; the historic sweep of the story and above all the infectious gaiety of the whole mean that no-one feels left out or short-changed.

Brahms and Simon wrote five more novels and a collection of short stories before Simon's death in 1948. He was taken ill suddenly after appearing on a television programme about bridge.

Caryl Brahms finished their final book, *You Were There*, alone and went on to write three more novels herself and three with me. From the 1950s she began to concentrate more on journalism and on writing for the stage and television. Together we made two attempts to produce *No Bed for Bacon* as a musical. One foundered at the Bristol Old Vic, the second at Golders Green after a try-out in Croydon. On the morning of her death on 5 December, 1982, we were due to start on another version, this time without music. She was eighty two.

Ned Sherrin, London 1999

'To my Wife,
My Second Best Bed . . .'

WARNING

TO SCHOLARS

★

This book is fundamentally
unsound

Chapter One

'Five o'clock of a fine summer's morning,' chanted the night-watchman. 'Five o'clock and all's well.'

He was an optimist. All over England people in furtive knots were conspiring against the Crown – also in Scotland, France, and the smarting and revengeful Spain. The Navy, which six years ago had defeated the Armada on an empty stomach, had not yet persuaded Lord Burghley to fill it for them and were getting restive about this. Rabbles, from Land's End to Dover Harbour, were bursting out like apple-bloom in Warwickshire, while at the Curtein Theatre Philip Henslowe was shaking his head over his account book.

'bowght the 10th of Ap'ell Xvj ownces of copelace bead wth sylver & gowld cop at viij ownce . . . x^{s}viij^d jtem for mackynge of the gherken & threed . . . iij^s iij^d.'

It seemed a lot of money. He wondered whether it would be cheaper to persuade the Puritans to close the Theatre and so put an end to competition, or alternatively to arrange with the Master of the Revels to behead, or at least to de-ear, the Burbages, father and son.

But the night-watchman cared for none of these things.
'A fine day,' he hallooed down the wind, turning his

back on Philip Henslowe and his troubles. 'Fine and lively. All's well.'

The heads of two traitors impaled upon the city gates nodded complete agreement.

The wind blew. A scatter of rain slid down the thatches, making them gleam and glisten and drip on to the passers-by. But the night-watchman shook himself and strode happily on.

'A quarter after five of a clear summer's morning. A fine, mild day,' he proclaimed obstinately.

Down the narrow streets over against St Paul's, the painted sign-boards wheezed and clanged and worked upon their hinges. The night-watchman liked them like this. He beamed approval as Bluff King Hal nearly leapt from his tavern sign in a spirited attempt to do something about the Virgin Mermaid wantoning next door.

'A fine warm summer's day,' said the night-watchman, blowing on his hands.

The mermaid was getting panicky. In her efforts to escape King Hal's bluff attentions, her behaviour grew wilder and wilder. Soon the creature would be quite unhinged. The night-watchman paused to await the outcome. He paused in front of a pair of stocks containing a proven witch fresh from her ducking-stool. Naturally she turned the Evil Eye on him.

But her powers were waning. The mermaid flew off her hinges and missed the night-watchman by inches. Instead she stunned the witch.

'A lovely morning,' said the night-watchman, gloating.

Down the empty streets he strode, chanting the hour. It was his first day at work and it was good to be alive. Only last week he had been a holder of horses, working for old Burbage outside the Theatre; and now here he was, a fully qualified and highly successful night-watchman. Soon he would be a town crier. And who knew but that he might end as a playwright on his own stage, playing on his audiences with fine words as a man might master the hautboy. After all, others had done it. What was that play he had so nearly wriggled into only last week? *A Midsummer Night's Dream*. That had been written by a one-time horse-holder, they said. That is why he had tried to see it.

'Six o'clock of a fine, promising summer's morning,' he shouted into the teeth of the gale.

The City was waking up. The merchants, their money-bags chinking from their saddles, were coming into Lombard Street. Dusty horsemen, carrying urgent messages, galloped recklessly past one another – hardly time to halloo – their coloured cloaks billowing out like wind-blown tulips.

From his lattice, Sir Walter Raleigh hung enviously out. It was high time, he decided, that he got himself a new cloak and put the Earl of Essex in his place.

With the eyes of Sir Walter upon him, the night-watchman redoubled his efforts. Who knew but a word in the right direction . . .

'Half after six of a glorious summer's morning,' he chanted blithely.

Sir Walter smiled.

Greatly daring, the night-watchman touched his forelock. People had been flogged for less.

But Sir Walter went on smiling. He was thinking of his new cloak. It should be made of rich velvet lined with cloth of gold. It should be fringed with sable. It should be cut Spanish-wise and he would sail out and grab a Frenchman to embroider it with squiggles. Sir Walter smiled blissfully. How Essex was going to hate that cloak!

The night-watchman tore himself away, and went down the street crying his greeting to the less fashionable quarters.

Less fashionable, but fascinating withal.

23

For here, walled round from the curious, stood the Theatre.

It was said that the Theatre was in a bad way. Though it had managed to outlive the threat of invasion, it was still beset on all sides by threats to its existence. First there was the fickle favour of the noble patrons – you could never be certain they would not lose interest and withdraw their patronage and purse-strings at the critical moment. There were the Puritans – they were always fidgeting to close the players down. Rival attractions: bear-baiting, cock-fighting, fairs, progresses, folk-dancing, risings, abatements, ex-ecutions, and harvesting all combined to cut down attendances. There were strolling minstrels and madri-gal meetings. There was a shortage of players and an abundance of playwrights. And even when all these things had been combated and a successful season begun, the plague might break out any time and close them down.

It needed courage to be a theatre owner. It needed enterprise and an optimistic heart. But most of all it needed private resources.

That is why the two fashionable theatres in London were owned by men of means. Philip Henslowe had a brothel and lent money. That is how he could afford to install his son-in-law at the Curtein.

Richard Burbage owned taverns and promoted bear-baiting. He could afford to indulge his son, Dick, at the Theatre – but only just. It was understood that the Theatre must pay its way or at least not lose too much.

Henslowe had money and friends at Court. But Burbage had a wizard playwright. Henslowe had craft, but Burbage had good sense.

In bad times they would work together, travelling from town to town, stopping in villages to play one-night stands to bewildered yokels, and sharing the proceeds. In good times they were enemies and would fight one another to the death.

At the moment they disliked one another very much. Both playhouses were doing well.

Henslowe at the Curtein was pouring magnificence upon magnificence, burning five hundred candles on one night without a thought. At the Theatre Burbage concentrated on new plays for old rather than turning old plays into new.

And when the players of the rival companies met they fell a-brawling.

The night-watchman stiffened. Voices loud and angry could be heard through the open roof of the Theatre, but there was no flag flying from the turret, so no performance was in progress. It could only be a rehearsal.

The voices rose to an hysterical pitch. Clearly it was a very good rehearsal. The night-watchman applied his eye to a chink.

Inside the Theatre all was tumult. The stage was alive with actors, all talking, all waving their arms, and all of them looking appealingly at a large man sitting at a table in the shadow. From a distance the boy players apprenticed to the company gazed at the quarrel in awe. To think that this was art!

The large man got up and strode to the centre of the stage.

'Enough of this,' he thundered. 'Back to the book, gentlemen.'

It would be an exaggeration to say that the effect was instantaneous. But bit by bit the group dispersed. The boy players stopped mouthing and aping and stilting up and down, and took up their positions on the scene. Two men rose from a box they had been sitting on and dragged it to the centre of the stage. It was marked:

A Street in Verona

An actor, wearing the voluminous pillows of a nurse, puffed out his cheeks and practised a rheumatic hobble. The prompter, who had been helping an understudy with his words, turned back the pages of his script.

'Enter Benvolio,' he announced portentously.

Nothing happened.

The large man waved his arms. 'Benvolio,' he thundered, 'where the devil are you?'

From behind the group of boy-players emerged an elegant figure, wearing a cloak Sir Walter Raleigh might have envied. The large man scowled at it.

'Master Melody,' he said, 'will it please you to stop sulking and speak your lines.'

The aesthetic young man's nostrils quivered. He took a deep breath.

'But, Master Burbage,' he said, 'I put it to you, as an artist, wouldn't you sulk if you had to speak these lines? Listen.'

He strode down stage. He drew himself up. He declaimed:

> *'The soughing yew doth darkle in the mound*
> *When the cold moon, Mercutio, owls her face.*
> *And mongrels mumble . . .'*

Burbage shuddered.

A hot argument broke out among the boy-players. Some thought the lines were good. Others didn't. Richard Burbage silenced them by knocking their heads together. But he could not silence the aesthetic young man.

'See,' said Master Melody triumphantly. 'Now is it fair to my public to ask me to speak a line like that?'

'Not ask,' said Burbage shortly. 'Require.'

'Mumbling mongrels,' said Master Melody with disdain. 'I demand that the line be altered.'

The company nudged one another.

'Not demand,' said Burbage. 'Ask.'

The company tittered.

'At the Blackfriars,' said Master Melody, 'we always

kept a hack at hand to alter any lines the actors could not speak.'

'Indeed,' said Richard Burbage coldly. He looked round the company.

'Is Will Shakespeare in the house?' he asked.

In a cold dark little room over against the back of the Theatre, Sir Francis Bacon was talking eloquently. Opposite him a melancholy figure sat tracing its signature on a pad.

> *Shakesper*
> *Shakspere*
> *Shekspar*

He always practised tracing his signature when he was bored. He was always hoping that one of these days he would come to a firm decision upon which of them he liked the best. He looked at them. He considered. He shook his head.

'Master Will,' said Bacon abruptly, 'I don't believe you're listening.'

Caught out, Shakespeare laid aside his pad. 'I heard every word,' he declared. 'You were saying something about a bed.'

'It is almost mine,' boasted Bacon. 'The next time the Queen goes on a Progress I am to have the first bed she sleeps on. The Master of the Revels has promised it faithfully this time.'

Shakespeare smiled.

'It was not his fault,' protested Bacon, 'that I did not get the bed on the Progress to Warwick. Sir Philip Sidney,' he explained, 'turned a graceful compliment at a vital moment and the rash Queen gave it him for nothing.'

'And the Progress to Cheltenham?' asked Shakespeare. 'What went wrong there?'

Bacon blushed. 'The arrangements,' he admitted. 'It was delivered to some place in Stratford. It was the second-best bed, too.' He sighed.

27

Shakespeare looked elaborately out of the window.

'There seems to be quite a mode for Gloriana's bed-steads,' he observed.

'Enormous,' said Bacon. 'Every noble in the land covets one to leave to his children. Prices are soaring daily.'

'Quite an investment,' said Shakespeare.

Bacon looked at him. 'And now to business,' he said coldly. 'I am here, Master Will, upon a delicate errand. Gloriana wants to see a play.'

Shakespeare leapt to his feet. He knocked over his chair. He beamed. He shook Bacon by the hand.

'Which one?'

'Er,' said Bacon.

'I know,' flashed Shakespeare. 'It is *Romeo and Juliet*. We will play her the balcony scene as it has never yet been seen.'

'No,' said Bacon.

'The Dream,' said Shakespeare. 'With real night-ingales,' he added ambitiously.

Bacon shook his head.

'The Shrew? Much Ado? Two Gentlemen?'

Bacon waved them away.

Shakespeare pondered. An awful thought struck him.

'Don't tell me,' he pleaded, 'that she's asked for Timon of Athens?

'No, no,' said Bacon soothingly. 'She did not ask for that. As a matter of fact she did not ask for any of your plays. She did not even,' he added, enjoying his moment, 'specify the author.'

'Oh,' said Shakespeare, dimmed.

'So,' observed Bacon with irritating charm, 'I thought I might trickle it your way.' He made a descriptive gesture.

The curtains parted. A little old man came diffidently into the room. He had the rather lost air of a clown out of his part. Seeing Bacon, he checked, won his victory with a visible effort, and advanced.

28

'Master Will,' he asked, 'are you very busy?'

'He is,' said Bacon coldly.

But Shakespeare smiled. 'What is it, Obadiah?'

The little man studied his toe. 'Just a thing I have been thinking about,' he said.

Bacon stirred restlessly.

'I could be very funny in it,' said the little man wistfully.

'Aha,' said Shakespeare. He leant back. 'Proceed,' he invited.

The little man broke into a babble. A mosaic of words, gestures, and mimicry filled the room. Soon the little man was acting all over it. Bacon looked at him in some disgust. It didn't even make sense. But Shakespeare was listening with that intentness that a wise playwright will never grudge his clown. From time to time he nodded. He did not need adjectives and verbs to translate the thought in a player's mind. He did not need rhetoric and couplets to tell him that his clown was offering him not only an interpretation but a creation. He had not yet made friends with this creation, but already he was making room in his mind to receive it. Yet like every author faced with the prospect of more work, his first comment was an objection.

'A grave-digger,' he said. 'How can I be funny about a grave-digger?'

'I will show you,' said Obadiah Croke eagerly. He mouthed a bit more. 'Master Will,' he pleaded, 'only give me a graveyard and together we will work out the business to crack the sides of the groundlings.'

'A graveyard,' said Shakespeare reflectively. He stroked his beard.

'A graveyard,' said Bacon, hoping to cut the argument short, 'is not comical.'

But Shakespeare rounded on him. This opposition had provided just the stimulation he needed.

'But it is hugely funny,' he said. 'A graveyard. Think of it.' He roared with laughter.

Obadiah Croke thought of it. He roared with laughter.

Bacon thought of it. ('Men feare *Death* as Children feare to goe in the darke.') He looked at the boisterous children before him. He marvelled.

'A graveyard,' repeated Shakespeare, wiping his eyes.

'With a grave-digger,' said Obadiah with relish.

'Two grave-diggers,' said Shakespeare, overcome at the thought.

They looked at the marvelling Bacon. They roared again.

Obadiah sobered first.

'That's a fine idea, Master Will,' he said. 'I could use a second grave-digger for a feed. A smaller part, of course.'

'Of course,' said Shakespeare. He pulled up a chair. 'Sit down, my good Obadiah,' he invited, 'I'll tell you how I see it.'

Obadiah sat down. Soon they were immersed in props and business.

Behind them Bacon paced restlessly up and down.

'But,' said Shakespeare some twenty minutes later, 'how do I get him off?'

Player and author looked at one another in dismay.

Bacon seized his opportunity. He took Obadiah Croke firmly by the shoulders and trundled him out of the room.

'Like this,' he said.

He came back. He sat down. He crossed his legs.

But Shakespeare had jumped to his feet and run to the doorway.

'Obadiah,' he shouted. 'I've got it! We won't take you off at all. We'll let you meet the hero. With a skeleton,' he promised.

A confused babble came down the passage.

Rubbing his hands, Shakespeare returned to his desk.

'He likes it,' he told Bacon happily.

Bacon spread his hands to heaven. These players!

'And now,' said Shakespeare cosily, 'what is it we were talking about, my friend?'

'And now,' Philip Henslowe was saying, 'what were we talking about?'

He was sitting in a dark, cold green-room over against the back of his theatre, the Curtein, and he was trying to keep his temper with his son-in-law. Granted, Edward was a good actor in a romantic kind of way and would reduce the groundlings to tears as quickly as the Earl of Essex could reduce his tailor. But what was wanted from him at the moment was a little common sense.

'My Faustus,' Edward Alleyn was saying, 'I was telling you how the audience ate it up.'

Henslowe sighed.

'Four recalls,' gloated Alleyn. 'And a laurel wreath.'

'You've got it with you,' said his father-in-law wearily.

Edward Alleyn picked it up and stroked it. 'Even Marlowe,' he said, 'was forced to admit that he had seen worse performances.'

'Tcha,' said Henslowe with contempt. 'An author.'

'It is a mistake to underrate your authors,' said Alleyn seriously. 'They are nearly as important to an actor as his supporting cast. A good author with a ready line and the wit to select that which is popular in someone else's work and mould it to my personality – why, he's almost worth the money you pay him.'

'Listen,' said Henslowe.

'For instance,' said Alleyn, 'take that author the Burbages have got. What's his name now?'

'Shakespeare,' said Henslowe grimly.

'Exactly. Now just look what he's done for the Burbages. Before they got him we never even used to notice what they were putting on at the Theatre. But now,' said Edward Alleyn with engaging candour, 'I get quite worried about it.'

'So do I,' said Henslowe. He glared. 'That is precisely what I have been trying to tell you for the past half-hour.'

'Not so much worried,' amended Alleyn, who had not been listening, 'as wondering. How does he keep it up? Why every time he writes a play Dick Burbage draws a full house with it.'

'What we want,' said Henslowe, 'is another Shakespeare. Then our threepennies might fill up.'

Edward Alleyn looked hurt. 'Fill up!' he said. 'Do I not overflow your floor?'

'Aye,' admitted Henslowe, 'but the threepennies are falling off.'

'Tcha,' said Edward Alleyn. 'The Earl of Essex never goes to the threepennies.'

But Henslowe was shaking his head. He had pulled open the drawer of his desk and was studying his account book.

Ruin!

'It's no use,' he said. 'If we are to survive ourselves there is only one thing for it. We'll have to have the Theatre closed.' He looked at his son-in-law. 'Put that damn thing down,' he snapped.

Edward, who had been trying on his laurels, jumped and hid the wreath guiltily behind his back.

'You were saying,' he said . . .

'We'll have to get the Master of the Revels to close the Theatre,' repeated Henslowe.

Edward Alleyn considered the point. 'Have a care,' he warned, 'that he does not close us as well.'

'No danger,' said Henslowe confidently. 'The Master of the Revels and I are like this.' He put his fingers together.

'Then that's all right,' said Alleyn, losing interest. 'Now tell me,' he asked, 'do you think I ought to take my recalls like this?' He held the laurel wreath on high and bowed to his father-in-law. 'Or like this?' He popped it round his neck like a halter.

'Like this,' said the exasperated Henslowe, and pushed him out.

He would have to grapple with this thing alone.

Back at the Theatre Shakespeare and Bacon were talking figures.

'A shipwreck,' said Shakespeare, tapping the list in front of him. 'An impersonation, three songs for a baritone, a sorting out, and a happy ending. That,' he decided, 'will be forty pounds.'

'Too much,' said Bacon promptly.

'Too much!' said Shakespeare. 'Forty pounds too much for a new play by Will Shakespeare!'

Bacon remained unmoved. 'Beaumont and Fletcher,' he said, 'would do it for a ten-pound note. What is more,' he pointed out, 'there are two of them.'

'Beaumont and Fletcher!' said Shakespeare. He picked up his quill. *Shakspaw*, he scribbled viciously. Clearly he was about to fly into a passion.

'Master Will,' said Bacon hastily. 'I was speaking only in terms of money. I was not, of course, in any way comparing their work with yours.'

'Ten pounds,' said Shakespeare, only partly mollified. 'It is an affront! Why my Lord of Southampton pays me more than that for a sonnet.'

'No doubt,' Bacon agreed. 'But all the same, forty pounds is too costly for Gloriana.'

Shakespeare got up.

'Master Bacon,' he said, 'you are reasoning like a child. For ten pounds Beaumont and Fletcher will give you any one of a dozen plays – each indistinguishable from the other. They have only to open a drawer – any drawer – and pick the first. But for my forty pounds I will give you,' he smiled, 'Illyria.'

Bacon nodded. 'But all the same,' he said, 'forty pounds.'

'What is more,' said Shakespeare generously, 'I will throw you in, without extra charge, a comic lord. I have the perfect name for him.' He beamed. 'Sir Toby Belch.'

'Good God,' said Bacon.

'Mind you,' said Shakespeare, 'I was reserving him for my Merry Wives, but for Gloriana I will transfer him to Illyria and make do with Falstaff.'

'You killed him off last week,' said Bacon. 'Hal Five,' he reminded him.

'So I did,' said Shakespeare, crestfallen. 'I remember – a' babbled of green fields. But no matter,' he brightened, 'he shall come to life again.' He sat down. 'I think I see exactly how I am to do it.' He picked up his quill. He was immersed.

Bacon took away the quill.

'Master Will,' he said. 'Back to your muttons, I beg. Let me remind you that I have not come here this day to act as audience to your grave-diggers, nor to aid you in resurrecting slain characters for Master Burbage, nor to stand mute while your genius uses up your paper and my time.'

'Mm,' said Shakespeare. He sighted another quill, pounced on it, and went on scribbling.

'But,' said Bacon, removing this quill also, 'I am here because the Queen has charged me with finding a diversion for my Lord Essex.'

'Essex!' said Shakespeare with strong disapproval. 'Why did you not tell me this earlier, my lord? Now,' he said firmly, 'the price is fifty.'

The curtains parted. Prometheus Melody inserted his head carefully between the folds.

'Your servant, sir,' he said, 'and can you direct me to the hack's room?'

'You have arrived,' said Shakespeare shortly.

'Indeed,' said Master Melody. He advanced into the room. He dusted a chair. He sat down cautiously.

'And which of you two gentlemen,' he asked, 'is the author?'

Shakespeare looked at Bacon, but Bacon was looking at the aesthetic Master Melody. Shakespeare smiled.

'I am the author,' he said. 'What is amiss?'

'This,' said Master Melody. He got up, pulled out the part he had refused to read at rehearsal, folded it to the offending lines, and thrust it into the playwright's hands.

'Young man,' he said, 'read me these lines, if you can.'

Shakespeare drew himself up.

'IF I CAN!'

A lesser man would have given ground. But not Prometheus Melody, the Essex of Blackfriars. He was not going to be cowed by a mere hack who did not even bother to wear a ruff in his workroom.

'If you can,' he challenged.

Shakespeare looked at him. He glanced at the lines. He declaimed them.

'This mumbling mongrel,' jeered Master Melody. 'Who,' he appealed to Bacon, 'has ever heard a mongrel mumbling?'

'Who indeed?' agreed Bacon courteously.

Shakespeare looked at them. His anger vanished. He smiled.

'Leave these lines with me,' he said. 'We will see what the hack can do with them.'

He read them over to himself. He tasted the adjectives. Clearly they could be used in that shining play these people would never give him time to write. *Love's Labour Won.*

'I think,' he said, 'we might cut them out of Romeo altogether.'

But Bacon and Melody had forgotten all about him. They were strolling out together and conversing amiably.

'By the way, Master Melody,' Bacon was saying, 'what are you doing after the play on Friday?'

Shakespeare smiled again. He sat down. He spread a fresh sheet of parchment. He reached for his quill. He wrote:

LOVE'S LABOUR WON
A Play in Five Acts by William Shakespere

He crossed out *Shakespere* and wrote *Shakspure*.

The curtains parted. Richard Burbage came in.

'Will,' he asked, 'are you busy?'

Shakespeare sighed and pushed his precious foolscap into a drawer.

'No,' he said, resigned. 'Not at all. Only a new part for Master Melody, a new scene for Obadiah, and a new play for Gloriana and my Lord of Essex.'

Burbage brushed these trifles aside.

'I've been thinking,' he said. 'I'd like to play a Dane – young, intellectual – I see him pale, vacillating, but above everything sad and prone to soliloquy.'

'I know,' said Shakespeare. 'Introspective.'

The curtains parted. Bacon had come back. He pulled out a sheaf of papers from his pocket and laid them on the desk.

'By the way, Will,' he said. 'I almost forgot. When you've got a moment to spare, you might polish up this essay . . .'

Chapter Two

The Palace at Whitehall was bone white under the discovering fingers of the early morning sun. It was five o'clock and the sentries had changed over. One of them was looking particularly smug. Only last week he had been a night-watchman, crying the hour to unresponsive ears, and now, here he was, Sentry to Elizabeth of England, guarding her from sudden death and Scotsmen. Privileged to challenge all who came to the Great Gates. In a uniform.

Even now the moment was upon him. His first challenge. Great heavens! It was Sir Francis Drake.

'Halt,' he commanded.

Drake looked at him.

'Who goes there?' he added weakly.

Inside the Palace the Court was waiting for Elizabeth of England to awake, and whiling away the time conspiring against her. Drake, making his way through a tracery of corridors, boomed greetings at successive treasonable groups, who at the sound of his voice edged away from each other and spoke loudly of their falcons. The more guilty among them tried to brazen it out by stopping Drake and telling him my Lord Essex's latest *bon mot*. But Drake was sick of the Earl of Essex. He was a blunt man and had a short way with traitors. He wished to God Gloriana would give him a free hand. He would ship the whole of the conspiring Court to Raleigh's new colony and see to it that no boat called to take them back again.

'Morning,' he growled to the mincing Master Bacon. 'Got your bed yet?'

Bacon hurried past him. As a matter of fact he had just heard that his promised bed had gone to the Earl of Southampton, and he was on his way to the Master of the Revels to register a protest.

In a little room Sir Walter Raleigh was bent over a chart of the harbour of Genoa.

'Greetings, Walter,' boomed Drake, slapping him on the back. 'How fares the new cloak?'

Raleigh beamed. 'Ah, Francis,' he said. 'The very man I wanted. When do you next sail for Italy?'

'Italy!' said Drake, who had come to try and persuade Elizabeth to give him enough money to get to 'the back side of Nueva Espana, north-west of California,' without having to rely on meeting a prize before he got there. 'What should I do in Italy?'

Raleigh smiled. 'Borgia,' he tempted, 'has a very fine beard for you to singe. Also,' he added, 'you might bring me back some Genoese velvet.'

'Velvet!' said Drake. 'Was it not last month that you boasted to me of the fine Flemish braid you had seized off the Netherlands and the great Cabuchon emerald you thought to make into a clasp?'

Sir Walter Raleigh shook his head sadly. 'I passed them to my tailor. But he, the fool, was conspiring. They quartered him yesterday.'

'And quite right, too,' said Drake.

'And the Crown has seized his stock. And,' said Raleigh bitterly, 'Elizabeth has taken my braid and given it to that bastard Essex.'

'And the emerald?' asked Drake.

'She has kept that.'

Drake looked pleased. 'Then she will be in a good humour.'

Raleigh looked at him. 'I would not make that hope my banker,' he said sourly. 'She snapped my head off last week and all I wanted was a rowing boat.'

'Ah,' said Drake, 'but then no doubt you were tact-less. Did you remember that with Gloriana one must speak first of the profits and only then of the cost?'

'Fool,' said Sir Walter Raleigh hotly. 'What profit is there to speak of in a rowing boat?'

A tremor ran through the Court. Gloriana had stirred. Any moment now and she would be yawning.

In the outer ante-room richly apparelled counsellors, princes, and sleepy, patient ambassadors separated themselves into an avenue that mingled hope with res-ignation. What mood would Elizabeth of England awake to find herself in this morning?

At the head of the procession Lord Burghley was reading a Sapphic ode. She would be difficult today. He knew it. A waste of time bringing up the matter of the Navy victuals that morning. Curse that playboy Essex for allowing his eyes to wander where the Queen could not fail to note their direction. Tcha, the fellow would never make a statesman! No self-control. The old man sighed.

In the inner ante-room the maids of honour were trembling. Lady Meanwell, mistress of the wardrobe, was particularly glum. It was her task to break the tidings to the Queen that her new overgown of cherry velvet trimmed with seed pearls had not yet been delivered. She had, of course, de-eared the tailor, but would the Queen be satisfied with that? Lady Meanwell sighed and envied the junior ladies of the Court, who had but to curtsy and to smile when Gloriana's progress led her in their direction, and could spend the rest of the day in dalliance, always provided of course that they did not dally with the Earl of Essex. And that reminded her. She must drop a word of warning to the young, unfledged, and tactless Lady Viola Compton.

She glanced across the room.

In a corner three maids of honour were failing to

39

tremble adequately. In fact, to look at them you would not suppose that they had their minds on the occasion of the Queen's awakening at all. Here was Elizabeth of England about to open an eye at any moment and not a pale cheek among the three of them! Their eyes were bright, their heads were together, and they were actually whispering.

'Essex called you his pigeon!' the first maid of honour was saying incredulously.

'I don't believe it,' said the second maid of honour.

They looked at Lady Viola Compton. They marvelled.

An honest, loyal, over-trusting, out-generalled, betrayed and so dismissed, heartbroken and now dead father had left Viola Compton orphaned in a Warwickshire manor. But his untimely end proved timely for his daughter, for, no sooner was he buried, than the Queen experienced one of her many changes of mood and selected his manor as a convenient resting-place on her Progress to Warwick. The conscience-stricken Gloriana had taken pity on the orphan, made her her ward, and brought her to Court. Already she was beginning to regret this. For two weeks at Whitehall had done nothing to pare off Viola Compton's natural directness. Indeed, she did not attempt to disguise her pleasure in her latest exploit.

'And what happened next?' asked the maids of honour.

'Next,' she said, 'he admired my gown. So I told him that I did not care so much for his cloak. It was not a patch, I said, on Sir Philip Sidney's.'

'You didn't!' gasped the first maid of honour.

'How did you dare?' breathed the second.

'And what did he say?' chimed in a third, who had added herself to the group.

'He told me to wait till I saw his new one,' said Viola Compton. 'Then he said that he liked my candour and patted my hair. Then he said that he liked maids who spoke boldly and took my hand.'

'Then?' asked the maids of honour breathlessly.

Viola Compton giggled.

'Then,' she said, 'the Queen came in.'

They gasped. Then, like young nightingales beguiled, they piped their mirth.

Scandalized, Lady Meanwell sped across the floor. But even as she drew her first outraged breath a smothered yawn came faintly from the Queen's bedchamber.

'Great heavens,' gasped Lady Meanwell, and, turning, sped in the opposite direction.

On her four-poster bed, curtained by damask taken from a treasure ship off Majorca, and blanketed with snow-ermine from Muscovy, Elizabeth of England was lying. She had the pale drowned face of a poet. A very bald poet. She was dreaming that she was forty-seven.

The curtain trembled. She opened her eyes. She wasn't. In fact, she was older than the silly hag now collapsing in front of her in a flurry of curtsies.

Lady Meanwell was babbling. Wishes for Her Majesty's continued good health jostled with the weather report, and bumped sharply against a treasure ship in Dublin Bay. Even the French Ambassador was dragged in. Anything – anything to ward off the evil moment with its inescapable absence of new dress.

'I trust,' said Lady Meanwell, casting desperately around for new topics, 'that you have slept well, M'am.'

She ought to have known better.

'Slept well!' said Queen Elizabeth. 'I assure you, Meanwell, I did not close an eye all night. First there were the nightingales. The place for nightingales,' said Elizabeth viciously, 'is on a platter for my morning breakfast.'

'There are nightingales for breakfast this morning,' said Lady Meanwell, delighted.

Queen Elizabeth waved this aside.

'Then there were rats in the wainscoting and the panel of the secret passage rattled all night.'

'I'm sorry, M'am,' said Lady Meanwell.

'And,' remembered the Queen, 'all night long there were messengers. In future,' she ordered, 'you will see to it that they gallop round by the back entrance.'

'Yes, M'am,' said Lady Meanwell.

Elizabeth of England stretched herself. 'And now,' she said, 'bring out my new dress.'

In another room of the Palace, Polonius Bounce, Master of the Revels, was thinking of getting up. By reason of his great age he was allowed to linger on in bed after the Queen had woken. But not very long after, of course. In fact, he reflected, gazing comfortably at the timbered ceiling, he ought to be getting up now.

The figure hovering round the bed was of the same opinion. In fact, it had been coughing for the last ten minutes.

Suddenly the Master of the Revels saw it.

'Go away, Dagglebelt,' he said.

But it was too late. The eager-eyed little man had leant forward.

'What is it,' he asked intensely, 'that stands on the roof at midnight and crows like a cock?'

The Master of the Revels blinked at him.

'Tom o' Bedlam,' said Dagglebelt, and cackled like a maniac.

The Master of the Revels sighed and turned his back to the wall. Who would envy him his job, supervising the amusements of the realm, extracting fees from rascally players, devising distractions for the Queen, and listening to every tomfool who thought he could help him to do it. And this particular perpetually bobbing-up tomfool wanted to be the Queen's jester. Even though the last jester had been caught by the heel and subsequently impaled for a shaft at Lord Essex, and no court jester within memory had lived to retire in happy melancholy on his pension.

Dagglebelt noticed the averted face. His cackling ceased. An expression of intense anxiety crossed his face.

42

'Would not the Queen think the riddle funny?' he asked piteously.

'No,' said the Master of the Revels with great decision.

Dagglebelt pondered. He turned the riddle over in his mind. It was still very funny. He began to cackle again.

The door opened. Philip Henslowe came in.

'What's the joke?' he asked.

Dagglebelt told him.

'Outside,' said Henslowe.

Dagglebelt went.

'Thank you,' said the Master of the Revels gratefully. He sat up and felt round for his pantobles. Henslowe found them for him. He sat down on the edge of the bed.

'I trust you slept well, Master Polonius,' he said.

The Master of the Revels shook his head.

'I did not close an eye,' he said. 'I could not forget the voyage of the *Golden Hinde* to Newfoundland and how the Admiral was lost.'

Henslowe was puzzled. 'The *Golden Hinde*,' he said. 'But that was long ago.'

'Ah,' said the Master of the Revels, 'when you have lived as long as I have it is not the time of the event that is important but that you can still remember it. Past and present are no longer definitions, for the past walks by my side in the present and the present is often more remote than the past.'

Henslowe tried to look as though he understood.

'Besides,' said the Master of the Revels, 'I have just been reading a tract by Master Hakluyt and he has taken down most movingly the whole impression. Listen.' He reached for a pamphlet.

'Munday the ninth of September, in the afternoone, the Frigat was neere cast away, oppressed by waves, yet at that time recovered: and giving foorth signes of joy, the Generall sitting abaft with a booke in his hand, cried out unto us in the Hinde

43

(so oft as we did approch within hearing) "We are as neere to heaven by sea as by land."

'The same Munday night, about twelve of the clocke, or not long after, the Frigat being ahead of us in the Golden Hinde, suddenly her lights were out, whereof as it were in a moment, we lost the sight, and withall our watch cryed, the Generall was cast away, which was too true. For in that moment, the Frigat was devoured and swallowed up of the Sea.'

His voice faded away. He blew his nose hard.

'It is most affecting,' he said, 'the way a ship goes trustfully through the oceans.' He turned the pages. 'See,' he said, thumbing the list of the ships that had ventured out on that voyage. '"The Golden Hinde of burthen, 40 tunnes. The Squirrill of burthen, 10 tunnes."' He blew his nose again.

Henslowe changed the subject.

'How goes the revenue for the sale of country bedsteads slept on by the Queen?'

'Ill,' said the Master of the Revels. 'The market is glutted.'

He was lying and he knew it. The demand for Gloriana's bedsteads had never been greater. Anyone who even hoped some day to own a country house was putting his name down on the waiting-list. And there was always Master Bacon. But by this time so ill was his mood that he was not going to admit this to a living soul.

'And the mop fair at that country village?' asked Henslowe.

'Stratford-on-Avon. Tcha!' said the Master of the Revels. 'We barely covered expenses. There is nothing to attract the crowds,' he explained.

'Ah,' said Henslowe.

'And that reminds me,' said the Master of the Revels. 'Judging by your returns nobody goes to your three-pennies either.'

44

Henslowe shifted uneasily.

'If you want my opinion,' said the Master of the Revels, easing himself into a doublet, 'you ought to get rid of your son-in-law. Can't hear him,' he said in a muffled tone of voice.

'If you want my opinion,' said Henslowe helping to extricate him, 'we want to get rid of Shakespeare. In fact, that's what I've come to see you about.'

'What, Will?' said the Master of the Revels. 'Our golden Will? Why he always fills our threepennies – even with Timon. What, pray, have you against Will Shakespeare, Master Henslowe?'

'He empties mine,' said Henslowe drily.

'All the world's a stage,' said the Master of the Revels richly, 'and all the men and women merely players. They come in and they go away,' he added a trifle muddled and looked meaningly to the door.

'*As You Like It*,' said Henslowe. 'A botched-up, countrified play. What a thing for the Burbages to spend their money on!'

'I liked it,' said the Master of the Revels firmly. 'Something in brooks, something in streams, something in stones, and good in everything,' he burbled.

Henslowe changed the tune of his attack.

'Master Polonius,' he said, 'have we not always been friends?'

The Master of the Revels adjusted his ruff. 'Yes,' he said warily.

'It is not often I ask of you a favour?'

'No,' said the Master of the Revels gratefully. He reached for his sword, and began to buckle it on.

'I want you,' said Henslowe, 'to close down the Burbages.'

The Master of the Revels struggled with his sword.

'Impossible,' he said.

'On the contrary,' said Henslowe, 'you can do it easily. Shut them down and blame it on the plague.' He gave a hand with the sword.

'No,' said the Master of the Revels puffing a little.

'Why not?'

The Master of the Revels pondered. 'I have just commissioned him to write a play for Gloriana.'

'I'll release Marlowe,' said Henslowe.

'Don't like Marlowe,' said the Master of the Revels. 'Prefer Shakespeare. Tomorrow and tomorrow and,' he paused. 'How does the line continue?'

'Don't know,' said Henslowe shortly. 'Will you or won't you shut up the Burbages.'

'I won't,' said the Master of the Revels. He fastened his ruff.

'Very well,' said Henslowe, straightening it for him. 'I'll go to the Puritans.'

'You can go to the devil,' said the Master of the Revels, losing his temper. He put on his cloak. Henslowe did not help him into it. He jammed on his hat. Henslowe watched him do it.

The door opened. Bacon came haughtily in.

'Out of my way,' said the Master of the Revels.

He strode crossly off to breakfast.

'Not a rag fit to wear,' rasped Elizabeth of England.

She was standing in front of a great wardrobe containing the ample folds of three hundred and sixty dresses. At the moment it also contained Lady Meanwell.

The Queen had received the news of her undelivered dress with rare calm. She had only torn her bed curtains, sworn lustily, and thrown a pantoble at Lady Meanwell. But now, as though to compensate for this unusual self-control, she was harder to please than ever in deciding what to wear instead. It seemed as though she would never make up her mind. The more popular dresses near the heavy doors of the cupboard had long since been rejected, and Lady Meanwell, urged by a steady torrent of abuse, was tunnelling her way into the stuffy recesses. Already her voice was a muffle.

'The cloth of gold?' she suggested.

'Speak up,' said Queen Elizabeth.

'The cloth of gold,' bawled Lady Meanwell.

'Can't hear a word,' said Queen Elizabeth.

The dresses rustled. Flushed and untidy, Lady Meanwell emerged into the open. She was carrying the gold gown.

'Fool,' said Elizabeth of England. 'I only wear cloth of gold in the mornings at a Progress. You ought to have known that. Put it back.'

Lady Meanwell tunnelled again.

'And don't crumple it.'

A heavy sigh came from the cupboard.

'The black with seed pearls?'

'Too sombre, dolt.'

'The saffron silk?'

'Not kind enough, numskull.'

'The tangerine damask?'

'I wore it last week.'

There was a knock at the door.

'Stay out,' said the Queen, rushing for her wig.

But the door opened. Drake came in.

'Oh it's you,' said Elizabeth relieved. She put down her wig. She extended her hand. 'My dear pirate . . .'

Drake knelt and kissed it.

'And now tell me,' said Queen Elizabeth. 'What shall I wear today to dazzle the French Ambassador?'

Drake considered. 'The cloth of gold I brought you from Cadiz.'

'Of course,' said the Queen. 'An admirable idea. Meanwell,' she ordered, 'go fetch it.'

Lady Meanwell disappeared into the stuffy wardrobe. She did not sigh heavily until she was well inside.

'Gloriana,' said Drake, 'I have been sitting in England a long time.'

The Queen looked at him. 'Well?'

'I would travel again. I would find, I would conquer and I would bring you back rich prizes for your coffers.'

'Ah,' said Elizabeth with evident satisfaction. 'And where do you plan to sail?'

Drake was forthright. 'The backside of New California.'

'Too far,' said the Queen. 'And too costly. No, you old weasel, if sail you must, a quick sortie to Boulogne maybe, but no further.'

'But the prizes . . .' said Drake.

'But the cost of getting them,' said Elizabeth.

They looked at one another.

'My ship is in Falmouth Harbour,' said Drake. 'It will cost but a trifle to make her seaworthy. All that I ask is a token payment for victuals and an order to your armourer for powder and shot.'

Queen Elizabeth pursed her lips. Clearly she was against it.

'Surely,' urged Sir Francis, 'great Gloriana gives this freely to her pirate, Drake?'

'Not so much as a drum,' said Elizabeth of England.

Drake sighed. 'Gloriana,' he said, 'be reasonable. Even Burghley is in favour of my voyage.'

There was a scuffle. From the cupboard, hot and exhausted, reeled Lady Meanwell.

'The cloth of gold,' she gasped, holding it out.

'Fool,' said Elizabeth. 'Put it back. I will wear my blue and silver. No,' she corrected, 'my cinnamon and sable. Stay,' she said, 'my parma violet.'

The door opened. Lord Burghley peeped in.

'The Earl of Essex,' he said, resigned, 'craves an audience.'

The Queen stood up. She laid her hand upon her heart. She melted.

'And I am not dressed,' she gasped. 'Burghley,' she said, 'see that my beloved pirate has what he wants, but be off – both of you.'

They bowed. They went.

'Meanwell,' said Queen Elizabeth, 'I've made up my mind. You may fetch me the cloth of gold,' she ordered, as one conferring a favour.

In the ante-room the maids of honour were getting above themselves. For a full hour the Earl of Essex had been closeted with the Queen. She was not expected to emerge this side of ten o'clock. Lady Meanwell had gone to the still room to supervise a dish of nightingales. Drake and Burghley had co-opted Raleigh and were immersed in charts and bored ambassadors had slipped away to refresh themselves with barbarian beer. In short, there was no-one here to keep the maids of honour in awe.

Gradually their whispering had become a chatter, their smiles giggles, and their fancies wild flights.

Viola Compton was seated bolt upright on the receiving throne.

'Meanwell,' she commanded in a vengeful croak, 'fetch me my cloth of gold. Stay, you fool. I've changed my mind. My traitor's tartan.'

A maid of honour giggled and started across the floor in the puffed out flurry of an agitated Lady Meanwell.

'Fool!' Viola Compton had turned to address a curtsying giggle. 'Why do you interrupt me now?'

'The Earl of Essex,' said the giggle, 'is here again. I mean craves audience.'

'The Earl of Essex.' Viola stood up. She put her hand on her heart. She melted.

The door opened. A pair of beady eyes fixed themselves on the make-believe Queen.

But Viola Compton was too rapt in her impersonation to see them. Her hands fluttered above a make-believe fard pot. She posed before a make-believe mirror. She put on an imaginary wig with hands that trembled.

'Does this become me?' she rasped.

'It does not,' snapped a much rawer rasp.

It was Elizabeth of England in ivory and ox blood. She was standing in the doorway.

Yet the world showed no signs of coming to an end.

*   *   *

In his room, breakfast finished, the Master of the Revels was settling down to pen a note to the Burbages. It was all very well for Henslowe to rely on his Edward Alleyn and a knavishly engendered lack of competition, but it wasn't right. The Puritans, might the blood dry in their bones – if they had any – would be only too delighted for a pretext to close down the Theatre. Burbage and Master Will filled the threepennies and made his coffers handsome acknowledgment of the fact. Right was right. And besides he liked the fellow's plays. He could follow them. None of your Marlowe nonsense . . .

'Master Burbage,' he began:

'I have the honour to warn you of a conspiracy which is even now afoot, and which is directed towards your undoing. The Puritans . . .'

Chapter Three

'Gentlemen,' said Burbage, looking at his company with distaste, 'at this rate we shall still be rehearsing when the performance is in progress.'

It was the morning of another anniversary of the Armada and the whole of England was preparing to celebrate it. Throughout the country fairs had sprung up overnight. In small villages sheriffs in their chains of office let prisoners out of stocks and allowed suspected witches to pass unducked. Toll roads were thrown open. Greens were garlanded. And squires were cheered and toasted in libations of their own pale ale and pommage.

From the outskirts of the capital serious celebrators streamed between the huddle of houses on London Bridge and into the city to line the route from the Palace to St Paul's along which Great Gloriana would progress on her way to give thanks to God for a timely change of wind.

At suitable pausing places stages had been erected, on which the many flattering events in the history of the nation were to be acted, while addresses and gifts from the rich guilds and city companies would be tendered to the Queen. So much for organized rollicking.

Later the lords and nobles would begin their banqueting. Outside their gates the rabbles would gather to regale themselves on the lukewarm remains of charity. That night the prentices would form torchlight processions in the streets – singing, reeling dragons breathing their flames from tavern to tavern.

England was pleased with itself.

At the Palace Queen Elizabeth was chivying Lady Meanwell through the wardrobe. Raleigh was regretting that his new cloak had not arrived in time for the Progress, while Essex, rising early, had rushed off on a special progress of his own. His public, he said, demanded it.

They were giving the *Spanish Tragedy* at the Curtein. They were giving *Henry V* at the Theatre. In short, the whole of England was one jubilating bubble of celebration. The invader had come, the invader had regretted it, they had turned away the face of danger in their stride, they were the salt of the earth and if anyone doubted it let them come, too, and test it out for themselves.

At the Curtein, Edward Alleyn was saving his voice in an impassioned soliloquy. But Henslowe was in too good a humour to pull him up. The Puritans had listened to him with sympathy. They had agreed that the plague, while discriminately passing over the Curtein, had settled itself round the Theatre. They had promised to close the Burbages down. So let Edward strut and mumble – the threepennies would still come to him provided they had nowhere else to go.

He made an amiable entry in his diary.

A notte of what charges my Soger petter
hath stode me in this yeare.

———

Jtem pd. hime 4 dayes traynynge .... Vs 4d
Jtem fownde hime Viij of powder for .... Viijs
Jtem pd for his levery & mony in his pursse Xiijs viid
Jtem fownd a head pesse wch coste me ...... Viijs
Jtem fownde a sorde & dager .... Viis
Jtem fownd a bealte & gerdell...................... Xijd
Jtem geuen at his gowinge awaye for
    powder & to dryncke................................ Vs.

A good lad Peter, in spite of his passion for 'finding' things, thought Henslowe, blowing on the ink.

At the Theatre Burbage was fast losing his temper. So was William Shakespeare. That was a fine fighting speech he had written for Hal Five, but not as it was being delivered by Master Melody.

'Master Prometheus,' he cried passionately.

Master Melody took offence at the interruption, strode forward and prepared to give battle.

'What is it this time?' he asked coldly.

Shakespeare remembered something. Was it not only this morning he had promised himself a holiday from temperaments? From the burning useless outpourings of artistic anguish that left him exhausted and incapable of concentration. Had he not decided that today should not only mark the anniversary of his coming to London (and, of course, the Armada), but that it should mark the beginning – the real beginning – of *Love's Labour Won.* He would be tolerant. He would speak quietly. He would show self-control.

'A trifle,' he said, and waved Master Melody on.

But Burbage waved him back.

'Master Melody,' he said. 'You are a Prince of England leading his men into battle – not my Lord Bacon begging for preferment. Will you try and remember that?'

Prometheus Melody looked vastly offended. He glared at Burbage. He glared at Shakespeare.

'Try,' said Shakespeare forgetting his resolution, 'and next week I will endeavour to cast you more suitably.' He reflected. 'Titania,' he suggested.

A titter passed through the company. But Master Melody looked pleased.

'Titania,' he said flattered. 'I have always wanted to play Titania. I am grateful to you, Master Will.' He turned to the fuming Burbage. 'Mark me, Master Burbage, I will have Titania in my contract.'

'Back to your speech,' said Burbage shortly.

53

With the air of a traitor forced to take an oath of allegiance Prometheus Melody stalked to the centre of the stage. He arranged himself. He threw back his head.

'Once more into the breach, dear friends,' he suggested . . .

Shakespeare shuddered. He tore his hair. He remembered something. He controlled himself.

He walked to a table in a corner of the stage and pulled out a batch of papers. He sorted them. He found the sheet he wanted.

It was headed:

LOVE'S LABOUR WON
by William *Shakespur*
Shakspire
Shikspar

He crossed them out. *Shacspore* he wrote.

He concentrated.

On the stage Mr Melody went on with his speech. He never went very far, for Burbage kept on hauling him back.

Act I, Scene I, wrote Shakespeare. *A solemn temple.* He looked at it. He shook his head. He crossed it out.

A gorgeous palace, he substituted.

He did not like that either. He looked at the stage for inspiration. He sighted Prometheus Melody.

'Then imitate the action of the tiger,' Master Melody was suggesting without much hope.

Even the crowd giggled. But Shakespeare took him at his word. He glared wildly. His mane stood on end. He leapt onto the stage and made as though he would tear Master Melody limb from limb.

'The tiger!' he snarled, thrusting his snout within an inch of Master Melody's taken aback nose.

'The tiger,' he repeated, stalking the retreating Master Melody round the stage.

'THE TIGER!' he roared with no self-control whatever . . .

*   *   *

The procession in the courtyard of Whitehall got clatteringly into its stride. It was glittering, it was spectacular and it was in a foul temper. Alderman and ambassador, sailor and soldier, and the entire Court rode through the gates, turned sharply to the right, and rode out in the direction of St Paul's, where a service of thanksgiving for the humiliation of the Spaniard was to be held.

At the head of the procession, mounted on a horse of clouded pearl, rode Elizabeth of England. She was wearing the cloth of gold. She was furious.

Not only was the Earl of Essex not riding beside her, but he had gone capering off on a progress of his own in an arrogant manner, snatching to himself the favour of the people and leaving her, a regal anticlimax, to trail her way past throats already hoarsened.

'Long live the Queen,' cried an honest housewife from an upper storey. Her voice was clear and fresh. She had only just woken up.

Gloriana raised her arm in royal salute. The housewife nearly swooned with ecstasy.

'And long live the Earl of Leicester,' piped a prentice from the gutter.

The Earl of Leicester smiled and waved his cap. He was furious. He knew that he was only riding beside the Queen because that puppy Essex had failed her. Granted old beacons can never be rekindled, but was it necessary for Gloriana to make such a madrigal and galliard about the business?

On the Queen's left rode the hero of the hour, the conqueror of the Armada, the trimmer of the King of Spain's beard, Gloriana's well-beloved pirate, the most idolized man in all the land, Sir Francis Drake. He called a bluff greeting to a knot of seamen roaring their delight. For a moment he almost forgot that he was furious.

'How well they love you,' said Queen Elizabeth.

That reminded him. He had set out that morning determined not to allow Gloriana to flatter him into a

55

good humour. She had changed her mind again when he was half way to Falmouth, she had sent after him and dragged him back to her side, his ship was still lying idle and unprovisioned in the harbour. She need not think that just because he loved her she was going to make a monkey out of him again.

Behind them a flourish of ambassadors condescended to parade before the barbarous English. They were furious. It was not reasonable to expect them to attend a thanksgiving service for a victory, not expected, not prepared for, and not deserved, which had upset the balance of power in Europe, and, by placing England on top, made diplomacy almost impossible.

'Long live the dagoes,' shouted the crowd amused.

The ambassadors practically unbent. They bowed. They almost smiled.

Behind them, mounted on a quiet chestnut, rode Lord Burghley, father of England. He was riding with Sir Francis Walsingham. He was going to speak to the Master of the Revels about this later.

The crowd roared their blessing as he rode a little slowly, a little gravely, on his way. He had kept England steady through perilous years. He had restrained the Queen when she would be rash and given her courage when she hesitated. He was the only man in the world who could persuade her to make up her mind.

Sir Francis Walsingham was aware of this.

'Listen,' he was saying, his ambassadorial suaveness brushed aside by his eagerness. 'You can convince the Queen that my plan is daring, breath-taking and proof even against fools.'

Burghley sighed. The trouble with Walsingham was that he had never grown out of his love of conspiring. Even a lifetime of failure had not cured him of it. He shook his head.

'But it is such a simple plan,' protested Walsingham. 'Why even Essex could hardly bungle it.'

'Indeed,' said Burghley coldly. He had not much

faith in his ward, but since the failure of the Anjou marriage project he had none whatever in Sir Francis Walsingham.

'Listen,' said Walsingham, eagerly. 'I will prove to you that my plan is a mathematical infallibility.' He edged his horse closer. 'Set the Irish against the Scots . . .'

Burghley sighed. If only he were riding with somebody silent like Sir Walter Raleigh.

Indeed, Sir Walter Raleigh was the only contented person in the whole procession. True, he was wearing his last year's cloak, but his new one was even now being cut out by a master tailor, a Portuguese, strongly recommended by Sir Francis Bacon, and would be ready in good time for the Ceremonial Tasting of the First Potato.

For weeks now the whole Court had been licking its lips over this appetizing prospect. But wheedle as they might, Raleigh would not even give them an inkling of the flavour of the rare root he had brought back from the Americas. Even the kitchen, in which the cook was being rehearsed in how to boil it, was guarded day and night.

Sir Walter had a moment of uneasiness. That new guard posted that morning – was he reliable? Only yesterday he had been a sentry guarding the Palace at Whitehall – but who wanted to be allowed to smell that? Would he be proof against the blandishments of Lady Meanwell or the hungry nose of Harry Hawkins?

Doubt seized Raleigh. But he could not turn back now.

'Have you completed your list of guests?' asked Sir Philip Sidney, riding beside him. He had been at pains to be extremely civil to the Master of the Revels to secure this place. Surely during this long and close-companioned journey Walter would weaken and drop him at least some hint as to the flavour of his unique root.

The Potato! Why the very name was appetizing.

'Will there be enough to go round?' he asked, anxiously.

Raleigh had been worrying about that too. Already the cook had used up two sacks in practice and he was still far from perfect.

'Who are you inviting?' asked Philip Sidney, going back to an earlier attack.

'Everyone,' said Raleigh. 'Southampton, Leicester, Essex, even the Master of the Revels.'

'And what of the Arts?' asked Sidney, interested.

'I have thought of them,' admitted Raleigh, 'but so far no name presents itself.'

'Bacon,' suggested Sir Philip.

Raleigh frowned. 'I do not care for his companions.'

'Pembroke?

'No palate,' said Raleigh.

'John Donne.'

Raleigh considered. He shook his head.

'Not done,' he confided.

Behind them, keeping his distance, alone and exquisite, rode Sir Francis Bacon. He was sulking. True he had managed to give his Portuguese tailor a quietus in the form of the custom of Sir Walter Raleigh, but as against this were many dark and lingering grievances. He held the procession in the objective mirror of his mind – what was he doing among these pirates on horseback, these senile counsellors who refused to die, these tactless red-faced generals more at home with a cutlass than a sword, this woman of a Prince? Why the only civilized elements in the whole procession were the foreign ambassadors – and how he hated them for the icy civility with which they cut him dead. Would that he were attending the Earl of Essex, sharing the cheers which my Lord generously paid for when he went on progress, instead of tagging along unheralded at the back of this fustian fit-out where not a single soul along the whole route had cried out 'Long live my Lord Bacon.' But it would not have been prudent to accept Essex's invitation and invite the anger of the

58

Queen. For there was no gainsaying it, Gloriana did not like him. He had done his best to alter this. He had smiled. He had worn cross-garters. And he had written her letters at every conceivable opportunity. But preferment, that most slippery of awards in Elizabeth's Court, became an eel in his hands. ('For light Gaines come thick, whereas Great come but now & then.')

Gloriana did not like him.

Only last week she had laid a booby trap for Burghley and ruined Raleigh's new cloak with a sack of flour balanced on a door, but, laugh it off as he might, it could not be denied that she had never so much as stuck out a foot to trip him up in playful affection.

He scowled. No bed for Bacon. It wasn't fair. He nearly burst into tears.

Polonius Bounce, Master of the Revels, seemed to have no fixed place in the procession. He was shooing and shepherding, restraining the impetuous, encouraging the stragglers, and cracking ancient jests with the ladies of the Court.

'What is it,' he asked Lady Meanwell, 'that stands on the roof at midnight and crows like a cock?'

The ladies of the Court reined their horses closer in.

'A Tom o' Bedlam,' said the Master of the Revels, and cackled like anything.

Lady Meanwell looked at him.

'Excuse me,' said the Master of the Revels, and galloped back down the line. The procession had turned a corner and he was in clear sight of Lord Burghley's expression as he listened to Walsingham's latest plot. There would be trouble about the riding arrangements. There was always trouble about the riding arrangements. He had never yet arranged a Progress without having to go into hiding afterwards for at least a month.

Looking down the years he saw his life at Court as one endless unmanageable chain of Progresses. It was hard to remember that once there had been a time

when a Progress was something exciting and signifi-
cant, and not just a sorting out of opposing ambitions
into more or less harmonious groups and batches.

He remembered his first Progress. How he had
ridden in the coronation train (with the arrangement of
which he was in no way concerned) of implacable,
righteous, unforgiving, Catholic Mary. He remembered
the little Jane Grey, walking backwards before her,
carrying candles to light her way. Her hair was in
braids, her face was freckled, she was nine years old.

He remembered her execution. How she had tied a
kerchief round her eyes and felt for the block, saying,
'What shall I do? Where is it?'

He felt depressed. He remembered something else . . .

Lady Viola Compton was getting restless. This was
only her second Progress but, in truth, it was nothing
but a repetition of the first.

Once again the Queen was stopping to receive an
address of welcome from yet another body of swollen
aldermen, upholstered with their own importance.

Viola pointed to a white wall capped with thatch in
the homely Dorset manner.

'What goes on there?' she asked Lady Meanwell.

Lady Meanwell pursed her lips. 'The Theatre,' she
said. 'Not a nice place. Players,' she explained. 'They
are not for you.'

Viola's father, guileless though he had been, could
have told Lady Meanwell that this was not the way to
curb his daughter's curiosity. 'Educative and instruc-
tive,' he would have said. 'You should visit it
frequently,' and returned to his supervision of his
Warwickshire pommage, secure in the knowledge that
his daughter would not gallop within a mile of it.

But Lady Meanwell did not know this.

'They are idle, wicked, worthless fellows,' she went
on, 'with only their voices to speak for them and only
their looks to leave as dowers for their children.'

'Players,' breathed Viola Compton. 'I have never
seen a play in a play-house.'

'I should hope not,' said Lady Meanwell. She drew her horse snubbingly ahead.

The aldermen, like swollen oes on spillikens, were taking their time. Viola looked at the Theatre. She must peep inside or die. And if the procession moved on she could always catch up afterwards. She saw a snub-nosed prentice boy. She dismounted. She threw him the reins. She gave him a penny.

'Wait here for me,' she said.

She slipped away into the dim entrance of the Theatre.

Rising and falling in its stirrups, the Court of Elizabeth of England continued on its progress.

Inside the Theatre the rehearsal of Hal Five, which had straggled itself all over the morning, had come to an end. This did not mean that the performance was perfect, the producer satisfied with it, or even that the actors knew their lines. It never does. But who cared? It would be all right on the night. Even the prentice boys could tell you that.

In the meantime there was that new play to be cast, rehearsed, and performed before the Queen and my Lord Essex – not to mention written. In order to do this they would need to spend time on it, a point everyone always overlooked – excepting the author. Secretly Shakespeare was a little flattered at the way his players took it for granted that he could supervise the rehearsals, rewrite the scenes, learn his own parts, alter everyone else's, be stool-shifter, prompter, and alarms heard off, keep an eye on the receipts, pay compliments to noble patrons, be available for any dinner-party in any part of the country, and, on top of this, extract a masterpiece, virgin and complete, from under his ruff the moment it was called for. But this morning he had put his foot down. He had made a scene. So Burbage had magnanimously allowed the playwright half an hour with his composer.

He was having it now while Will Kempe took the

61

boy players through the Bergomasque they would be needing for *The Dream*, and Burbage inspected a rostrum the carpenter was assuring him would be quite steady for Mark Antony's oration, provided he was careful.

Burbage was doubtful. He mounted the rostrum with great care, he advanced gingerly to the edge, he threw an imaginary toga round his bosom.

'See,' said the carpenter triumphantly. 'It is steady.'

Gaining confidence Burbage planted his feet firmly apart and pointed an accusing hand at Lady Viola Compton.

Viola shrank back into the shadows. But it was all right. Mark Antony had not seen her.

'Friends, Romans, countrymen – um—' he was saying blindly.

Viola congratulated herself. Like a flash she darted up a flight of stairs and hid herself in the first balcony. This was too charming a world to be turned out of. She did not understand what all the passion was about, but she liked it.

First there was plenty for her eyes to take in. The jigging apprentices, the actors hearing one another's words, the argument between the stubborn carpenter and the prostrate Mark Antony.

But gradually her attention was drawn to a dark man with intent brown eyes and a trim beard which Sir Philip Sidney might have envied. What attracted her particularly were his eloquent hands. At the moment he was waving them at an exquisite young man with an offended expression.

'Speak the speech trippingly, as it were – on the tongue,' he was saying.

The young man opened his mouth.

'Stay,' said Shakespeare. 'I will speak it myself.' He looked round. Viola shrank back into the shadows. But he had not seen her.

'Is Master Byrd in the house?' he asked.

'Master Byrd,' said a patient voice, 'has been standing

beside you for the past seven and a half minutes.'

'Splendid,' said Shakespeare, absently. 'The very man I want. Now listen carefully Master Byrd, for we give this play to the Queen and if she does not care for it she will assuredly de-ear us both.'

Byrd clapped his hands to his ears. He was never of that school which preferred to con its madrigals by a score rather than hear them sung by lovely lads in taverns.

'Look you,' said Shakespeare, 'the play opens to the sound of your lutes and viols. What I want is a few bars – not too many – of haunting music to set the scene.'

'Ah,' said Byrd.

'It is a palace in Illyria,' explained Shakespeare. 'I am a Prince crossed in love. I am waiting for news of my cruel she. I walk up and down. I listen to the music. And I say:

> 'If music be the food of love, play on;
>   Give me excess of it, that, surfeiting,
>   The appetite may sicken, and so die.
>   That strain again! It has a dying fall:
>   O! It came o'er my ear like the sweet sound
>   That breathes upon a bank of violets,
>   Stealing and giving odour . . .

'These words cut through your music, Master Byrd,' he explained.

'I will set it in eight parts,' said Byrd, raptly.

'You must keep it in the background while I speak,' said Shakespeare, oblivious. 'So now you understand exactly what I want.'

Byrd nodded. '"Greensleeves",' he said. 'It is a new northern ditty and will lend your Illyria something of our native vigour – and melancholy.'

'Sing it,' commanded Shakespeare.

Byrd cleared his throat. But from the gallery a clear fresh voice came floating down.

'Who's that?' asked Shakespeare, peering across the

63

sun-flooded court into the shadows of the recessed gallery.

'She sings the note truly,' said Byrd approvingly. He listened.

Shakespeare blinked. 'It must be one of the boy players. I will reprimand him later.'

Byrd shook his head and went on listening.

'No matter,' said Shakespeare, obliviously. 'It is a good tune. It will set the note admirably. What say you Master Byrd?'

'She's stopped,' said Byrd.

'Good,' said Shakespeare. 'Now in the next scene . . .'

The Morris dancers had broken up. Will Kempe was talking to a new arrival.

'What is the matter Master Kempe?' called Shakespeare.

In a funny little jig that combined the essence of ruefulness with a trained precision, Will Kempe crossed the stage.

'Bad news, Master Will,' he said. 'Richard Greene has been most grievously hurt in a tavern brawl.'

'Dead?' asked Byrd.

'He is dead,' said Kempe and jigged sadly away.

Shakespeare looked after the doleful jigging back. He did not see it. Dick Greene had been no friend to him in life. He had tried to block him in his work and he had pilloried him in his plays. But they spoke each other's language, they plied the same trade. And people who worked beside you ought not to die. They were not exposed to the incidence of war. Plague should not touch them. There should be an infinite store of time for them to draw upon. Because for them there was work to do.

He shook himself free. He turned to his composer.

'Come,' he said. 'There is much to be done.'

'Hurry,' said Philip Henslowe, 'there is much to do.' The rehearsal of the *Spanish Tragedy* dissolved. In its place the company went to work on *Volpone*. All save

Edward Alleyn. He was at the moment looking at last night's receipts in his father-in-law's great ledger.

Receat the french comodey xxviij s.

'Only twenty-eight shillings,' he lamented. 'And I was so good in it.'

'Superb,' said Henslowe, absently.

'An Edward Alleyn,' moaned Edward Alleyn. 'And we only take twenty-eight shillings. It is an insult.'

Henslowe slapped him on the back.

'Cheer up,' he said. 'We are attending to the insult. Within a week the Puritans will close down the Theatre.'

'Ah,' said Alleyn. He flicked the ledger over absently. He pointed. 'What is this?' he asked.

Henslowe looked over his shoulder. His face lit up.

'It is a magical recipe,' he said. 'Your wife sent it from the country.'

'Indeed,' said his son-in-law. He spelt it out.

> *To make a fowle ffalle downe*
> picture yt in paper & when yt is makinge leat one say m·a·n to the eand wth battes blude behold her with a pyne & she will falle downe jmedyateley.

'Tcha,' he said. 'It will never work.'

Henslowe looked annoyed. He was always annoyed when anyone doubted his spells.

'Find me a bird,' he said, 'and I will prove it.'

Alleyn pointed out of the window where a large goose was exploring the grassy verge of the courtyard like a Cecil seeking fresh avenues for taxation.

'A goose,' said Henslowe doubtfully. 'I had pictured something smaller. But no matter – we will try it.'

He seized a piece of paper. He began to draw.

'A bad likeness,' said Alleyn, critically.

Henslowe looked up. 'Lend me a pin,' he demanded.

The players who had abandoned *Volpone* to witness this interesting experiment searched themselves. They found several. Henslowe selected the longest and poised it over the head of the pictured goose.

'Now,' he said and jabbed.

The audience gasped. Then they broke into applause. Outside, the goose, with a despairing squawk, had fallen down.

'Now do you believe me?' asked Henslowe, triumphantly.

From round the corner came a stealthy figure. It gazed furtively around, grabbed the fallen bird, stuffed it into a sack and made off, the booty slung across its shoulders.

The players sighed and went back to *Volpone*.

At the Theatre a grumbling carpenter was erecting yet another rostrum for the eloquent Roman. But Burbage had ceased chivvying him. He held a letter in his hand and he was looking stricken.

'Will,' he called. 'Come here a moment.'

'Just a minute,' said Shakespeare.

'Just a second,' said Byrd.

They put their heads together again. They were absorbed. Even Master Melody, hurrying up that moment to discuss his interpretation of Titania, hesitated and halted. Clearly this was not the moment.

'Master Will,' called Burbage again.

Up in the gallery Viola Compton hugged herself. This utter and rather charming absorption in the matter to hand was something quite new to her. She longed to plunge into it. At home her father had always been a little vague about everything. At court everybody could think of three things at once, if necessary, in their sleep – it was an essential condition of remaining there. But here, though there were quarrels, conspiracies and all the other lovely amenities to be found at court, they concerned not internal preferment or foreign policy but the presentation of a play.

'Master Will,' called Burbage sharply.

Shakespeare started off in his direction. He was still talking to Byrd. Will Kempe seized his opportunity and jigged over to intercept.

'Master Will,' he said. 'I have come across a suite of dances in an old book.'

'Ah,' said Shakespeare cordially and tried to pass on.

'They are the very thing,' said Will Kempe, neatly barring his way with a little jump, 'for your new diversion for Gloriana and the Earl of Essex.'

'That's different,' said Shakespeare. He waved to Burbage. 'I come anon,' he said.

Will Kempe began to speak. It was not so much a speech as a demonstration. He jumped, he kicked, he stamped, he slapped his heels on his behind, he leapt, he twinkled.

'Will!' called Burbage in anguish.

Conscience-stricken Shakespeare side-stepped his ballet-master, dodged a wrestling match, avoided a fairy with a grievance, and had almost reached home when a little boy with a pale face clutched at his sleeve.

'Master Will,' he said beseechingly. 'I want to drown myself.'

Even Shakespeare looked startled. He patted him on the head.

'There, there, Salathiel,' he said. 'It will pass.'

Salathiel Pavey did not appear to hear. 'But first,' he announced raptly, 'I wish to go mad.'

'Indeed,' said Shakespeare, interested in spite of himself.

'And sing wild songs,' added Salathiel eagerly.

Shakespeare relaxed. He understood.

'A mad maid who drowns herself. It is an idea.' He tasted it. 'It is a very good idea, Salathiel.' He tasted it again. 'Dramatic.'

'That's what I thought,' said Salathiel Pavey, delighted. 'But first,' he said, 'I shall need to be betrayed.'

Shakespeare nodded. 'Naturally.'

'And before that,' said Burbage, interrupting, 'you will have to find a new management. Come.' And linking one arm firmly in the playwright's, while warding off a carpenter, an enraged lute-player and Prometheus Melody with the other, he led him firmly to the corner table.

'Will,' he said, 'I have received a secret warning from the Master of the Revels.'

'Master Polonius?' said Shakespeare. 'What has he to say?'

'Plenty,' said Burbage. 'We are to be closed.'

Shakespeare looked at him. 'You jest. The plague has abated.'

'The Puritans will have it so,' said Burbage. 'They will come and, because we are within the confines of the city, they will close us down.'

Shakespeare stroked his beard. 'Because we are within the walls of the city they will close us down. They will stamp out our flourishing theatre and our patrons will have to make do with Ben Jonson.'

'Exactly,' said Burbage grimly.

'Because we are within the walls of the city,' said Shakespeare thoughtfully. He leapt suddenly to his feet. 'But, Dick,' he cried, 'we must be crazy. It is so clear, so simple, this thing that we have to do.'

'What?' asked Burbage.

'Do you not see,' said Shakespeare, in his excitement beginning to stride up and down as though an obstinate scene were at last starting to shape itself. 'We must move our theatre outside the walls, move it in its entirety, rafter by rafter, bench by bench, brick by brick.'

Burbage looked at him.

'Let's go,' said Shakespeare.

He picked up an inkwell.

Lady Viola Compton rejoined the procession very late. Her companions teased and twitted her and made mischievous enquiries about her rendezvous. She answered them at random. She was thinking of something else.

Chapter Four

Three soldiers were galloping down Cheapside. Their armour was polished, their stirrups adjusted, and their swords reassuringly sheathed in their scabbards. Their expressions ranged from the enigmatic to the ferocious.

In front of them, righteous as Catherine of Aragon, pale as the King of Spain, stern as Sir Roger Ascham when the infant Princess Elizabeth refused to lisp her Greek, and bolt upright, rode a Puritan Father. People had no right to enjoy themselves. He was going to stop them. His cause was a just one and he knew it. He was enjoying himself.

A little behind the cavalcade, but equally well polished, rode another soldier. His expression was a mixture of pride and sorrow. You could see them struggling with one another. True, he had much to be thankful for. It could not be denied that he was making progress in his career. Only last week he had been stationed outside a kitchen, guarding the potato Sir Walter Raleigh had brought from overseas, and here he was, a soldier with a mission, on a horse – not quite so fast as the others, but on the whole very willing – riding to close down a playhouse. His face lit up.

But at the cost of going against his conscience. His face fell.

He liked the Theatre. When he had been a holder of horses, before he had been a night-watchman, before he had been a sentry, before he had been chosen to guard Raleigh's root, before they had given him a horse, he had often thought he had it in him to write a play. His colleagues had scoffed at him – but then no doubt they had scoffed at Shakespeare when he had been among them. True his concentration on his career now kept him much too busy to write his play immediately, but one of these days, when he had time . . .

His face brightened.

But he was on his way to close down a theatre.

His face fell.

Even if he did find the time to write a play it was doubtful if Burbage would ever consent to put it on after this. It was very doubtful.

His face fell even further.

Still he reminded himself, he must look on the bright side. Only two weeks in the army and he had been preferred above his comrades to ride on a mission with a City Father. That he did not care for the mission to which he was galloping must not be allowed to interfere with his ambition. An ambitious man had no room for sentiment. In a few moments they would have arrived and he must do his duty.

He looked keenly in the direction of his objective.

Good heavens! He had lost the cavalcade.

Meanwhile the cavalcade, sweating and spurring, had rounded the corner to pull up in front of nothing. Where the Theatre had been was an empty space surrounded by a thatched wall.

'Damn,' said the Puritan. He corrected himself.

Two men came tottering out of the yard bearing between them a heavy beam. Beside them walked an exquisite young man. He was carrying a mirror.

The Puritan called to him.

Prometheus Melody halted. He realized the Puritan. He inspected him.

'Kill-joy,' he said, and walked quickly off.

The two men lowered the beam and sat down on it.

70

They tore off their ruffs. They fanned themselves.

'Obadiah,' said one of them, 'while we are resting hear me my words.'

'Willingly,' said Obadiah Croke.

He listened.

The soldiers looked at them. They looked at the Puritan. The Puritan remained motionless.

A little man came jigging out of the courtyard. He was carrying two baskets filled with wigs. He looked as though he might start juggling with them at any moment.

The Puritan called to him.

'Where are you off to?' he asked.

'Well, ultimately,' said Will Kempe, 'to Norwich.' He jigged over to the Puritan. He executed a beat. He lowered his basket. He bowed.

The Puritan felt he was being jibed at, though he could not put his interfering finger on the exact spot. He waited.

'But not immediately,' said Will Kempe. 'First I must get into condition. It is a long way to jig to Norwich,' he explained, 'even for a wager.'

'Betting,' said the Puritan, side-tracked, 'is evil. Besides,' he added weighing up the chances, 'you will never do it.'

'What will you bet?' said Will Kempe promptly.

'A shilling,' said the Puritan. He remembered himself.

'We have come,' he said sternly, 'to close the Theatre. Where is it?'

Will Kempe smiled. 'We have carried it away. We have borne it outside the confines of the city.'

'Have you?' said the Puritan.

'Brick by brick,' said Will Kempe triumphantly, 'beam by beam, every one of us from the prentice boys to Master Will himself. Even the Governor,' he boasted, 'came to lend a hand with the flag-pole.'

'You surprise me,' said the Puritan.

'And now,' said Will Kempe gloating, 'it is all safe on

the other side of the river – the Bankside,' he pointed out, 'where your grasping, meddlesome, intolerant, liberty-destroying, short-sighted, inartistic, soulless, senseless, crass, and stupid fingers cannot meddle with it. We open on Friday sennight with Hal Eight. I shall not put a stool at your disposal. Good morning.'

He picked up his baskets. He bowed. He jigged away.

In the background a soldier laughed. He had forgotten his career.

Chapter Five

The Palace at Nonsuch was pointing its dissimilitude of chimneys at the cloudless sky. In the knot garden two counsellors of state were pacing up and down absorbed in a problem of great moment.

'I wonder,' Lord Burghley was saying, 'what it will taste like?'

'Don't expect too much,' warned the Master of the Revels. 'Remember black olives.'

Burghley shuddered. 'How was I to know,' he said, 'that it would have a stone in it?'

'For myself,' said the Master of the Revels, 'I am always suspicious of stones in foreign roots. I shall bite my potato most carefully.'

Burghley nodded. 'Even if it hasn't got a stone in it,' he concurred, 'it will probably have pips.'

They had reached in their pacing a garden of pruned trees; squat doves throwing podgy shadows, elegant peacocks with spreading tails, a sugar loaf, a great orb, a miraculous swan with a crown on its head.

Burghley pulled up in front of a green and very prickly armchair.

'And that reminds me,' he said. 'Have you arranged the seating order yet?'

The Master of the Revels shook his head. 'It has nothing to do with me,' he said, 'and with the Queen in her present humour I am glad of it.' He shook his head. 'It is Raleigh's own banquet,' he said comfortably, 'and he must attend to the details.'

'I hear,' said Burghley, twitching peevishly at an old bit of sable, 'that he is to wear a magnificent new cloak that will put us all in the shade.'

The Master of the Revels cackled. 'He will need it, for there will be little left of his conceit after the banquet.'

Burghley pondered this. 'You fear the potato will be tart?'

'As to that,' said the Master of the Revels, 'I have no opinion. But I do hear that he has not found a satisfactory cook and regrets bitterly that he did not import a savage along with the root.'

'Careless,' said Burghley. 'No attention to detail.'

'Exactly,' said the Master of the Revels. 'I know for a fact that he has not even started to consider the problem of precedence for his guests. Seems to think,' he marvelled, 'that it will take care of itself. It would not surprise me,' he finished with all the contempt of the professional for the amateur, 'to find the guests seated all anyhow.'

'Drake next to the Spanish Ambassador,' suggested Burghley.

The Master of the Revels cackled. 'Southampton and Lady Meanwell.'

'The Earl of Essex and Lady Viola Compton.'

They roared.

'All the same,' said Burghley, wiping his eyes, 'the Compton chit constitutes a menace. She enmeshes the Earl of Essex, which enrages the Queen, which hinders the Government of the country.'

'Tcha,' said the Master of the Revels. 'She looks like a young lad. No volume, no,' he curved the air with his hands, 'voluptuousness.'

'But she is a nuisance,' said Burghley discontentedly. 'She plays on my young ward as Master Dowling plays on his virginals.'

A pumpkin came sailing through the air. Automatically the father of England stretched out a hand.

74

'Well held, sir,' said the Master of the Revels approvingly.

Burghley examined his capture.

'Bruised,' he said discontentedly. 'Unfit for eating. I will throw it into the lake.' He wound up his arm.

'Stop,' cried an agonized voice.

The counsellors turned.

From behind a green giraffe came Dagglebelt the jester. His sleeves were rolled up. His hair awry. He was carrying two pumpkins.

'Go away,' said the Master of the Revels crossly. 'This is no time for jokes.'

But Dagglebelt held his ground. 'I have come to ask you to give me back my pumpkin,' he said earnestly. 'It slipped out of my hand,' he explained.

'Three pumpkins,' said the father of England indulgently. 'What a supper you will have tonight.'

'He must be fond of pumpkins,' decided the Master of the Revels. 'Give it to him, Burghley.'

Dagglebelt almost snatched the held-out pumpkin in his eagerness. His big chance had come.

'Now just watch me a minute,' he pleaded.

He planted his feet in an open fourth. He threw up one pumpkin. He threw up another. He threw up the third.

'Juggler,' explained the Master of the Revels.

Breathing heavily Dagglebelt caught the first pumpkin. He clutched at the second. He missed the third.

'A bad juggler,' said Burghley disappointed.

'It was an accident,' said Dagglebelt. He picked up the pumpkins. He tried again.

'Dolt,' cried a raw voice from an upper storey. 'Run away and practise while you still have hands to do it with.'

Dagglebelt gave one glance. He abandoned his pumpkins. He ran.

Elizabeth of England withdrew from the window. She was smiling. Only at her delectable Nonsuch did yellow pumpkins come floating over giraffes, and foolish counsellors find nimble hands to catch them. And to think that only yesterday she had been on the point of leaving it. And the day before that. And the day before that. And the day before that she nearly hadn't come. In fact, if she had not caught that sweet-speaking, false-swearing, fancy-veering, philandering, smooth-cheeked, good-for-nothing Robert Devereux exchanging glances with the Compton chit she might have stayed on in London where Burghley would almost certainly have talked her into giving Drake his provender. Indeed, she was certain that he had followed her here in order to cozen a grant for her beloved pirate. He should have it, of course, but all in good time. Let Burghley so much as mention a single victual today . . .

In the garden, their hands behind them, and looking like two naughty boys caught stealing pumpkins, the counsellors of State looked at one another.

'She's in one of her moods again,' said the Master of the Revels.

Burghley nodded. 'Don't think I'll mention those victuals today,' he confided.

It seems to me,' said the Master of the Revels moodily, kicking a piece of grass, 'you can't mention anything to the Queen these days.'

Burghley sighed. 'At times,' he said, 'she reminds me of her father.'

'A grand musician,' said the Master of the Revels with appreciation.

'That's not what I meant,' said Burghley crossly. 'I was referring to her conduct in affairs of State.'

'Ah,' said the Master of the Revels. He lost interest.

Not so Burghley.

'Managing monarchs,' he began comfortably, 'is like forecasting the weather. We Cecils have been doing it for centuries. One has to take into account the hot breath of favour, the cooling wind of diminishing affection, the rising tides of ambassadors, the ebb of preferments, the threatening clouds of insufficient revenue . . .'

'And the tornadoes of rage,' put in the Master of the Revels, well pleased with himself.

'I was going to say something quite different,' snapped Burghley. He paused. 'Now you've put it out of my head,' he said pettishly.

'A woman,' said the Master of the Revels, oblivious. 'That's what the Queen is. It would be much easier,' he pointed out, 'if she were a man.'

Burghley looked at him. 'Indeed,' he said coldly. 'And why?'

'No man,' said the Master of the Revels, undaunted, 'however weak-willed, would change his mind quite so often.'

'And no man,' said Burghley, 'could take the imagination of the people like the Queen. Why, three-quarters of the realm are in love with her.'

'And the other quarter,' retorted the Master of the Revels, 'are plotting against her.'

Burghley waved away the other quarter.

'My friend,' he said, 'you do not understand the Queen, you do not measure the love the people have for their Gloriana, nor yet the courage that has commanded it. You have not even grasped that her constant, inexplicable, infuriating changes of mind are not weakness but the strongest weapon of diplomacy that England has ever possessed.'

'As to that,' began the Master of the Revels confused . . .

Burghley ignored him. 'It has been my privilege,' he said, 'to counsel the Queen through the tricky years of long-armed peril to the prosperous harbour of her . . .' He paused. He pushed aside the term 'old age.' Even to himself he would not admit that his Sovereign was an aged woman. 'Mellow days,' he finished.

The Master of the Revels nodded.

'I have seen her,' said Burghley, 'on the eve of the Armada, gathering her courage into her frail hands. I was with her when she nerved herself to sign the death warrant of her cousin, Scots Mary. I have seen her facing the thread of sedition with a stubborn conceit. I have watched her dragging the red herring of her marriage across the conflicting seas of foreign politics. I have seen her failing to make up her mind, hesitating and hesitating till she had gained the time she needed, keeping the whole of Europe at bay with no other weapon than that weak will of yours. Besides, she is a great Prince and a great Woman.'

'But wilful,' said the Master of the Revels stubbornly. 'There may be expediency in political vacillation,' he conceded, 'but I ask you, Master Burghley, what merit can there be in substituting eight hairy pirates for eight slender virgins?'

Burghley blushed. 'No doubt,' he said, 'the Queen had her reasons.'

'It ruined my chief effect in the Progress to Greenwich,' complained the Master of the Revels. 'Eight virgins were to bear Gloriana in her palanquin. Why,' he rounded on Burghley, 'did the Queen have to wait to change her mind till I had scoured the country to find them?'

Burghley shrugged. 'You were lucky to have your Progress at all. The Queen was in such a passion that day that it took all my influence to persuade her to embark, and then she did not start until the morrow.'

'Aye,' said the Master of the Revels, 'and I had already paid the bellringers two shillings and sixpence to peal all day. And this they did though the Queen was not there to hear them. Why,' he rounded on Burghley again, 'did you not bring your influence to bear earlier?'

'Master Polonius,' said Burghley reasonably, 'would you start off on a progress carried by eight virgins if you had just happened upon your prettiest maid-of-honour teaching the spinet to the man you loved?'

The Master of the Revels pondered. 'So that was what was ailing the Queen that morning.'

'Viola Compton,' said Burghley. 'A chit of a girl. No volume, no voluptuousness, no manners . . .'

'But what a talent for mimicry,' sighed the Master of the Revels.

'Granted,' said Burghley, a connoisseur of acting. 'But that is beside the point. It is a week now since I have been waiting to find the Queen in a humour to discuss victuals for Sir Francis and the moment has not yet come.'

'I would not wait to speak to the Queen,' advised the Master of the Revels, from the depth of disappointing experience. 'Why do you not address yourself to the chit?'

'You are right,' said Burghley. 'I must speak to Mistress Compton. Candidly,' he admitted, 'I had considered this gambit already. But it was not a move to be undertaken lightly. The handling of infatuated virgins, dazzled by elegant striplings . . .'

'Look,' said the Master of the Revels, who had not been listening. He pointed.

In some annoyance Burghley swung round. His annoyance transferred itself.

Up the avenue of resplendent yew trees came, one might almost say strutted, a resplendent figure. It admired itself in the pond. It tried out an attitude. It smirked. It was not the Earl of Essex.

Sir Walter Raleigh was wearing a new cloak. The sun, as though conspiring with him, brought out the rich colours of the velvet and shone back from the elaborate gold squiggles.

'Gaudy,' said Burghley, twitching peevishly at the bit of old sable round his neck.

'Ah,' said the Master of the Revels keenly, 'all is not gold that glistens.'

How right he was.

From over a giraffe a golden orb came sailing out of its juggle. The counsellors ducked. Not so Sir Walter. The pumpkin caught him squarely on the jaw. He took a step back. He sat down in the pond.

The counsellors were delighted. They rushed to the pond.

'Lost your balance,' beamed the Master of the Revels.

'Ruined your cloak,' pointed out Burghley with great satisfaction.

From his squatting position Raleigh glared at them. 'Give me a hand,' he growled.

The two old men consulted together. They advanced gingerly to the edge of the pond. They held out their hands. Raleigh grasped them. They began to heave.

From behind the giraffe another golden orb came sailing out of its juggle. It passed over the stooped backs of the counsellors of State, but it caught the rising Raleigh on the left ear. Raleigh stopped rising. He sat down in the water. The counsellors of State staggered a little and sat down with him.

From behind the giraffe came a disconsolate figure.

It was Dagglebelt in search of his pumpkins. He scanned the landscape. He saw the Government of England sitting in the pond. He saw his precious pumpkins floating beside them. How to get them back?

He must turn away their wrath. He must bring to their notice the brighter side of the situation. He must make a tactful approach.

He came nearer. From the pond the Government of England glared at him.

Dagglebelt lost his head.

'I' God's name, masters,' he babbled. 'How come you to take a bath?'

In her room Elizabeth of England was scowling out of the window. How she hated Nonsuch. To think that she might have left it yesterday. Or the day before. Or the day before that. And the day before that she need not have come at all. How she hated the maze in which Earls could triumphantly lose themselves with maids-of-honour she ought never to have brought from Warwickshire. Robert Devereux, drat him, would certainly swear he had no idea the Compton chit was there. Elizabeth gritted her teeth. She wouldn't be tomorrow.

The curtains parted. Lady Meanwell came bustling in. She curtsied to the Queen, she picked up three discarded gowns, she almost danced with them to the wardrobe. Clearly she was on top of the day. As a matter of fact she had just discovered her oldest friend conspiring in a manner that would almost certainly lead to her undoing and was filled with delight at the prospect. She even hummed a little.

'You are in a good humour, Meanwell,' said the Queen drily.

Lady Meanwell almost giggled. But it was too early to warn the Queen. A conspiracy needed time to mature.

'Answer me,' said the Queen peremptorily. 'What has pleased you?'

Lady Meanwell thought furiously. Nothing came.

'It is a riddle-me-ree,' she said at random.

'Tell it to me,' ordered the Queen.

Lady Meanwell concentrated. She could only remember one, but it seemed suddenly to be a very funny one. She began to shake with laughter.

'What is it,' she asked, 'that stands on the roof at midnight and crows like a cock?

There was a silence. Lady Meanwell did not notice this. She was wiping her eyes.

'Well,' said Elizabeth of England, 'what is it?'

'A Tom o' Bedlam,' said Lady Meanwell, doubled up.

Elizabeth of England looked at her. She snatched off her wig. She threw it.

'Get out,' she said savagely.

Lady Meanwell fled.

Elizabeth of England spat. She returned to her desk. She picked up a quill. She selected a piece of parchment.

To the Bishop of Ely, she wrote. She had a fine flowing scholarly hand. At the moment it was quivering with rage.

Proud Prelate,

You know what you were before I made you what you are now. If you do not immediately comply with my request I will unfrock you by God!
                                    ELIZABETH.

Downstairs the seat of Government had transferred itself to Burghley's dressing-room.

'Try this,' said the Master of the Revels encouragingly. He held up a pair of embroidered breeches.

Sir Walter Raleigh, who had been standing in his underwear, failed to brighten. Even at this distance they looked a bit threadbare. Still he must not hurt Lord Burghley's feelings, especially while he was borrowing his clothes.

'Admirable,' he said, and stretched out a hand. But Burghley, also in his underclothes, got to the breeches first. He held them up. Two diamond patches were clearly visible.

'Tcha,' he said, 'they are hardly worn at all. The very thing for country wear. I shall put them on at once.'

He did so.

The Master of the Revels sighed. He was getting quite cold hanging about in his underclothes. He crossed to the wardrobe. He peered.

'Stop trying things on,' said Burghley crossly. 'I'll find you something presently.'

But the Master of the Revels had got hold of a doublet. It was made of emerald green and ermine. It was falling to pieces. Not even Burghley could wear it in the country.

'What about this?' he asked.

Sir Walter Raleigh winced.

But Burghley had been unable to control himself. He snatched.

'Oh, no, you don't,' he said. 'This is my favourite doublet. I've had it for years.'

'Ah,' said Raleigh.

'I was just going to put it on,' explained Burghley. He did so.

Raleigh had caught sight of a cloak in the fustian depths of the cupboard. It was grey with age, it was lamentably fashioned, the moths had made a fine meal of the astrakhan collar. He picked it up and, holding it well away from him, moved to put it across the shoulders of the Master of the Revels.

But Burghley, moving very quickly, arrived first.

'It's mine,' he said. 'I was just going to get it out.' He fumbled with the rusty clasp.

'See,' he said, 'I am nearly dressed. Didn't take me long, did it?'

Appealed to, his two companions glared at him. They were still in their underclothes.

'Now all I want,' said Burghley, oblivious, 'is a hat.' He rummaged.

'Burghley,' burst out Raleigh. 'Answer frankly. Do you purpose to lend us clothes or are you leading us on?'

'Presently, presently,' said Burghley. He had found a hat, flat as an oyster, with a peacock's feather, almost intact, stuck on top of it. He was trying it on. It seemed a little small. He wondered if it had shrunk.

'I remember,' he said suddenly. 'It belonged to young Essex. He was actually throwing it away,' he told Raleigh, unbelievingly.

Beside himself, Raleigh snatched up a coverlet and dashed out of the room.

There was a scream in the passage. Lady Meanwell, flying from the Queen's displeased presence, had collided with the coverlet.

'Out of my way, woman,' thundered Raleigh. He swept Lady Meanwell aside and, pulling the coverlet closely around him, stalked awfully away.

'He's taken my quilt,' mourned Burghley.

Chapter Six

Over on the Bankside Mr Burbage's players were very active. They were rebuilding their theatre and trying to rehearse in it at the same time. Carpenters carrying beams tripped over actors mixing mortar. Actors bearing benches shouted their cues from various parts of what had been assembled of the house. The Burbages were bobbing up everywhere, exhorting, encouraging, and testing. A put-together stool seemed too flimsy a thing for a well-upholstered Wolsey. Burbage said as much. The carpenter denied it. Other carpenters rallied to his support. Burbage proved his point by sitting on it.

In the middle of it all the immaculate Master Prometheus Melody was accosting anyone he could to hear his words. Few had time to listen to more than a stanza, for even the boy-players were busy with whitewash and scrubbing brushes.

In a space that later was to be the retiring room, two clowns, mounted on short ladders spanned by a trestle, were whitewashing a newly erected wall. They were looking very serious.

'I shouldn't tell him, Obadiah, not if I were you,' said William Tarleton. 'Not yet awhile.'

Obadiah Croke looked rebellious. 'And why not? Were they not the closest friends?'

'Not since *The Merchant of Venice*,' said Tarleton, dipping his brush into the bucket. 'Master Will could not abide Thomas Kyd since the row about that.'

Obadiah Croke covered the wall with bold strokes. 'Then why not tell him Kyd is dead?'

'You are a simple creature, Obadiah,' said Tarleton, dabbing the doorway delicately. 'Have you not noticed how it upsets Master Will to hear of the death of a playwright? Squeamish,' he explained.

Obadiah Croke nodded. 'I have noted,' he said, 'that he works twice as hard after such tidings.' He glanced over his shoulder. The bucket wobbled a little. 'You are right, Master Tarleton. It would be a shame to disturb him now. See how happy he is.'

Tarleton turned round. His elbow caught the bucket. The bucket lurched. Tarleton grabbed at it. So did Obadiah Croke. The trestle heaved. The bucket rotated. The whitewash spurted forth to smother the bobbing Burbage, who had come up to congratulate the clowns on their progress.

Blinded, Burbage staggered into the ladders. The erection came down.

So did the decorators.

The clowns picked themselves up. They looked at the spluttering actor-manager. They shivered.

But Burbage was laughing heartily.

'Very comical,' he chuckled. 'Very comical indeed. By my troth,' he said, 'we must get Master Will to write us in a whitewash scene. It has great commercial potentialities.'

The well-groomed Master Melody was gliding across. He was almost hurrying. Burbage picked up the bucket and hurled the whitewash over him.

'See what I mean?' he said.

The clowns hugged one another. So did the player-boys. Even the carpenters unbent so far as to smile. Only Master Melody was not amused.

Burbage was the first to pull himself together.

'That's enough now,' he commanded. 'Back to work all of you. Tarleton,' he said, 'go and mix some more whitewash. Obadiah, assist Master Melody to his feet. Salathiel, bring me a towel.'

Gradually the players went back to work. Soon the Bankside was filled with the sound of energetic hammers and busy saws. Once again Carpenters were hurrying all over the place, boy-players were clambering up and down, and Mr Burbage was personally supervising the hoisting of the flagpole on whining winches.

In the middle of it all, lying on his stomach, with an inkwell before him and an overturned table shielding his back from the wind, William Shakespeare was at work.

'*Love's Labour Won*,' he wrote. 'Act I. Scene I. A castle in Spain.' A wisp of wind made its way round the table and under his neck. He frowned. He crossed out the Spanish castle. 'A windy heath,' he wrote.

And while he worked, brick by brick, his Globe Theatre was growing up all round him.

'You are losing your grasp,' said Edward Alleyn, at the Curtein, crossly. 'Our threepennies will be empty again next week.'

Philip Henslowe laid aside his papers. 'Why?' he demanded.

'They are opening across the river on Friday.'

'With Hal Eight,' said Henslowe defensively.

'Ah,' said Edward Alleyn, 'but Shakespeare has written a new scene for *Catherine of Aragon*.'

'A new scene is not a new play,' said Henslowe defiantly.

'And a farewell speech for Cardinal Wolsey,' said Alleyn, determined not to spare his father-in-law. 'And what are you doing about it?'

'I am spending a lot of money,' said Henslowe bitterly. He picked up a sheaf of papers, sorted them, and handed them to Alleyn.

'See,' he said, 'what I am about to spend on your art.'

Edward Alleyn looked over the sheets. He read:

'The contractor, Katherens, is to take down the

existing structure, and to build in its place another game house or plaie house fit for players to play in and for the game of bears and bulls. There is to be provided a tyre house and a frame to be carried or taken away and to stand upon tressels, sufficient to bear such a stage. It is agreed to build the same of such large compass, form, wideness and height as the playhouse called the Swan in the liberty of Paris Garden. And the said playhouse or game place to be made in all things and in such form and fashion as the said playhouse called the Swan, the scantling of the timbers, tiles and foundations as is aforesaid without fraud or covin.

'1. Two staircases without and adjoining the play-house of such largeness and height as the said playhouse called the Swan.

'2. "Heavens" over the stage to be borne and carried away without any posts or supporters to be fixed or set about the stage. Gutters of lead needful for carriage of water that shall fall about the same.

'3. Two boxes in the lowermost storey, fit and decent for gentlemen to sit in, and shall make the partition between the rooms as they are at the said playhouse called the Swan.

'4. Turned columns upon and over the stage.

'5. Principals and forefront of the playhouse to be of oak; no fir to be used in the lowermost or under stones, except the upright posts or the back part of the said stones, all binding joists to be of oak.

'6. To new tyle with English tyles all the upper roof of the said playhouse.

'7. Also a louvre or storey over the said play-house as it now is.'

'That's all very well as far as it goes,' said Alleyn, only partially mollified, 'but who is going to write the play for my opening?'

'Drayton and Dekker,' suggested Henslowe. 'See,' he pointed to an entry in his account book. It read:

'Lent unto m^r [willso] drayton and m^r dickers in pt of a boocke called Haneballe & Hermes otherwisse called worse feared than hurt the some of xxx s.'

'Tcha,' said Alleyn. 'They are no Beaumont and Fletcher! A pity,' he said, 'that with all your plottings that go askew and all your plannings that go awry, you have never fallen upon a scheme to persuade Shakespeare to write for us.'

'You wrong me,' said Henslowe, hurt. 'For days I have been thinking of nothing else. And now at last I have the perfect plot.'

'Master Will is loyal,' said Edward Alleyn, unconvinced. 'You cannot bribe him out.'

'Ah,' said Henslowe, with his finger against his nose. 'But I can burn him out.'

'Witchcraft?' asked Edward Alleyn scornfully.

'No, stagecraft,' said Henslowe. 'This time,' he added, 'I must make certain.'

Chapter Seven

Elizabeth of England looked out of the window.

She froze.

On the terrace, Mary, Queen of Scots, pale and composed and about to die, was staring into nothing. She was looking straight at the spot where the Dean of Peterborough should have been standing offering her the consolations of a Protestant Church.

'Master Dean,' she was saying, 'I am settled in the ancient Catholic religion and mind to spend my life in defence of it.'

'Not quite so passionate, my child,' said the Master of the Revels. 'You are more resigned than defiant.'

Mary, Queen of Scots, relaxed and became a very young girl.

'I will try it again,' said Viola Compton meekly.

In the weeks before the Court had moved to Nonsuch, Lady Viola Compton had been haunting Master Burbage's new theatre on the Bankside. True, it was not yet open to the public, but Viola was in no mood to wait. No sooner had they re-erected the balcony than she had taken to hiding in it to watch Master Will rehearsing his improved version of Hal Eight. She could swear she knew the play by heart. Soon she was acting Catherine of Aragon before her mirror. From there it was but a step to Anne Boleyn. And after that The Forbidden One, whose name must never be mentioned, followed inevitably.

There was one man at Court who could be relied on to furnish her with every detail of the death of Scots Mary. Master Polonius Bounce would not only remember but might be coaxed into forgetting that he was forbidden to speak her name. So she had gone in search of the Master of the Revels just as he and Burghley were setting out in search of her.

The two old men had decided that, unconstitutional though this might be, they would seek out the chit and offer her some fatherly advice. It was not tactful, they had agreed to tell her, that one so young should so dispose herself as to attract the attention of a certain nobleman for whom it was well known that the Queen had much affection.

But somehow they had quite forgotten to chide the chit. For Polonius Bounce had been one of the few present at that tragic scene at Fotheringay and soon he had begun to remember.

'It was a winter's night when the two Earls arrived with the warrant for Mary Stuart's execution,' he began. 'You sent it,' he told Burghley accusingly.

Burghley blushed. 'Political expediency,' he muttered, automatically.

It was the sentence with which he had kept on warding off the Queen's fury when he had ended twenty years' indecision by dispatching, without the Queen's knowledge, the warrant she had so unwittingly signed.

'How did she receive the news?' he was impelled to ask in spite of himself.

The Master of the Revels considered. 'She seemed not to be in any terror from aught that appeared from any of her outward gestures of behaviour,' he remembered.

'That soul is unworthy of the joys of heaven for ever whose body would not in this world be content to endure the stroke of the executioner for a moment,' said Mary, Queen of Scots, in a brave voice.

The Master of the Revels nodded. 'After that, child,' he said, 'she wept bitterly and remained silent.'

'Like this?' asked Viola Compton, hiding her face with a lawn handkerchief.

'Like that,' said the Master of the Revels, 'but with less passion. I regret to tell you, child, that for weeks now she had been deprived of a confessor and when she asked for one now they offered her instead the Dean of Peterborough.' He turned on Burghley. 'Your doing!'

'It wasn't me,' said Burghley defensively.

The Master of the Revels looked doubtful.

'You wouldn't even,' he said accusingly, 'give her the consoling assurance that her tired body would rest in the kindly earth of France.'

'Politically inexpedient,' said Burghley. 'I made arrangements,' he pointed out, 'that her servants should be restored to their homes.'

'You could hardly do less,' said Viola Compton severely.

Burghley was silenced.

'She spent the night,' said the Master of the Revels, 'taking care of the nerves and emotions of her household, her little flock. She bade them hasten supper for she had much to do. She ate as usual, abstemiously.'

'But she spoke cheerfully to her physician,' broke in Viola, 'and before rising pledged her little company.'

'So she did,' remembered the Master of the Revels. 'We all marvelled at it.'

'She was in many ways a great woman,' said Burghley uncomfortably.

They ignored him.

'Having laid aside the robe and petticoat and wimple, which for the last time expressed her queenly state, she sat down with an inventory, dividing her clothes and jewels and property among her servants. She was an excellent woman of business,' remembered the Master of the Revels approvingly, 'and anxiously exact in matters of debt.'

'Her money she divided into little bags,' said Viola, inspired, 'with the owner's name written on each.'

91

''Tis true,' said the Master of the Revels, impressed, 'without advisers, papers, or account book this remarkable woman drew up her will.'

'And a lot of trouble it gave me, too,' said Burghley. They waved him away.

'She wrote letters,' suggested Viola.

'She wrote to the King of France,' remembered the Master of the Revels, 'commending her servants to him and asking him to spend the night in prayer for her.'

In spite of himself, Burghley sighed.

'By this time,' said the Master of the Revels, 'it was two o'clock in the morning and her servants entreated her to take some rest. It was her custom to have the lives of the Saints read aloud to her before she went to rest. That night Jane Kennedy was the reader. Mary bade her look for the life of a Saint who had been a great sinner. She stopped her,' said the Master of the Revels, 'at the life of the penitent thief.'

'In truth,' said Mary, Queen of Scots, 'he was a great sinner, but not as great as I have been. I wish to take him for my patron for the time that remains to me. May my Saviour have mercy on me, and remember me, and have mercy on me as He had on him at the hour of his death.'

'Very good, child,' said the Master of the Revels. 'Very good indeed.'

'But less passion,' said Burghley defiantly.

'She lay on her bed for some hours,' said the Master of the Revels remembering.

'Her ladies were already in mourning dresses,' pointed out Viola, 'and knelt about the room with lighted tapers, weeping or telling their beads.'

'But Scots Mary lay quite still,' said the Master of the Revels, 'and they thought that she was praying.'

'Very like, very like,' said Burghley uncomfortably.

Viola Compton was swept into the flow of the narrative. 'One of the servants,' she said, 'carried the ivory crucifix from the altar in front of her. The rest followed weeping.'

'But,' said the Master of the Revels, 'when the weeping servants reached the door of her apartment they were turned back.' He glared at Burghley. 'Your doing!'

Burghley made no answer.

'So now Mary carried the crucifix and the folded kerchief in her own hands,' said Viola.

'At the foot of the stairs she met Andrew Melville, her steward,' remembered the Master of the Revels. 'He was to take the news of her death to Scotland. "This will be the sorrowfullest message that I ever carried," he sobbed. Poor fellow, he was very much upset,' said the Master of the Revels.

'But she comforted him,' said Viola.

'Good Melville, today thou seest the end of Mary Stuart's miseries and that should rejoice thee.'

'Very good child,' approved the Master of the Revels. 'But a little more conviction.'

But Viola Compton was lost in her story. She drew herself up. Her voice rang out.

'She bade him tell her friends that she died a true woman to her religion, a faithful Scottish woman, and a true French woman.' She looked straight at Burghley.

Burghley twitched unhappily at his ancient ermine.

'Before she entered the hall,' said the Master of the Revels, 'she spoke again about her servants, begging that some of them might attend her on the scaffold and when they demurred she added with her old womanly charm, "Alas, poor souls, it will do them good to bid me farewell and I hope that your mistress, being a maiden queen, in regard of womanhood, will suffer me to have some of my own people about me at my death." And she undertook for her maids that they would neither weep nor make a commotion.'

'From her gentlemen,' he continued, 'she chose Melville, Burgoign, Gorian the apothecary, and Balthazar Holley, an old man.'

'Of her maids,' said Viola, 'Elizabeth Curle and Jane Kennedy, and with these following her she moved into the hall.'

'A fire burned in the large fireplace of the hall,' said the Master of the Revels, 'and near a platform was hung all round with black. The two executioners, masked, in black clothes and white aprons, stood motionless on the platform. There was a black-draped block and a stool. And the axe was leant against the balustrade.'

'I'm going,' said Burghley abruptly. He went.

They did not see him go.

'While the Queen's commission was being read,' said the Master of the Revels as though to himself, 'Mary Stuart sat collected and indifferent as if what she heard concerned her not at all. The Dean of Peterborough approached that august and disdainful presence and, bowing low, got four times as far as "Madame the Queen's most excellent Majesty."'

'But Mary Stuart stopped him firmly,' said Viola Compton.

'Master Dean, I am settled in the ancient Catholic religion and mind to spend my life in defence of it.'

'Very good, child,' said the Master of the Revels vaguely. 'Then,' he said, 'while we all joined in prayer for Mary's repentance, for a blessing on the Queen's Majesty, and confusion to her enemies, Mary began to recite aloud the penitential psalms in Latin, praying with great fervour. With very great fervour,' remembered the Master of the Revels.

'When the rest had finished,' prompted Viola, 'she continued her prayers, praying especially for Elizabeth of England – that she might serve God aright.'

'She held the cross in her hand,' said the Master of the Revels, 'often striking it against her breast. Lord Kent,' he shook his head, 'could not moderate his zeal and cried, "Madam, settle Christ Jesus in your heart and leave these trumpery things."'

'But the crucifix meant much to Mary,' said Viola. 'As she ended her prayers she kissed it and said, "Even as thy arms were spread here upon the cross so receive me into the arms of thy mercy."'

'So receive me into the arms of thy mercy,' repeated the Master of the Revels. He stopped. 'I can still hear her voice,' he said.

'And then?' said Viola. 'What happened then?'

'Then,' said the Master of the Revels, 'the executioner approached to help her undress.'

Viola shivered.

'She pushed him away,' said the Master of the Revels. 'One could almost have sworn she pushed him playfully. "Let me do this," she said. "I understand this business better than you. I never had such a groom of the chamber."' He blew his nose hard. 'What a woman,' he said in awe.

'Then,' said Viola, 'she beckoned to her two ladies to help her?'

The Master of the Revels nodded. 'Aye,' he said, 'and the familiar service moved them beyond bearing and they began to sob aloud.'

'But Mary placed her finger on their lips?' said Viola.

'Aye,' said the Master of the Revels. 'And she said with the old authority, "*Ne criez pas, j'ai promis pour vous.*"'

'*J'ai promis pour vous,*' repeated Viola. 'And then she kissed them and made the sign of the cross over them.'

'She was still a noble and comely woman as she stood in her crimson underdress,' sighed the Master of the Revels. 'Elizabeth Curle, weeping, kissed the kerchief and bound it round her eyes.'

'Bind my eyes,' said Viola.

The Master of the Revels fumbled.

'Then,' he said, 'she sat down on a stool, raised her head and stretched her neck, expecting the sword stroke, for such was the privilege of royal persons condemned to death in France. But no stroke came,' said the Master of the Revels. 'You could have counted ten and still no stroke came. Instead a confused sound of voices and the giving of new directions. The strain on her poor nerves!'

He sighed.

'The executioners helped her to rise and to arrange her head on the low-lying block.'

Viola sank to the ground and laid her neck upon a boulder.

'Like this?' she asked.

'More simply,' said the Master of the Revels.

With eyes darkened, but with hand clasping the Cross of Christ, through the terrible silence of that crowded room, she cried with unfaltering voice, *'In manus tuas Domine commendo animam meam.'*

Then the axe fell.

'And what do you think you are doing?' rasped an awful voice.

The Master of the Revels lowered the silly little stick he had raised shoulder high. Viola Compton scrambled to her feet and tore at the kerchief round her eyes.

They turned to face Elizabeth of England.

She stood before them, her beady eyes darting venom, a witch haunted by the shadows of her own misdoing. If she had not been a Queen of England you would have sworn that she was trembling.

'Fools!' she screamed. 'How dare you . . .'

She broke off. She controlled herself. She signed to Viola.

'Child,' she said. 'Follow me.'

The Master of the Revels was left holding his stick. He looked vaguely at the boulder where the white neck had lain.

'She had a little dog,' he muttered. 'She had concealed it in her petticoat. Now it lay beside the dead body and could not be induced to leave it.' He pointed. 'Just there.'

In the manager's office over on the Bankside, Burbage and his playwright were in conference. They were sharing Hal Eight's throne, using Juliet's coffin as a table, and the canopy from Hal Four had been hurriedly moved into position to keep a sudden shower off their heads.

They were collaborating.

'Tell you what,' said Burbage, 'we'll call it the Court.'

'C-a-u-t,' wrote Shakespeare. 'No,' he said firmly, 'that is no name for a theatre.'

'It is very appropriate,' said Burbage, hurt, 'for it is maintained by favour and surrounded by conspiracies.'

'And nobody goes there if they can avoid it,' said Shakespeare. 'No – we will not call our theatre this.'

Burbage thought again.

'Let us,' he suggested, 'call it the Bankside.'

'B-y-n-k-s-y-d,' wrote Shakespeare. He shook his head. 'It is too local. Master Burbage, I have a better idea. Let us call our theatre the London.'

'L-u-n-d-u-n,' wrote Burbage. 'Master Will, I have a better idea still. Let us call it England. Merrie England,' he added.

Shakespeare did not attempt to spell this out. 'Old-fashioned,' he said. 'Stinks of Hal Eight. The theatre,' he explained, 'must be living, universal, and should speak for all men at all times.'

They concentrated.

'The English Channel,' muttered Burbage. 'The Indian Ocean.' He shook his head. 'The Seven Seas.' He frowned.

'Tell you what,' said Shakespeare inspired. 'We'll call it the Globe.'

'G-o-l-b,' wrote Burbage. He nodded, well satisfied.

The collaboration had arrived at a successful conclusion.

'Take your time, child – consider. Do not make up your mind too quickly. It is a dangerous habit. I never make up my mind quickly,' said Elizabeth of England.

Viola, who had followed the Queen in too great a state of terror to know where she was going, began to recover her senses. She was beginning to realize that she had not been beheaded, that her ears were still intact, and that she was not even in a torture chamber being strapped onto the wheel, but in the Queen's own boudoir, sitting on quite a comfortable stool.

'I do not know,' she said. 'I had never thought . . .'

'Take your time, child,' repeated Elizabeth. 'You must leave the Court and you must leave it as soon as we return to London, but it is for you to decide what you wish to do. And I,' she pledged her word, 'will help you to do it.'

Alone with Viola Compton, Elizabeth of England had not raved. She had not cursed, spat, thrown her pantobles, or spoken shrilly. She had not even boxed the chit's ears. She had been too shaken by what she had seen acted down on the terrace below to do any of these things.

It had taken her twenty years to nerve herself to sign the death warrant of Mary Stuart, which even then she could not bring herself to dispatch. She had thought she would die when they brought her the news of her cousin's execution. She had thought she would behead everyone connected with it. Beginning with Burghley. But time had passed and though in the end she had forgiven them all she had never forgiven herself. Though the name was never mentioned, she often found herself thinking of the French woman and then quickly thought of something else.

She was going to forget that scene on the terrace just as quickly as she could.

The chit must go.

Her mind was made up on that point. In record time.

But she would not treat the child unkindly, she decided as she looked at the young girl trembling before her. She was young and alone.

'Sit down,' said Elizabeth, pointing to a stool.

Years ago Elizabeth of England had herself sat at the feet of her Queen on a suppliant stool. She had not been Elizabeth of England then. She had been the unfortunate fruit of her father's second and therefore non-Catholic marriage and there had been much doubt in the Queen's, her sister's, mind whether she should be allowed to live. Indeed, even now when she thought of Bloody Mary, Elizabeth was surprised to find her head still on her shoulders and her ears intact. She tried not to remember those helpless years – even at this day she would seek forgetfulness of them in pleasant company; her charming pirates, dear old Burghley, romantic Sidney, or that rascal Essex, drat him.

Yes, the chit must go.

She applied herself to the task of speeding her as painlessly as possible.

But the chit seemed to have no idea where she wanted to go or what she would do when she got there. Extraordinary.

'You would like to marry?' suggested Elizabeth, helpfully.

Viola shook her head. 'No, thank you, M'am, I do not think I should care for that,' she said.

'You may be right,' said the virgin Queen wisely. She considered. 'You would care to travel? I could send you,' she pondered, 'to Ireland.'

'Not Ireland, M'am, please,' said Viola. 'It is so far away.'

'Paris, then,' suggested Elizabeth. 'They live quite well there I hear.'

'But that is farther still,' said Viola obstinately.

Elizabeth took off her pantoble. But no, she would be patient. She slipped it on again.

'What is the matter with you, child?' she asked. 'Why is it that you do not wish to go away? What is it that you do not wish to leave?'

Viola was silent.

'Who is it that you do not wish to leave?' said Elizabeth. 'Is it a man?' she asked more shrilly.

'Oh, no, M'am,' said Viola.

Elizabeth relaxed. 'What is it then, child?' she asked.

'Come, take your courage in your hands and tell me.'

Viola took a deep breath. She gathered her courage in her hands.

'It is the Playhouse,' she said.

The Queen looked puzzled.

'It is so exciting, so important, so different,' said Viola, trying to explain. 'Whenever I watch the players I forget all about the Court. I wish,' she finished in a rush, 'I could be a girl boy-player.'

Gloriana looked at her. Viola put her hand over her mouth. What had she said!

'A girl boy-player,' said Elizabeth. 'Ridiculous. Never heard of such a thing.'

'I'm sorry, M'am,' said Viola humbly.

'Preposterous,' said Elizabeth. 'Out of the question. How could you do it anyway?'

A gleam of hope appeared in Viola's eyes.

'I could disguise myself as a boy. I make a very good boy,' she added hopefully.

Elizabeth looked at the young flushed face, the dark lad's head, the slender figure, the almost invisible hips.

'Tcha,' she said comfortably, 'no voluptuousness.'

'But I don't have to be voluptuous to be a boy,' pleaded Viola.

'Silence, child,' snapped Elizabeth. 'That's all you know.' She looked at her again. 'So you want to dress up as a boy and go play acting?'

'If you please, M'am,' said Viola humbly.

Elizabeth of England thought it over. 'It is an idea, by God,' she decided. 'And you would be better employing your talent for mimicry at a playhouse than at my Court. Already,' she said severely, 'Mistress Meanwell has complained to me that she can get no obedience from my ladies-in-waiting since you have been imitating her walk.'

Viola eyed the Queen warily. But the Queen was not looking altogether displeased at Lady Meanwell's discomfiture.

'But she has such a funny walk,' said Viola. 'See.' She broke into a wobble.

'Stop it, child,' commanded Elizabeth. 'Stand still and attend to me.'

Viola stood still.

'Have you ever,' asked Elizabeth sidetracked, 'noticed the peculiar progression of Master Bacon?'

Viola had. She demonstrated.

'Very good, child,' approved Elizabeth. 'But a little more languor.'

Viola giggled. 'Please, M'am,' she dared, 'are you ever going to let the poor man have his bed?'

'Of course not,' snapped Elizabeth. 'Why should I?' she asked defiantly.

She returned to the matter in hand.

'Philip Henslowe,' she said, 'will do anything for money. They tell me his brothel over by the Clink is not doing so well since the plague. I could, if I wished, apprentice you to him as a boy-player.'

'So please you, M'am,' said Viola, 'I would like to go to Shakespeare.'

'Master Will?' said Elizabeth. 'Impossible. He is writing me a play and you will distract him.'

'Nothing can distract him,' said Viola. 'He can write his plays while they build a theatre round him. He will take no notice of me. Besides,' she added, 'he will think I am a boy.'

'That's what I meant,' said Elizabeth. 'Have you,' she asked at a tangent, 'ever seen the Earl of Southampton? Never mind, child,' she added, noticing that Viola looked puzzled, 'you will learn about these things soon enough.'

She rose to her feet and made a gesture of dismissal. 'That will be all, child. You may go.'

'But,' said Viola, 'you have not told me. May I go to Master Shakespeare? Is it settled?'

'Settled!' said Elizabeth of England. 'Have you taken leave of your senses, child? Do you expect me to settle a thing like that in a flash? I must have time to make

101

up my mind. It always takes me a long time to make up my mind. Remind me to tell you some day,' she said, 'about those years when I was making up my mind whether to marry.'

If she had not been a Queen of England you could have sworn that she was boasting.

Chapter Eight

A fine clear morning. Sir Walter Raleigh's new servant laying out his master's new cloak nearly added 'and all's well.' It reminded him of the time when he had been a lowly night-watchman and had greeted Sir Walter, leaning out of the window, with just this information. And now here he was on the inside of that window. Why, only last week he had been riding to close the Theatre and now here he was trying on his master's new satin cloak.

He surveyed himself in front of the mirror. He raised his arm. Why, he was the very living image of the Earl of Essex. Not quite so dissipated, of course, but every bit as haughty.

A sparrow mocked him from the window-sill. He strode over. The sparrow, jeering defiantly, flew away. He threw an apple after it. It hit an old man.

Sir Walter's servant withdrew hurriedly. The Queen alone knew what was the penalty for hitting the Master of the Revels on the crown with an apple.

The Master of the Revels sat up and rubbed his head gingerly.

'What happened?' he asked.

The dark lad gazing at him as one who sees the dead quicken, who, up to this moment, had been all high spirits, burst immediately into tears.

'Oh,' he said, 'you are not dead. I am so glad.'

The Master of the Revels struggled testily to his feet.

'Stop crying,' he ordered. 'Young lads do not cry.'

But the sobs went on.

The Master of the Revels looked embarrassed. 'Here,' he said, 'have an apple.'

The young man bit into it doubtfully.

'Better?' asked the Master of the Revels. 'Then let us hurry on.'

The young lad dried his eyes. 'You are a darling,' he said, and hugged the old man.

Sir Walter's servant, scandalized, turned his back on them. The Master of the Revels ought to be ashamed of himself. In the street, too!

But the Master of the Revels was patting the young lad with every evidence of enjoyment.

'There, there, my dear,' he was saying. 'You are a little over-excited. It is only natural. I remember,' he began, 'how I felt the first day I went to my old tutor, Sir Roger Ascham . . .'

'God bless you, Master Polonius,' said Viola Compton. 'But remember it another time.' She tugged at his sleeve. In her impatience she was the prettiest lad you could wish to see.

'We shall be late,' she urged. 'The rehearsal will have started.'

As they went down the street the voice of the Master of the Revels could be heard remembering his old tutor's advice.

'Lutinge and singinge,' he was saying, 'take awaye a manlye stomake.'

Prometheus Melody, too, was in a hurry. He had woken up far too late to allow himself that comfortable margin for elegant dressing that was expected of the Essex of the Globe Theatre. But he had not so much overslept as underslept. He had been with the Earl of Southampton and they had sung madrigals and ballets far into the night. Their voices had blended so well. But perhaps it was a good thing that Master Bacon had taken himself into the country. Indeed, Master Melody trusted that he would never hear of it.

But he must not be late for the rehearsal. Master Burbage was so unkind if you were late.

And he must not disturb Dame Quickly down below. He owed her three weeks' rent. Dame Quickly was so unkind when you owed her three weeks' rent.

He tiptoed to his bedroom door. All quiet. He lifted the latch. Not a sound. The door swung slowly inwards.

'Good morning, Master Melody,' said Dame Quickly.

She was standing outside the door barring the way down the passage. One arm was akimbo. The other held by the ear a surly, churlish, red-headed oaf.

Master Melody took a step back.

'Tonight,' he babbled. 'After the performance. They are going to pay us.'

Dame Quickly looked at him grimly. Clearly she had heard this speech too often from too many lodgers to be deceived.

'Master Melody,' she said, 'I offer you three choices. You can pay me my money and go. You can owe me my money and stay locked in this room. Or,' her mouth set in a grim line, 'you can do me the trifling favour I have asked you so often.'

Master Melody looked at the trifling favour wriggling in its mother's grasp. He paled.

'You can take my son,' said Dame Quickly inexorably, 'and you can apprentice him to Master Burbage.' To emphasize the point she gave the ear an extra tweak.

'Why are you so reluctant?' she demanded of the rooted Prometheus. 'Have you not often agreed with me that he will make a fine boy-player? Take him.' She pushed the trifling favour forward.

Master Melody was jerked into life.

'Not now,' he pleaded. 'Tomorrow. You see, I'm in a hurry.' He tried to duck, but a massive arm swung him round and the trifling favour meanly kicked him in the pants.

'Make up your mind,' said Dame Quickly. 'You have only yourself to please.'

Prometheus sought wildly for escape. The window – too high. Stay cooped in this room while some other actor stole his applause – not while he lived. But to present, as his prodigy, this hulking lout, so plainly of the people, whose only vices could never be anything but obscenely natural . . .

At the Globe Theatre nearly everything was ready for the opening. True there was no thatch to the tiring rooms, the second gallery still needed a few more props, and Master Byrde had been too busy with his Mass for Five Voices to rehearse the musicians in their new fanfare.

Still he was attending to that now.

Added to this noise there was a frantic hammering on every side. Cartloads of stools were being dragged into their positions and curious passers-by were being dragged out of theirs. A platform was being erected for Catherine of Aragon's trial scene, and Catherine himself, bepillowed and protesting, was being made to mount it. The boy-player kept on pointing out that he still lacked the tremendous new speech Master Will had finally got round to writing, but nobody worried about that. 'First,' said Burbage curtly, 'let us discover whether you can stand on this platform. Later we will decide what you are to say on it.'

Catherine of Aragon spat.

Burbage was in a bad temper. It was not that the opening night was preying on his nerves. It was not the fact that the whitewash was laid on too thick and the thatch too thin. That Cardinal Wolsey's new robes had not arrived, that the carpenters were threatening to strike, that none of the actors knew their lines, and that large parts of the play still remained to be written. That the costs were running high and his resources low and that all around people were plotting against his success. The plague, the Puritans, and the machinations of Philip Henslowe had long since accustomed him to accept all these things as an inescapable routine.

No, an event of far greater moment was disturbing him.

It bade fair to alter his whole life.

Doctor Lopez had forbidden him his ale.

It made it no better to reflect that it was his own fault, for going to a clever foreign physician instead of staying with his regular English saw-bones, who could be relied on to prescribe nothing more alarming than leeches.

No ale!

Suffering Spaniards! He was thirsty already.

He looked sourly at the beaker of milk he had brought with him.

William Shakespeare at work on a much-crossed-out revision of Catherine of Aragon's speech looked up in search of inspiration. He saw Burbage looking at the milk. This would never do. He must coax him into a better humour or Hal Eight would suffer.

'Cheer up, Dick,' he said. 'Are there not other drinks in this brave new world?'

'What other drinks?' asked Burbage. He could not think of any.

'Mead,' said Shakespeare. 'Sack. Pommage.'

'Pommage!' said Burbage dangerously.

Shakespeare tried another angle. 'It may be difficult at first,' he said winningly, 'but presently it will come easier and soon you will not be missing it at all.'

He ducked.

'Besides,' he added, coming up, 'think of the money you will save.'

'Ale money,' said Burbage. He laughed bitterly. 'Alms for oblivion.'

'By God!' said Shakespeare. 'That's good. That's genius!' He took up a quill and held it poised above his paper. 'What for oblivion?' he asked.

'Alms,' said Burbage. He spelt it.

Through an unhinged gate, past a half-built wall, underneath some flapping canvases and over a pile of thatching straw, came two noblemen. They were clad in sapphire and scarlet, their cloaks were ermine trimmed and embroidered in gold, their bolster trunks were the last word in fashionable wear for men, and their shoes were befurred, coloured, and pointed. It was a pleasure to look at them as with practised ease they trod their way through the rubbish that led to the stage.

Unfortunately nobody had time to do this.

They were Sir Philip Sidney and Sir Francis Bacon.

Bacon was broody and sullen. But something seemed to be pleasing Sidney.

'Good morning, Master Burbage,' he said. 'How well your theatre progresses. Good morning, Master Will. How goes the new play?'

'Move away, Sir Philip,' said Burbage. 'You are standing on the trap-door.'

'New play,' said Shakespeare vaguely affable. 'Which one do you mean?'

Bacon frowned. 'The play for Elizabeth of England,' he said. 'You should be thinking of nothing else.'

'Master Bacon,' said Burbage. 'Don't stand there, please. You are obstructing my actors.'

'You wrong me,' said Shakespeare, hurt. 'I think of nothing else. See what I have already written.' He rummaged.

'*Love's Labour Won*,' he read. 'Act I. Scene I. No, no,' he said hastily, 'this is not for you.'

Sir Philip Sidney smiled. 'Like the bed – eh, Bacon?'

Bacon scowled at him. 'It is no joke this,' he said. 'It is not funny to ride to Stratford-on-Avon on a false rumour.'

Shakespeare put down his papers. 'You went there,' he said. 'Why?'

'He is credulous,' said Sidney, seating himself. 'They told him he would find his bed there.'

'Get up, Sir Philip,' said Burbage urgently. 'The glue on that stool is not yet set.'

'The Queen's bed that was meant for me,' said Bacon. 'Her second best bed. They told me that a woman called Ann Hathaway would direct me to it.'

Shakespeare smiled grimly to himself. 'And would she?'

'How can I tell?' snapped Bacon. 'I could not find her.'

He kicked savage against a brick. The brick won.

'Put that brick back,' said Burbage sharply. 'It is a cue for the stage hands.'

'I asked everyone,' said Bacon, hopping slightly, 'but nobody seemed to know where her cottage was.'

'Ah,' said Shakespeare. 'Then you are still bedless. A pity.'

'It will not be for long,' said Bacon coldly. 'I saw Polonius this morning. I was very firm with him. And I am to have the bed from the Queen's next Progress. He has promised faithfully.'

'What again?' said Sidney, sympathetically.

Bacon looked worried. An awful thought had presented itself. Was the Master of the Revels not altogether sincere in his protestations?

('He that seeketh to be Eminent amongst Able Men hath a great Taske'.)

Was he leading him by the nose? Was he, in short, making a fool of him?

His fist clenched. He took a step back. There was a sound of ripping.

'Look out,' said Catherine of Aragon, 'that was my skirt.'

Burbage was fidgeting impatiently. 'Master Will,' he broke out, 'will you have the goodness to get your friends out of here and leave me with my actors.'

'But I have so much to do,' protested Shakespeare. 'You amuse them, Dick. Take them to the Mermaid. Give them some ale.' He put his hand over his mouth.

Cardinal Wolsey, seeing the group conversing so amiably and judging that the moment was ripe, hurried over and drew Shakespeare aside.

'Master Will,' he said, 'I want to be a ghost.'

Shakespeare looked at him evilly.

On their right an epidemic of hammering had broken out. On their left a great deal of hoisting, whoa-ing, steadying and 'there-lads' was going on. Cardinal Wolsey felt that perhaps he had not made himself clear.

'A ghost,' he repeated.

'A ghost,' said Shakespeare, looking at him with hate. 'You are going the right way about it.'

Cardinal Wolsey backed. Perhaps he had not chosen the right moment.

'You misunderstand me,' he said. 'I speak of a stage ghost, who talks most chillingly, a perturbed spirit who walks at midnight and urges his son to avenge him.'

'What for?' asked Shakespeare impatiently.

Cardinal Wolsey was confused. 'I had not thought so far,' he confessed. 'I am not a Dekker.' He caught sight of Master Will's face. 'A Shakespeare,' he amended hastily. 'You could write a fine speech for a ghost,' he tempted.

'Indeed,' said Shakespeare.

'And I,' said Cardinal Wolsey, feeling he might be fighting a losing battle, 'can groan most horrid.'

He groaned.

'Will,' shouted Burbage. 'Stop making those noises. I have an opening on my hands at four o'clock, I have a theatre to complete half an hour before, and I have your guests to get rid of at once . . .'

'My guests,' said Shakespeare, furious.

The rest of the speech was lost in a crash. The beam had stopped steadying and whoa-ing, but it had come down. It had come down with a rush that had caught a swinging door and neatly penned Master Bacon into an unswept and very small corner. To get him out they would have to unhinge the door and carry away the beam, an operation for which, as Burbage pointed out, there was simply no time at the moment.

'Take it easy, Master Bacon,' advised Shakespeare. 'Stop shouting. I promise that we shall have you out in time for the performance.'

'And anyway,' said Sidney, soothingly, 'you can see quite well from there.' He stood on his toes and craned.

'In the meantime,' said Cardinal Wolsey, helpfully, 'I will fetch you some ale.'

'Ale,' said Burbage, dangerously. He advanced on the once more backing Wolsey, but broke off to gaze incredulously at the doorway.

Advancing towards him was a quartette calculated to prove the last straw to any busy impresario. From one side came that boring old weasel, the Master of the blasted Revels, bringing with him some unlucky stripling who doubtless could not escape. From the other side came that unbearable puppy, that temperamental cry-baby, that Essex of the Globe Theatre, that unmitigated nuisance, Prometheus Melody. Would to God that he were rid of him! And anyway he was late. And what the hell did he mean by bringing in his horse-holder by the ear with him.

Burbage froze into a rock of managerial dignity as the quartette approached – a rock loaded with dynamite. By instinct everybody in the theatre stopped whatever it was he had been doing at fever pitch. All was silent save Master Bacon bleating pathetically behind his beam.

With perfect breeding Master Melody averted his eyes from the painful spectacle. Taking a firmer grasp on Master Quickly's ear he pushed him forward.

'Master Burbage,' he piped into the silence, 'I have brought you an actor.'

Burbage swelled. He swayed slightly. He controlled himself.

'By a coincidence,' said the Master of the Revels, well pleased with the surprise he was about to spring, 'I, too, have brought you an actor.'

Burbage swivelled round. He saw the Master of the Revels. His eyes fell on the stripling. He clenched his fists. He controlled himself. He took a deep breath.

'Now let me get this clear,' he said in a quiet but penetrating voice. 'You,' he pointed at Master Melody, 'have brought me an actor. You,' he swung round on the Master of the Revels, 'have brought me an actor. You have both brought me an actor. That,' he counted them on his quivering fingers, 'makes two actors altogether. Two untutored, cluttering-up, wide-eyed oafs I am to be saddled with on the day of the performance.' He took a step forward. His self-control broke.

'Take them away,' he roared.

Viola turned pale. She clutched the Master of the Revels by the arm. Yet if she had not been a bit of a girl you could have sworn that she was steadying him, the spit of her royal mistress.

But the oaf had no such affection for Master Melody. He wriggled himself free and fled.

'I must look for him,' babbled Master Melody. 'I must bring him back. I owe his mother three week's rent.'

He fled.

'You frightened him,' said the Master of the Revels reprovingly.

Burbage looked at him. He swelled. He swayed slightly. Could he hit an old man? He saw red. Easily.

Sir Philip Sidney acted quickly. He pushed the Master of the Revels out of the way, then snatched the foaming beaker Salathiel was offering Master Bacon and thrust it on Burbage.

'Take it,' he said. 'Your need is greater than his.'

Burbage gulped it down. He wiped his mouth.

'Ah,' he said.

Thus encouraged the Master of the Revels emerged from behind Sidney's back. He took the slowly evaporating Burbage gently by the arm and led him aside.

'It is the Queen's wish,' he said.

Watching the resigned shrugging of Burbage's shoulders, Viola could feel the way the conversation was going. She became aware that Sir Philip's eyes were on her. She turned away. She found that Shakespeare was looking at her.

It was a most peculiar look. Viola was used to men looking at her admiringly in Court. It was nothing like that. There was in it the measuring glance of a painter, the appraising eye of a cook, the shrewd measurement of a buyer at market and a little of Lady Meanwell inspecting them upon parade. He walked twice around her, he walked away from her and towards her again, he nodded, well satisfied, he reached for a piece of paper and thrust it into her hands.

'Read this, boy,' he ordered.

Viola looked at the sheet.

'Aloud, boy,' said Shakespeare impatiently. 'Read it aloud.'

'*Love's Labour Won*,' read Viola. 'Act I. Scene I.' She shook her head. It was very puzzling.

'My fault,' said Shakespeare. He snatched the sheet away and hugged it to him. 'It is my new play,' he explained.

'I like it,' said Viola politely.

'You think it good?' said Shakespeare pleased. 'There is much to be done yet. But you are right. It will be the best play I have ever written if,' his face fell, 'I ever write it.' He sighed. He shook off his depression and looked at Viola benevolently. 'What is your name, boy?'

Viola tried to remember what it was she had decided to call herself.

'John Pyk,' she said and laughed.

Shakespeare picked up his quill.

'P I G G E,' he wrote. He looked at it. He tore it up. He rummaged among the papers on his table.

'Master Pyk,' he said. 'Do me the pleasure of reading me these lines.'

Viola glanced at the sheet. She read the lines over to herself.

'But they are lovely,' she said.

Shakespeare beamed. 'They should be spoken to music,' he said, 'but no matter. Read them boy.'

Viola's eyes grew dark.

> 'Fear no more the heat o' the sun,
>   Nor the furious winter's rages;
> Thou thy worldly task hast done,
>   Home art gone, and ta'en thy wages
> Golden lads and girls all must,
>   As chimney-sweepers, come to dust.'

'Dick,' called Shakespeare urgently. 'Come over here. I have found you an actor.'

> 'Fear no more the frown o' the great,
>   Thou art past the tyrant's stroke;
> Care no more to clothe, and eat;
>   To thee the reed is as the oak;
> The sceptre, learning, physic, must
>   All follow this, and come to dust.'

On the other side of the stage a bunch of clowns stopped working a gag and drifted over to listen. A carpenter laid down his hammer.

> 'Fear no more the lightning-flash,
>   Nor the all-dreaded thunder-stone;
> Fear not slander, censure rash;
>   Thou hast finish'd joy and moan:
> All lovers young, all lovers must
>   Consign to thee, and come to dust.'

The Master of the Revels turned to Burbage. 'What did I tell you?' he said.

> 'No exorciser harm thee!

114

> Nor no witchcraft charm thee!
> Ghost unlaid forbear thee!
> Nothing ill come near thee!
> Quiet consummation have;
> And renowned be thy grave!'

Viola looked up. She saw a group of intent faces. The Master of the Revels was nodding gently. One of the clowns was weeping a little. There was an expression of awe on Shakespeare's face.

Viola looked at him.

'By God,' said Shakespeare, speaking almost to himself. 'I had genius then.'

Viola looked at Burbage.

'Very good, boy,' said Burbage, 'but a little less passion.'

Sir Walter Raleigh sat at his desk before his open lattice overlooking his garden, writing a poem. He was wearing a cloak of rich satin with an historic occasion painted on its back. It showed Queen Elizabeth, carried in a palanquin and surrounded by her entire court, presenting him with a bed.

The artist had done his work well. You could see Master Bacon quite plainly.

All around the desk lay crumpled pieces of paper. But Sir Walter's face wore a pleased expression.

> 'Give me my scallop-shell of quiet,
> My staff of faith to walk upon,
> My scrip of joy, immortal diet,
> My bottle of Salvation,
> My gown of glory, hope's true gauge,
> And thus I'll take my pilgrimage.'

By God! he was writing well now.

'My Gown of Glory.'

He stroked it lovingly. What an effect it was going to make when he entered to greet his guests at the ceremonial tasting of the first potato. Philip would be impressed, Drake would be stunned, and Gloriana would grant him that monopoly in performing bears he had been hankering after. He could almost feel sorry for poor old Essex in his wretched cloak of gold.

Time for a rest and a smoke. He reached for his long pipe. He filled it with weed. He lit up and puffed – long, luxurious puffs.

In the garden, his new servant, busily clipping bushes, smelt the Virginia tobacco. Rack and Thumbscrews! His Master was on fire!

He grabbed a bucket. He ran.

At the Bankside order had been restored. That is not to say that the Theatre was completed, the costumes ironed out, or the new speeches written and learnt. But tempers had been soothed, actors and stage-hands sent about their business, Sir Philip Sidney had tactfully remembered an appointment, and Master Bacon, extricated from his beam, was being coaxed into a good humour by the busy playwright.

It was a simple matter to coax Master Bacon into a good humour. All you had to do was to listen and admire. It was difficult this time, for Bacon was busy teaching him all about stagecraft, but Shakespeare thought he could manage by concentrating on polishing up Wolsey's speech in his head. Master Bacon could, with a sneering whisper, curdle the commission of his new play for Gloriana. He must be placated and beguiled. He must be made to feel important. Blast the fellow – one must treat him as an equal – almost.

'This,' said Shakespeare with a wave of the arm, 'is one of our most extravagant productions.'

Bacon shrugged. 'It is still Hal Eight,' he said. 'Old stuff.'

'I have written two new speeches,' said Shakespeare with some heat, 'and if it were not for untimely visitors, Master Bacon – but no matter.' He pulled himself up. 'We have conceived the production on a lavish scale and there are many new scenes.'

Bacon smiled. By a lucky chance he had been jotting down a few notes on the theatre and now he could use them to impress. He pulled out a parchment and held it negligently in his hand.

'Alterations of Scenes,' he said, 'so be it quietly and without Noise, are Things of Great Beauty and Pleasure.'

'Thank you,' said Shakespeare. 'We have also,' he added, 'a procession of cardinals and quires placed one over the other.'

'Acting in unison,' said Bacon, 'especially in dialogues hath an extreme good grace, and the Voices would be Strong and manly, a Base and a Tenour. No Treble,' he pointed out.

'Oh,' said Shakespeare, uneasily.

'And the Ditty,' continued Bacon. 'High and Tragicall – not Nice or Daintie.'

Shakespeare shook his head. 'I doubt if the three-pennies would stand for that,' he said.

'As to the scenes,' said Bacon, now well into his stride, 'let them abound with Light, specially coloured and varied.'

Shakespeare pondered. 'I think,' he said, 'you will approve our effects with the candles in the Court scene.'

'The Colours that show best by candle-light,' said Bacon, taking a quick peep at his notes, 'are White Carnation and a kinde of Sea Water Greene.'

'We have no sea water green,' said Shakespeare sadly.

Bacon ignored him. 'And Oes or Spangs,' he went on, 'as they are of no great cost so they are of most glory. Rich embroidery,' he pointed out, 'it is lost.' He waved it aside.

Viola Compton, who had been hovering about the stage unable to decide which focus of fascination to attach herself to, came rushing up.

117

'Look,' she said, pointing to a line of heralds. 'Real trumpets.'

Interrupted, Bacon glared at her.

'These things,' he said in some annoyance, 'are but Toyes to come amongst such serious observations.'

Obadiah Croke shuffled diffidently up.

'Not now, Obadiah,' said Shakespeare. 'I will read you my grave-digger's scene some other time. I have almost got round to writing it,' he added encouragingly.

'It is not that, Master Will,' said Obadiah. 'I bring you a letter from your wife.'

'Oh!' said Shakespeare. He stuffed it into his pocket and smiled at Obadiah.

'I have thought out some pretty business for you with a skeleton,' he said.

Viola was quite shocked. She had known that actors were absorbed in their work, but surely a man ought to take just a little more interest in a letter from his wife. Why this was exactly the way that husbands behaved at Court. She wondered what Master Will's wife was like. Somehow it had never occurred to her that he might be married.

'I trust,' said Obadiah, who had failed to observe that Shakespeare had not opened the letter, 'that Ann Hathaway is well.'

Bacon looked up sharply. The exquisitely phrased sentence he was trying to sort out of his notes slipped back into its muddle.

'Ann Hathaway!' he said. 'You know her?'

Obadiah Croke opened his mouth. The next moment he had seized his toe and hopped away.

'Ann Hathaway,' said Shakespeare casually. 'Why, I know her very well. But,' he added quickly, 'I have not heard from her since she changed her cottage.'

'The Courier,' said Obadiah hopping back, 'tells me they had a great deal of trouble moving-in a bed.' He broke off in some astonishment to look at Master Bacon, who had picked up his toe and was hopping.

118

'How clumsy I am today,' said Shakespeare reproving himself.

Burbage, distraught and his hair ruffled, passed by them. He saw Viola and eyed her speculatively. She made to smooth a fold in her skirt, remembered and put her hands behind her back.

'Boy,' said Burbage. 'Come over here.'

He led her to a corner of the stage and signed to her to sit on the stool beside his table.

'Boy,' he said, 'I have decided to start you at once.'

Viola jumped up from her stool. 'At once. This afternoon!'

'Sit down,' said Burbage. 'You fidget me. I have a part for you. Do you think you can learn it in time?'

Viola trembled. Visions of being called upon to play Catherine of Aragon at the least floated before her. Could she do it? Through her hauntings of rehearsals in the upper gallery she knew most of it already, but it was one thing speaking lines in front of a mirror and quite another thing to remember them in front of an audience. Could she do it?

She must.

'Yes,' she hissed.

Burbage looked a little surprised. He rummaged among the papers on the table.

'Listen attentively, boy,' he said. 'The scene is a hall in Blackfriars where they are about to try the Queen.'

Viola swallowed. It was – it was Catherine of Aragon! She had felt it all along.

'There is a fanfare,' said Burbage, 'trumpets, sennets and cornets.'

'Real trumpets,' breathed Viola.

Burbage nodded approvingly. 'Then,' he said, 'there is a great procession.' His eye took on the look of one lost in admiration of his own production. 'First come two vergers with silver wands, next them two scribes in the habits of doctors; after them the Archbishop of Canterbury. He,' said Burbage, 'walks alone.'

Viola fidgeted. How did that speech go? 'Sir, I desire you do me right and something . . .'

'He is followed,' said Burbage lusciously, 'by the bishops of Lincoln, Ely, Rochester and St Asaph. I'm a bit nervous about St Asaph,' he added. 'Next them, at some small distance, follows a gentleman bearing the purse with the great seal and a cardinal's hat, then two priests bearing each a silver cross, then two gentlemen bearing two great silver pillars. Cardinals, noblemen, and the Sergeant-at-Arms bearing a silver mace. Then,' said Burbage, dropping his voice dramatically, 'the King takes his place under the cloth of State.'

'And then,' breathed Viola, 'the Queen takes her place some distance from the King.'

Jerked out of his vision, Burbage resumed rummaging. He found a parchment and handed it across.

'Here is your part,' he said. 'Do you think you can do it?'

Viola gulped. 'I'll try,' she vowed.

She looked at the parchment. One sheet. It seemed very short for Catherine.

'You are the scribe,' said Burbage. 'You have two cues to learn.'

'Two cues,' said Viola faintly.

'Two,' said Burbage encouragingly. There was no mistake. 'You have two speeches. First you announce in a bold voice, "Henry, King of England, come into the Court!"' he looked at Viola enquiringly.

'Henry, King of England, come into the Court,' repeated Viola dutifully.

'Next,' said Burbage, 'you announce clearly so that all may hear: "Catherine, Queen of England, come into the Court."'

'Catherine, Queen of England,' said Viola miserably, 'come into the Court.'

Burbage nodded. 'A little more passion,' he said.

Meanwhile Sir Francis Bacon was still talking about stagecraft. He was talking very beautifully, very eloquently, and hardly referring to his notes at all. But Shakespeare had given up listening. He knew that if he listened he would argue, and if he argued he would lose his temper. And if he lost his temper he would lose his show at Court. And if he lost his show at Court Philip Henslowe would get it for his players. Already he had secured the Masque for the Ceremonial Tasting of the First Potato. 'Potato.' A lively word. He made a note of it, in the margin of Cardinal Wolsey's speech.

Good God, he hadn't finished it yet.

Would he never be rid of this pale, selfish, garrulous, dilettante, influential eel? No matter, he would concentrate on finishing Wolsey's speech while he was talking.

'But,' Bacon was saying, 'all is Nothing except the Roome be kept Clear and Neat.' He averted his eyes from the littered stage.

'Farewell,' muttered Shakespeare through his teeth. 'A long farewell to all my greatness.'

Over the house-humped Bridge a coloured cloud was approaching. It was made up of dancing prentices, gaping loafers slouching curiously along, a scatter of rude little boys and a great deal of dust. In the centre of it a team of horses were hauling two cannon.

Cannon! It was rumoured that these were the very cannon that had been set up to repel the Armada. The crowd had been following them for some miles. Now they followed them into the yard of the Globe Theatre.

The driver's face wore a satisfied smirk as he pulled the horses to a sidling halt. Only this morning he had been sacked from Sir Walter Raleigh's service for a perfectly natural mistake, and here he was with a new job already. You couldn't keep a good man down.

He cracked his whip jauntily. Then he pulled hurriedly at the reins. He had overlooked the effect on the horses.

He whistled to the fringe of faces that were looking

out at him from an almost finished lattice.

'Is Master Burbage within?' he called.

A clown came curiously out. He looked at the cannon. He beckoned.

More clowns came out. They beckoned. Soon the whole cast and several carpenters were clustering round the cannon while Will Kempe was trying to balance himself on a barrel.

'What is this?' asked Shakespeare from the doorway. 'Cannon – by God!' He pounced.

'Now,' he said happily, 'I can write a play about the Siege of Calais.'

Burbage pushed his way through the crowd.

'Cannon,' he said delighted. 'Why, they're the very thing for our performance this afternoon. Drag them in, boys. Careful, Master Kempe,' he called as the clowns rushed to obey his order.

The driver made frantic efforts to unhook his team, while the clowns got hopelessly mixed up with the horses.

The motion proved too much for Will Kempe. He gave up his attempts at balancing, planted himself astride and slid down the barrel.

A thought struck Burbage. He turned to Shakespeare.

'By the way, Will,' he said. 'I wonder who ordered them?'

'I forgot,' said the driver. He unbuttoned his jersey. 'I have a letter for you.' He rummaged and produced a piece of parchment.

Burbage unrolled it. Shakespeare looked curiously over his shoulder.

'Jtm. Pd for goinge by water. dii.j.'

They looked at one another. They shrugged.

'Try the other side,' suggested Shakespeare.

Burbage turned the parchment. There, in a fine flowing handwriting, an inscription was written.

122

To Master Burbij:
    Wyth Beste Wyshes for a Plausant Oppenynge
    Pfmnce.

PHILIP HENSLOWE.

Burbage blinked.

'He's spelt your name wrong,' said Shakespeare disapprovingly.

Chapter Nine

The public, like coloured currants, had sifted themselves all over the Bankside and were milling and
sieving round the Globe Theatre. Over London Bridge
and across the commons more coloured atoms came
jolting and even galloping. From St Paul's, from
Westminster, from the Temple, and as far back as
Cheapside, Dick Burbage was draining London of its
inhabitants. Clearly the opening was going to be a riot.

Dressed as Hal Eight, Burbage was bestriding his
little world, a Tudor Colossus. Contrary to dark
prophecy, the Globe Theatre was erected and complete
to the last drop of glue. Indeed, as the first client
arrived to proffer his threepence the gatherer had just
hammered the last nail into the box he held out to
receive it. And the early arrivals among the
groundlings were rewarded with a fascinating glimpse
of carpenters gathering their belongings and being
chased off the stage by an urging Hal Eight.

The crowd at the gates thickened. Slowly the theatre
began to fill. This was because there were only two
gates for the public to get in at and also because one of
the gatherers had arrived with no change. Outside
horse-holders were doing a brisk trade. One enterpris-
ing Elizabethan, though already in charge of three,
decided he could hold a fourth – an unruly black mare
with a nasty look in her eye.

He couldn't.

Inside the Lords' boxes began to fill. From the back of the stage excited chirrups could be heard from the musicians' gallery. The three galleries were agog with bobbing heads while the groundlings amused themselves by singing madrigals.

In his room, ignoring the curious heads peering at him over the half-built wall, Shakespeare was working furiously. Only one speech left to write!

Now a pickpocket, with greedy fingers, got to work among the groundlings. He moved furtively from impassioned tenor to concentrating bass, taking here a handkerchief, there a copper. But he came to grief over a golden dubloon in the pouch of a pirate singing a sea shanty. Hardly altering a note the pirate spun round, grabbed his wrist and handed him over to justice.

The groundlings were all for tying him to the cannon. But Burbage would have none of it. The cannon, he promised them, was going to be fired. So they contented themselves with the usual punishment for pickpocketing and tied the thief to posts of the platform that supported the raised apron stage. Here he was doomed to stay for the whole of the performance, like it or not, with his back to the clowns and stage effects, unable to dodge any missile that might be hurled at him.

In the most magnificent of the Lords' boxes, hardly smelling of glue at all, Burbage had set out a stool of honour. It was for Philip Henslowe, the generous donor of the stage effects. But Henslowe had been detained. Instead, he had sent an evil-looking oaf, who was an expert in firing cannon.

He thought of everything.

A cloud drifted over the sky. The groundlings looked up at it warily. But those in the galleries felt superior. Even though the rain poured down they had their cover.

From the flagstaff a pennant fluttered. From the turrets four trumpeters sounded a fanfare. Martial music burst from the musicians' gallery.

From the wings Prologue came striding on.

He looked at the audience. He frowned at them.

'I come no more to make you laugh,' he told them ominously.

The show was on.

Philip Henslowe closed his account book with a snap.

> *Lent upon iij payer of worsted stockens the (ii) 25 od decembr 3 to be payed with one moneth next the some of . . . xs.*

From the way he had been lending money to his company lately one might imagine he was doing it for love of them. True, he had always lent them money, but today he did not seem able to concentrate on getting a fair rate of interest for it. All day long he had been lending too much and too cheaply, and all because of Burbage's first night.

He hoped the accident would go off all right.

He could not pretend to himself that the plot was watertight. As conspiracies go he had thought of many neater ones. Firing a cannon to fire a theatre involved a strong element of risk. The gunner's aim might be bad. The tampin or stopple might fail to lodge in the thatch.

But he must concentrate. He must keep his accounts in order. He opened his book.

> *John Henslowe. Layd owt mony to by hime a clocke. xvij.*

He looked at his nephew's account and sighed. Who did the spendthrift think he was? Sir Walter Raleigh?

On the stage Anne Boleyn was talking to an old lady. She was talking slowly and taking up as much time as possible with business, for she knew that the scene that followed took a lot of preparation. Not only were there the cannon, with a strange man who had not been at rehearsal in charge of them, but the entire procession had to be straightened out into the correct order. Even as the old lady wheezed her responses at her, she could hear Burbage shouting off.

Burbage was getting excited again. One of the heralds had forgotten his trumpet, while the sounder of the sennet was complaining that he could not get a note out of it. A verger was having a quarrel with a cardinal over the order of precedence, the Bishop of Ely, who was doubling with the Earl of Surrey, was complaining that Master Will had forgotten to give him time to change. Catherine of Aragon had entered into a bout of fisticuffs, and Cardinal Wolsey was conning his farewell. And the gunner kept on rushing up and asking whether he couldn't fire his cannon into Anne Boleyn's apartment.

Viola had got herself into a terrible state. She knew her lines – both of them.

'Henry, King of England, come into the Court.'

So far so good.

'Catherine, Queen of England, come into the Court.'

Word perfect.

But would she remember to get them in the right order?

Anne Boleyn had finished telling the sceptical old lady that she did not wish to be a Queen. The boy-players made their exit to a smattering of applause.

Heavily disguised as the Bishop of St Asaph, Will Shakespeare nodded. On the whole the scene had gone better than he had expected. Now for the procession.

This was going to smash 'em.

This was going to knock 'em cold.

This was going to bowl 'em over like a row of ninepins.

This was going to set the house on fire!

If Catherine of Aragon let him down he'd wring her neck.

> '*Which of your friends have I not strove to love*
> *Although I knew he were mine enemy?*'

'If you don't get that line over,' he scowled, 'I'll brain you.'

Viola started. She redoubled her efforts. 'Henry, King of England . . .' she muttered frantically.

There was a fanfare of trumpets, the procession moved ponderously forward and out onto the apron.

There was a gasp from the groundlings, a roar of applause.

The Bishop of St Asaph glared at the gunner fussing around the cannon. Let him as much as drown one syllable of those lines he had polished up . . .

The gunner was taking aim.

Cardinals, Bishops, Ushers and Attendants paced majestically to their places on the stage. The Bishop of St Asaph tripped and collided with the Sergeant-at-Arms, but that was only because he was looking over his shoulder at something that was happening in the wings.

Henry the Eighth, waiting to make his entrance, shook his fist at him. Just like Will to ruin his own scene. Would there were some way to stop him acting.

'Count twenty,' he hissed at the gunner in charge of the cannon, 'and then fire.'

The gunner spat.

Henry the Eighth ignored him. He stepped grandly forth onto the stage.

The cannon went off.

'Too early,' thought Henry the Eighth crossly. 'Never gave the groundlings time to cheer.'

The cannon had gone off. The noise had half-deafened the audience, but such was Burbage's presence that they never noticed that the tampin or stopple had lodged in the thatch. Only the gunner spat on his hands and made off quickly.

Moving with measured tread, Henry the Eighth took his place under the canopy of state. The two cardinals disposed themselves one on each hand.

A thin plume of smoke was rising from the thatch. The groundlings had no eyes for it.

For now Catherine of Aragon, clad all in black, was crossing the stage.

The Bishop of St Asaph looked at her approvingly. It was not for nothing that he had stormed at her during rehearsal. She moved quite well for a lad of eighteen.

The thatch was beginning to burn merrily. But the enthralled audience never took their eyes off the stage.

'Let silence be commanded,' said Cardinal Wolsey.

But the wood was beginning to crackle. The actors gazed at one another uneasily. What could be the matter with the groundlings? What were they muttering to one another about? Some of them were not even looking at the stage!

Viola's knees felt like waving corn-stalks. Hal's speech was nearly over. At any moment now the Cardinal would give her her cue.

'Be't so,' said Cardinal Wolsey. 'Proceed.'

Which was it? Oh God! Which was it?

'Henry, King of England,' piped the scribe. 'Come into the Court.'

There now! She had got it out.

But, dear God, she had never thought it would have such an effect. The whole house was in an uproar. The nobles were on their feet, the groundlings were scuffling and pushing, and even the actors had got out of formation.

She looked up helplessly.

Dear God! The theatre was on fire.

The Globe Theatre was on fire. You could see it from the other side of the City.

The audience, streaming out of Henslowe's theatre, commented on it, marvelled at it, and made for it to a man.

The thatch and timber burnt quickly. A ring of flame licked its way round the walls. It was indeed a miracle that the audience and actors had got themselves out uninjured through the two small gateways. There was only one casualty and that to a pair of trousers. Even the pickpocket tied to the posts had been liberated in time to ply his trade outside.

Onlookers and actors had joined themselves into a chain, filling buckets from the river, passing them up and down, emptying them onto the flames, waiting hopefully for the orange of the flames first to turn blue, then die down, then to disappear and, disappointed, calling for more water.

The clowns had contrived to drag out a chest. They were bending over it now, examining the contents, seeing what each had saved with the reflection of the flames flickering over them.

Burbage, still dressed as Hal Eight, had been working like a lunatic saving his people and salvaging his goods. Now he leant wearily against the cannon.

'We can do no more,' he said. 'Let it burn.'

Beside him a soot-covered, breathless and very tired Bishop of St Asaph sighed and shook his head.

'A pity,' he said. 'The play was going so well, too.'

'Poor Will,' said Burbage. 'All your work wasted. My poor actors – how can I pay them now? Poor Master Pyk,' he turned to the white-faced Viola, who was trying very hard to keep from crying: 'Your first lines and no-one listening to them.'

Viola sobbed.

'Master Burbage!' Philip Henslowe, followed by his son-in-law, thrust his way through the throng. 'I have only just heard. What a misfortune!'

'Tragic,' said Edward Alleyn.

Burbage forced a smile. There was nothing to be said.

'How did it happen?' asked Henslowe, all sympathy.

'It was the tampin,' said Burbage.

'The stopple,' corrected Shakespeare.

'The stopple,' said Burbage, 'lodged in the thatch.'

'The tampin,' corrected Shakespeare.

'It set fire to the thatch,' they agreed.

'Unfortunate,' said Henslowe.

'Tragic,' said Edward Alleyn.

Burbage managed a smile. 'We must be thankful it was no worse,' he said. 'No lives were lost, and nothing of value has been left to burn.'

'Good God,' cried Shakespeare. He dashed away.

'Will,' cried Burbage, as he vanished into the flames. 'You must be mad. Come back! Come back at once! Will, do you hear? Come back!'

'He will burn,' said Viola. 'Why did you let him go?'

'He is possessed,' said Henslowe. He fumbled for his book of spells.

A heavy beam fell with a crash to the ground. There was a shower of sparks. Through them dashed a wild figure, uttering cries of triumph and brandishing a piece of parchment.

'See,' he cried, thrusting the parchment into Burbage's hands. 'I have saved it.'

'Love's Labour Won,' read Burbage. 'Act I. Scene . . .' The rest was burnt.

Burbage looked at his playwright. His cheeks were black, his hands were blistered, but the smile on his face was one of child-like content.

'Oh, Will,' he said. 'You are a fool.'

Chapter Ten

'Well, well, well,' said Philip Henslowe. 'So, Master Borne, you have had your portrait painted.'

William Borne nodded gloomily. 'It seemed a good idea at the time,' he muttered.

'And now,' said Henslowe sunnily, 'your wife doesn't like it, I won't have it outside my theatre, and Tassoe is pressing you for payment.'

William Borne nodded again. 'And I have no money,' he said.

Henslowe leant back and put the tips of his fingers together.

'Well, well, well,' he said. 'We must see what we can do about it – eh, Edward?'

Edward Alleyn, who had been admiring himself in a robe of Hercules, looked over his shoulder.

'What's that?' he asked vaguely.

'See,' said Henslowe, 'my son-in-law agrees with me. Very well, Master Borne, you shall have your money. There!' With a magnificent gesture he flung a handful of silver on the table.

William Borne blinked at the pile. 'At what interest?' he asked suspiciously.

'No interest at all, my dear fellow, no interest at all,' said Henslowe largely. 'Only too delighted to oblige a member of my company. All pull together. Identity of interests, one large happy family,' he gloated.

William Borne blinked again. He saw the money

lying on the table. He concentrated on the one concrete fact in this phantasmagoria of miracles.

He grabbed it and ran.

Still smiling, Henslowe picked up his pen.

'Lent vnto Wm Borne for to geue the paynter in earneste of his picter the some of   vs.'

Edward Alleyn came strutting past. Henslowe actually smiled at him. Today he came very near to liking his son-in-law.

'Well,' said Edward Alleyn. 'We've settled old Burbage now.'

Henslowe allowed the 'we' to pass.

'Burnt to the ground,' he said. 'Not a timber left.'

'No stage,' gloated Edward Alleyn. 'No dressing-rooms.'

'No box office,' said Henslowe, 'and I'll be buying back those cannon cheap.'

They rubbed their hands.

'Poor Dick Burbage,' mused Henslowe. 'It's tough on him when you come to think of it.'

'Indeed it is,' agreed Alleyn. 'He has a fair degree of talent too,' he added generously.

'A useful actor,' agreed Henslowe. 'Half a mind to offer him a job.'

'I wouldn't do that if I were you,' said Alleyn quickly. 'Difficult to work with,' he explained.

'Ah,' said Henslowe. He frowned. 'A pity. I would have liked to do something for the son of my old friend. No theatre! What a tragedy.' He sighed. 'Poor Dick.'

'And no costumes,' said Alleyn. 'I hear they were all burnt. Poor Dick.' He sighed.

'And no playwright. Poor Dick,' said Henslowe. 'For now Shakespeare will certainly come to us.' He shook his head.

'Poor Dick,' said Alleyn. 'And no company. Already two of them have come to me to beg for parts, poor fellows!'

'No actors,' said Henslowe sadly. 'Poor Dick.'

'Poor Dick,' said Alleyn. 'And no friends. They are leaving him like rats.' He took out his handkerchief.

'And no credit,' said Henslowe. He wept.

'I am depressed,' said Edward Alleyn. 'Let us go and drink some ale.'

'A good idea,' said Henslowe. He blew his nose hard. 'Just one moment.'

He made an entry in his diary.

'Leant Edwd Alleyn for to bye a robe to playe hercolas in the some of   xxxxs.'

'Cheap at the price,' said Alleyn. 'See how it becomes me.' He flourished it. 'I shall wear it in the Masque of Hercules for the Ceremonial Tasting of the First Potato,' he boasted, 'and I wager it will have no need to blush before the cloak of My Lord Essex himself.'

Henslowe looked at him. 'Well, well, well,' he observed, returning to abnormal, 'we will say no more about it.' He rose to his feet. 'Come, let us go to the Mermaid Tavern.'

'Not the Mermaid,' said Edward Alleyn with marked distaste. 'Ye Olde,' he pointed out.

'"Tis a very fine eleventh-century inn,' said Philip Henslowe. 'And what is more the landlord owes me money. Come.'

They went.

In the centre of the Mermaid a hack writer was scribbling furiously. He had to get his account of the burning of the Globe Theatre ready for the printer next week.

'No longer since than yesterday while Burbage his companie were acting at the Globe the play of Hen 8. And there shooting of certayne chambers in way of triumph, the fire catch'd, and fastened upon the hatch of the house and there burned so furiously as it consumed the whole house and all in less than two hours, the people having enough to save themselves.'

In another corner Sir Henry Wotten was writing to his nephew. He always found writing to his nephew difficult, but today he had been greatly helped by a timely fire that had destroyed the Globe Theatre and given him matter for a page or so.

'Now to let matters of state sleep. I will entertain you at the present with what hath happened at the Bankside. The King's Players had a new play representing some principal pieces of the Reign of Henry the 8th which was set forth with many extraordinary circumstances of Pomp and Majesty, even to the matting of the stage, the Knights of the Order, with their George and Garter, the Guards with their embroidered coats and the like sufficient in truth within a while to make Greatness very familiar if not ridiculous. Now, certain canons being shot off, some of the Paper or other stuff wherewith some of them were stopped, did light on the Thatch, where being thought at first but an idle smoak, and their eyes more attentive to the show, it kindled inwardly and ran round like a train, consuming the whole House to the very ground.

'This was the Fatal period of that virtuous Fabrique, where nothing did perish but Wood and Straw and a few forsaken cloakes. Only one man had his breeches set on fire, that would perhaps have broyled him if he had not by the benefit of provident witt put it out with bottle ale.'

At a table surrounded by deep drinkers a young man was biting his quill. He, too, was writing about the fire, but ale had made him ambitious and he was trying to express it in verse.

'All you that please to understand
Come listen to my story . . .' he was muttering.

At another table John Chamberlain was writing to Sir Ralph Windwood.

'But the burning of the Globe or Playhouse on the Bankside cannot escape you which fell out by a peal of chambers that I know not upon what occasion, were to be used in the play, the tampin or stopple of one of them lighting in the thatch that covered the house did burn it to the ground in less than two hours, with a dwelling-house adjoining, and it was a great marvel and fair grace of God that the people had little harm having but two narrow doors to get out at.'

Watching the concentrated quills wagging around him, Edmund Howe, consuming his seventh glass of ale, had a sudden pang of conscience. What sort of historian was he, sitting at the Mermaid, drinking ale, just as though the Globe Theatre had never burnt down at all! Just as though he had never promised Master John Stow that he would conscientiously continue and augment with matters foreign and domestique, ancient and modern, the *Annals and General Chronicles of England.* 'You began it, John, and I will finish it,' he had vowed. They had shaken hands on it. And here he was drinking ale!

He put his pewter on the table and called loudly for quill and parchment. As an afterthought he called for more ale. Soon he was deep in composition.

'If I should have set down the several terms and damages done this year by fire, in the very many and sundry places of this Kingdom, it would contain many a sheet of paper, as is evident by the incessante collections throughout the Churches of this realm for such as have been spoyled by fire. Also upon S. Peter's day last, the playhouse or Theatre called the Globe, upon the Bankside neare London, by negligent discharging of a peal of ordinance close to the south side, the Thatch thereof took fire and the wind sudainely disperst the Flame round about and in a very short space the whole building was quite consumed and

136

no man hurt, the house being filled with people to behold the play, viz. *of Henry the 8.'*

Edmund Howe looked at his manuscript and pursed his lips. There was something definitely wrong about it. He held it up to the light, he held it upside down, he examined it from all angles. He shook his head. It was still wrong.

He decided to get another opinion.

He kicked over his stool and made an impressive progress to a table where a red-faced man was writing intently.

'Ben,' he said. 'How do you spell suddainely?'

Interrupted in his composition Ben Jonson glared.

'I don't know,' he said. 'Ask anyone. Ask Shakespeare.'

Edmund Howe continued to waver above him. He might be drunk but he knew when he was being insulted.

'Master Jonson,' he said acidly. 'You are asking the impossible. William Shakespeare is not here.'

'He will be sooner or later,' said Jonson. 'You mark my words.'

The door swung open. But it was not Will Shakespeare who came in with such a doleful air. It was Sir Walter Raleigh. Without any cloak whatever.

From the other end of the tavern a sailor noticed him. He was a very fat sailor and there was a look of speculation in his eye.

Sir Walter Raleigh glanced moodily around the room. How he hated everybody in it! A fine hand-painted cloak ruined!

'Good-evening,' said Master Howe, swaying slightly before him. 'How, in your opinion, would you spell suddainely?'

Sir Walter considered. 'S-A-D,' he began doubtfully.

Edmund Howe waved him to silence. 'Do not

137

trouble yourself,' he said. 'I perceive that you are not Master Shakespeare.'

Raleigh stared.

'But do not be perturbed on my account,' added Howe quickly. 'He is coming – I have been assured of that.' He bowed. 'I go now to wait for him.'

He steered off and settled suddenly on a stool in the doorway.

The door opened. Edmund Howe rose expectantly to his feet.

But it was Sir Philip Sidney. Muttering and disappointed Edmund Howe sat down again. Another minute and he was fast asleep.

Sir Philip Sidney looked around him. He sighted the cloakless Raleigh and smiled joyfully to himself.

'Ah, Walter,' he said. 'Come to drown your sorrows in drink? I hear it was such a beautiful cloak, too,' he sympathized.

Raleigh glared. 'I've come to talk to Master Ben,' he said coldly. 'Only sensible man among you.'

Ben Jonson pushed aside his composition. 'Sit down, Master Raleigh,' he invited, 'and drown your sorrows in good Mermaid ale.'

'Drown!' said Raleigh. He did not seem to care for the word.

At the table surrounded by deep drinkers the young man had stopped chewing his quill and was writing like one possessed.

At Ben Jonson's table Sir Philip Sidney was taking the sulking Raleigh to task.

'Stop brooding, Walter,' he was saying. 'There are worse misfortunes in the world. Take the Burbages.'

'Poor Burbage,' said Ben Jonson. 'He's ruined.'

'So is my cloak,' said Sir Walter Raleigh.

'A terrible fire,' said Ben Jonson. 'All the water in the Thames could not have put it out.'

'They brought me one bucket,' spat Raleigh, 'and that was too much.'

'Cheer up, Walter,' said Sidney. 'You can always get another cloak.'

'Burbage cannot get another theatre,' Ben Jonson pointed out.

'It was hand-painted,' said Raleigh obstinately.

'Burbage,' said Ben Jonson, 'built the Globe Theatre almost with his own hands. I went down to help him one day.'

'How did you fare?' asked Sidney, interested.

Ben Jonson fidgeted a bit. 'Well, I somehow never quite got round to helping him,' he admitted. 'You see,' he explained, 'I started arguing with Will about a sonnet.'

There was a shout from the deep drinking-table. The poet had ceased writing and jumped on it.

'All you that please to understand,' he declaimed,
'Come, listen to my story,
To see Death with his rakering brand,
Mongst such an auditorye,
Regarding neither Cardinal's might,
Nor yet the rugged face of Henry the eighth.'

There was a stir round the doorway. The rugged face of Henry the Eighth appeared in it. Behind him came the Bishop of St Asaph. Taking care not to disturb the sleeper by the door they advanced upon Ben Jonson.

The room was awed to complete silence. How to chatter in the face of such great grief?

The silence was broken with a thwack.

It was Burbage walloping Ben Jonson on the back.

'What ho! you beer-swilling old dragon,' he roared.

Shakespeare's arm was already raised to thwack Sir Walter Raleigh. Just in time he pulled it back.

'Good evening, Master Raleigh,' he cried, trying his best to imitate Burbage's deep boom. 'Come to drown your sorrows?'

Raleigh leapt to his feet.

'Too much of water have I had, O Shakespeare!' he announced passionately.

'A pentameter,' said Shakespeare approvingly. 'Iambs. Anapestic substitution.' He made a note with much flourish.

The tavern gasped. Here indeed was the right kind of courage to bear outrageous fortune.

'Boy,' boomed Burbage. 'Ale. For everyone,' he added largely.

'You are very generous tonight,' said Ben Jonson.

'And why not?' roared Burbage, draining his pewter and holding it out for more. 'The doctor has forbidden me ale, but what do I care tonight? Tonight I would drink with the whole world, I would drink with you, I would drink with Master Polonius, I would even drink with Philip Henslowe. Ah, here he comes.' He waved a welcoming arm. '*À moi*, you plotting old weazel!'

Philip Henslowe looked slightly surprised. He advanced warily.

'He called you a weazel,' hissed Edward Alleyn, advancing warily behind him.

'Hist,' said Henslowe. 'Admit nothing.'

They came forward.

'Drink, Master Henslowe,' boomed Burbage, passing a pewter. 'Refresh yourself at my expense. You will not even have to make an entry in your account book.'

Edward Alleyn sniggered. His father-in-law's account book was easily the most unpleasant feature of his life.

'Drink deep, Master Henslowe,' said Shakespeare. 'Fear not. It is no Greek who brings you this gift.'

Henslowe blinked. He had always been given to understand that Master Will was weak on the classical side.

'Drink deep, Master Alleyn,' said Ben Jonson, puzzled, but unwilling to be left out of the conversation any longer. 'It is good ale – I can vouch for its quality, even if I do not understand why it is offered.'

140

'Maybe,' said Sir Walter Raleigh sourly, 'they have poisoned it.'

Edward Alleyn dropped his pewter. Henslowe, whose nerves were stronger, merely stopped drinking.

'I have great news,' boomed Burbage, clambering on to the table. 'I want the tavern to drink a toast with me.'

There was a pushing back of stools. The tavern had arrived at its feet. The pot-boy tried to prop up Master Howe, asleep by the doorway, still waiting for Shakespeare to arrive, but the task was beyond him.

'Gentlemen,' said Burbage, lifting up his pewter. 'I give you my new playhouse, I have acquired the Whitefriars Theatre.'

They drank.

If ever a look said 'Silly old bungler – I told you so,' it was the look which Edward Alleyn shot at his father-in-law.

'Great news,' said Ben Jonson, clapping Shakespeare on the back. 'I rejoice for you. There is not a playwright in the theatre,' he assured him, 'whose talent pleases me more. Provided,' he added severely, 'you keep off sonnets.'

Shakespeare smiled. 'And you, Master Jonson,' he said, 'take my advice and stop writing plays. *Volpone!*' he roared.

'Congratulations, Master Burbage,' said Henslowe, holding out his hand. 'I am very glad to hear of your good fortune.' Already his conspirator's brain was turning over at high speed seeking for schemes to wreck it.

'Congratulations, Master Burbage,' said Sir Philip Sidney. 'Raleigh and I will come to your opening. In a new cloak – eh, Raleigh?'

The chaff was getting on Raleigh's nerves. 'Never again,' he muttered, 'shall I go forth without my cloak.'

'C-L-O-K-K,' muttered Shakespeare.

'Not in a sonnet, Will,' warned Ben Jonson.

But Shakespeare was already searching round for parchment and quill. 'It is the very line I needed to begin one – ah!' He pounced on the blank side of Jonson's composition.

'Not that, Will,' said Ben Jonson quickly. 'I don't want you to read that.'

Shakespeare promptly turned it over. 'What is it?' he asked. 'A play?'

Ben Jonson fidgeted. 'No, Will,' he said. 'It is an epitaph.'

'My epitaph?' said Shakespeare.

He read it.

> 'This figure that thou here seest put,
> It was for gentle Shakespeare cut;
> Wherein the graver had a strife
> With Nature to outdo the life:
> O, could he have but drawn his wit
> As well in brass, as he hath hit
> His face: the Print would then surpass
> All, that was ever writ in brass.
> But, since he cannot, Reader, look,
> Not on his Picture, but his Book.'

He read it again. He frowned.

'Is it not good?' asked Ben Jonson uneasily.

'It is good,' said Shakespeare. 'But untimely.'

Out in the courtyard the prentice boys were waiting, lovely lads singing to tavern lattices. Their voices, like fledgling bells, came floating through the open window and hushed the babble of congratulation that had been surging round Burbage.

> 'Drink to me only with thine eyes
> And I will pledge with mine.'

'Listen,' said Ben Jonson. He pushed aside his pewter.

The voices sang on.

> 'I sent thee late a rosy wreath
> Not so much honouring thee

142

As giving it a hope that there
It could not withered be.
But thou thereon didst only breathe
And sendst it back to me
Since when it grows and smells, I swear,
Not of itself but thee.'

The voices died away.

'O rare Ben Jonson,' said Shakespeare. He was weeping.

Ben Jonson nodded sadly

'God,' he said. 'What genius I had then!'

Now it was growing late. In twos and threes the guests had departed from the Mermaid. Now there were only a few groups left and Edmund Howe dozing in the doorway. The despairing pot-boy had long since given up all attempts to wake him.

Sir Walter Raleigh had elected to stay behind. A mood of melancholy had his simple soul in its grasp. What was the good of anything? Everybody was happy except him. Burbage had his new theatre, Sir Philip Sidney had a new joke. It was even rumoured that Bacon was going to get his bed. And he had nothing. Not even a cloak. He felt as though he would never get a cloak. He kicked moodily at a stool and contemplated a sonnet to Despair.

The fat sailor in the corner, who had been watching Raleigh since his entrance, decided that his moment had come. He walked over and bowed.

'Master,' he said. 'I am newly arrived from the Flemish coast in a ship laden with many rich materials.'

Like a flash Sir Walter Raleigh was himself again.

'Show me,' he said.

With the most matter-of-fact air in the world the sailor began to undress himself. He took off his jerkin, he took off another. He was wrapped all round with plum-coloured plush.

143

'Ah,' breathed Sir Walter.

Thrusting one end of the roll into Raleigh's hands the sailor began to unwind himself. Farther and farther towards the other end of the room he progressed, while Raleigh lovingly gathered in the rich material.

The sailor came back. He was now a medium thin sailor. Sir Walter Raleigh threw him a bag of silver, folded his purchase tenderly, and with the air of one who takes his loved one to him, bore it away into the night.

In the doorway Master Howe sat up with a jerk. He looked round the empty inn. What a long time Master Shakespeare was coming.

He went to sleep again.

Chapter Eleven

All over London there was only one topic of conversation. It was not the unrest in Ireland – the public was tired of that. It was not the rebellion in Scotland, for was not the Crown practically secured for their James VI, still hiding in France in case it wasn't. It was not the rumour that Spain was trying to build a new Armada. It was not that the plotting Walsingham had over-reached himself in Holland – they had been waiting for that from the moment they heard he went there. It was not even the whisper that Bacon, having by skilled legal circumnavigation saved the Crown an annuity on a citizen since beheaded, was going to get a bed at last. No, it was none of these things that had caused heads to nod, mouths to water and a crowd to gather outside the Guildhall.

It was, in fact, the Ceremonial Tasting of the First Potato.

The entire capital was one vast stomach. It was rumoured that after the flower of England had been regaled, Sir Walter Raleigh was going to release some supplies to the poor outside the gates. Optimists had even brought their platters with them.

It would not be long now.

Since early morning idlers had been arriving in ones and twos, by afternoon the trickle had become a torrent and now it had congealed into a rabble. Even

Gloriana's Progress to Tilbury had hardly brought out a greater company.

In a candle-lit room in the Guildhall, before a great mirror, a famous figure was being arrayed and raising all hell about it.

'Where is my rouge pot?' called a querulous voice.

There was a patting-in of too high a colour, a wiping-off of too much cream, and a starting all over again.

'Fetch me my busks. Lace me into them. Not so tight, you fool!'

The servant fumbled.

'Fetch me my robe. Hurry, you sluggard!'

The servant scuttled into the cupboard. A pantoble followed him.

The figure before the mirror threw up its arms.

'Why does everyone conspire against my looking my best tonight?' it demanded of the frescoed ceiling.

The candles guttered.

The servant came timidly back with an embroidered garment over his arm.

'Not that one, you fool,' screamed the figure beside itself. 'My robe of Hercolas.'

The servant sighed. Only last week he had been a hauler of cannons for Philip Henslowe and here he was, promoted to be manservant to his son-in-law.

'My pantoble,' screamed Edward Alleyn. 'I've only got one on.'

Sighing heavily, the manservant went back into the cupboard. Promotion – yes, but he was not at all sure he was going to be able to hold this job down.

The door opened. Philip Henslowe came lovingly in. On his face was an encouraging smile and his whole bearing was redolent of an impresario's idea of a bed-side manner. He looked at Edward Alleyn. His hands flew out in an ecstasy of admiration.

'Charming,' he said. 'Very charming.'

'I'm not dressed yet,' snapped Edward Alleyn. 'Can't find my pantoble. Hurry,' he cursed the wobbling behind that could be seen jutting out of the cupboard.

The behind wobbled more furiously.

'How are you feeling?' asked Henslowe, trying his hardest not to smile at the scene.

'Frightful,' said Edward Alleyn. 'Look at the material I have to put across tonight before the Flower of England and the Queen herself.'

'The Masque,' said Henslowe stiffly. 'Do not tell me that you are dissatisfied with that – it was at your request that I paid Master Jonson thirty shillings to devise it.'

Edward Alleyn waved the thirty shillings aside. 'Look at the supporting cast,' he grumbled.

Henslowe sought to change the subject. 'Burbage,' he said, 'would give his ears to play before the audience you will have tonight.'

'Burbage,' retorted Edward Alleyn sulkily, 'has a very nice new theatre.'

'He has no audience,' said Henslowe. 'It is too far for them to go. And the plague draws nearer and nearer to it. Only yesterday the Master of the Revels was telling me that if his returns do not improve he might have to consider taking away his patent.'

'Hold this candle,' said Edward Alleyn. 'I think my wig is awry.'

'Further,' said Philip Henslowe, holding up the candle-stick, 'I have this day arranged with a gang of cut-throats to waylay and rob such hardy spirits as might venture on the journey to the Whitefriars Theatre. Take my word for it,' said Philip Henslowe complacently, 'Burbage is finished.'

The manservant emerged with a pantoble. Edward Alleyn slipped it on. He stood back. He wrapped the robe of Hercolas around him. He admired himself.

'How do I look?' he gloated.

Henslowe examined him.

'Marvellous,' he said. 'But your pantobles don't match.'

*　*　*

147

'How do I look?' asked Elizabeth of England.

Lady Meanwell looked at the bald head, the scraggy neck, the blackened teeth, the grim shoulder blades.

'Wonderful,' she said.

Elizabeth of England picked up a pantoble and threw it at her.

'Fool,' she screamed, 'do you think you can deceive me with your sweet-tongued flattery? I know that I am an old hag, that none of you loves me, that you are all afraid.'

Lady Meanwell caught back a sob. She held out a whalebone stomacher. 'See,' she said, 'the waist of a stripling lad.' She laced the Queen in.

Elizabeth of England smoothed her hips.

'Not bad, Meanwell,' she said. 'Not at all bad for a woman of – ah well, no matter.'

'And now for the cheeks,' said Lady Meanwell. Deftly she patted in the rouge. 'It is not every skin,' she admired, 'that can stand this exotic colour.'

Queen Elizabeth peered into the candle-lit mirror. 'You are right there, Meanwell,' she said. ' My colouring has always been good.'

'And now the frock,' said Lady Meanwell. 'White silk with pearls,' she fondled them, 'the size of beans – a present from your beloved pirate.'

'Ah, Drake,' said Queen Elizabeth. 'My thoughtful Drake. There, Meanwell, is one who really does love me. He shall have his victuals. I shall speak to Burghley tonight – or maybe tomorrow. Come, Meanwell, help me into it.'

'And now,' said Lady Meanwell some ten minutes later, 'the coiffure.'

'I am a little doubtful about this,' admitted Elizabeth. 'Is bright red really suitable do you think?'

For once Lady Meanwell dared to speak the truth.

'Suitable, no, ma'am,' she said. 'But entirely lovable.'

Queen Elizabeth patted her on the shoulder.

'Meanwell, you whore,' she said affectionately, 'you flatter me.'

Lady Meanwell turned away to pick up a pantoble. She was crying.

'How do I look?'

The Master of the Revels woke up with a jerk. Viola Compton, the lad's disguise discarded, was dancing round the room in skirts.

'Dear me,' said the Master of the Revels, 'you remind me of pretty little Kitty Howard the night Hal asked her to dance.'

Viola took off her pantoble and threatened him with it.

'I believe,' she said, 'you are as old as the devil himself.'

'Older,' said the Master of the Revels sadly. 'Much older.'

From the banqueting kitchens of the Guildhall arose a smell. A smell unlike any of the smells known to Londoners. And Londoners were connoisseurs of smells. It was a soggy smell, a flat and depressed smell, a smell that was trying to warn you not to expect too much.

The quick-witted in the crowd nudged one another.

'The potato,' they said. 'Delicious,' they added loyally.

Sir Philip Sidney riding into the courtyard turned to Sir Christopher Hatton.

'Do you smell anything, Kit?' he asked.

Sir Christopher Hatton sniffed. He shook his head. 'I have a cold,' he explained.

The crowd cheered. Sir Philip Sidney waved a hand. He was gone.

The crowd shifted to another foot and settled down to await the next comer.

Now the guests began to arrive more quickly, the flower of the land with their women-folk beside them. Drake came with Grenville, Leicester with the Earl of Surrey, and the Earl of Southampton, elegant and scowling and alone.

149

And now the crowd became jocular. For here, asked at the last moment, but assuring each other that no-one would realize this, came the Bacon brothers.

'Greetings, Master Robert,' they shouted. 'How goes the law?'

'Greetings, Master Francis. How goes the bed?'

Sir Francis Bacon tried to look confident. It was a sorry effort. He essayed a cheerful smile.

But the crowd had lost interest in him. For here was old Father Burghley, who had England in his care and loved every mother's son of them, clad as usual in a cloak not one of them would be seen dead in. Beside him the Master of the Revels, by contrast, was a figure of splendour. As usual they were deep in conversation. What grave secrets of State occupied their attention?

'For my part,' Burghley was saying, 'I intend to bite my potato most carefully.'

But now the crowd took a deep breath. The Queen was coming.

First came the gentlemen, Barons, Earls, Knights of the Garter, all richly dressed and bare-headed. Next came the Chancellor, bearing the seals in a red silk purse, walking between two stalwarts, one of whom carried the Royal Sceptre, the other the sword of State, in a red scabbard studded with golden fleur-de-lis, point upwards.

Next, borne high on a palanquin by ten bearded pirates, came Elizabeth of England, proud and glorious, surrounded by her attendants, twenty ladies of the Court, very handsome and well-shaped and dressed in white. The Queen's bosom was uncovered, as all the English ladies had it till they married, and she had on a necklace of exceeding fine jewels. She had in her ears two pearls with very rich drops. She had red hair. Upon her head she had a small crown. She was dressed in white silk, bordered with pearls of the size of beans, and over it a mantle of black silk, shot with silver threads; instead of a chain she had an oblong collar of gold and jewels.

What a Queen! How they loved her! How they would die for her!

The crowd let out a roar.

In his tiring room at the Guildhall, Edward Alleyn was fuming. He had put on his cloak of Hercules four times and taken it off five and still the backing behind in the cupboard had been unable to produce his pantoble. True he had produced a pair of fur-lined boots, an armoured knee-cap, and a warrant for the execution of ... with the name left blank, but none of these seemed to be quite suitable to adorn his other foot.

'Hurry,' fretted Edward Alleyn, 'or I shall be late for my first entrance.'

He need not have worried. Before a Prince of England, balanced on plots and surrounded by jealousies, conspiracies and the bitterly smarting Spain, could eat, there were certain ceremonials, founded on common sense and heavily disguised with court regalia, to be observed – no matter how hungry the monarch or how appetizing the tit-bit.

First a gentleman had entered the banqueting hall bearing a rod, and along with him another who had with him a small army bearing a giant table-runner, which after they had all knelt three times with the utmost veneration they spread on the long banqueting table and, after kneeling again, they all retired from the empty room.

Then came two others, one with a rod again, the other with a salt cellar, a plate and bread. This was for the Queen. When they had knelt as the others had done and placed what was brought upon the table they, too, retired with the same ceremonies as performed by the first.

With less ceremony, but quicker, an army of salt cellars appeared on the long table. These were for the flower of England. It seemed unlikely that anyone should wish to poison them all and the seating order had been kept a secret, not so much for reasons of State, but because the hard-pressed Sir Walter had only just worked it out. He hoped it would turn out all right.

Last came an unmarried lady, we are told she was a countess, and with her a married one, we feel sure it was Lady Meanwell, bearing a tasting fork. The former was dressed in white silk, who, when she had prostrated herself three times in the most graceful manner, approached the table and rubbed the plate with bread and salt with as much awe as if the Queen had been present and not peering at her through the curtains.

When they had waited there a little while the Yeomen of the Guard entered, bare-headed and clothed in scarlet, with a golden rose upon their backs, bringing in at each turn a course of twenty-four dishes, served on plate most of it gilt – the Spanish galleon had sunk too quickly for Drake's pirates to salvage the lot.

These dishes were received by a gentleman in the same order as they were brought – he very seldom got muddled – and placed upon the table. Lady Meanwell gave to each of the guards a mouthful to eat of the particular dish he had brought for fear it should be poisoned. Lady Meanwell, who had a private feud, waited hopefully as the seventeenth guard from the left munched his tit-bit. She was ever hopeful when the seventeenth guard munched the Queen's dishes, but, as usual, he obstinately remained alive.

During the time the guard, which consisted of the tallest and stoutest men that could be found in all England (being carefully selected for this service), were bringing dinner, twelve trumpets and two kettle-drums were making the hall ring for half an hour together. Through this heartening fanfare, the Flower of England, hungrily waiting in the anteroom, bawled small talk at one another.

'I always say half an hour is too long,' shouted Burghley. 'Five minutes would be more than enough.'

'In Harry Tudor's time,' said the Master of the Revels, 'it was an hour and a half. Sometimes,' he remembered, 'Hal would get impatient and would pick up a fowl and start.'

'No manners,' said Burghley.

'Ah,' said the Master of the Revels, 'but a fine musician.'

The drums and trumpets modulated themselves into a boastful triumph.

Decoratively disposed about the anteroom, in attitudes originally learnt from posing to exigent painters, the flower of England was chatting affably in loud tones.

The potato, exciting and unknown, was the main source of discussion, but one or two scandalous sidelines were developing quite promisingly.

'I wonder,' said Sir Philip, in a loud aside to the Earl of Southampton, 'what has happened to my Lord Essex?'

'He isn't coming,' announced the well-informed Master of the Revels.

'Essex isn't coming!' The news sped round the room. Heads nodded, knowing smiles flickered from face to face, and in the corner farthest from Gloriana winks were openly exchanged.

Essex was out of favour. Gloriana was definitely displeased with him.

As the trumpeters blew themselves into a martial air, everyone was busy passing on rumours.

'Scolded like a naughty boy!'

'Banished from Court!'

'No potato for him!'

'Answered her back!'

'Beheaded if he isn't careful.'

'She's confined him to his room,' the Master of the Revels told the sulking Earl of Southampton. 'Alone.'

The Earl of Southampton scowled heavily. He was

very cross about this. He and Essex were the closest of friends. They had arranged to taste the potato together and later to compose sonnets to one another to commemorate the occasion. The Earl of Southampton had cheated slightly and commissioned his in advance. Even at this moment Will Shakespeare, invited by the Earl's influence to represent the Arts, was showing his gratitude by taking himself to a corner, ignoring the Flower of England milling around and staring with concentrated intensity at a piece of parchment. The Earl of Southampton hoped that the blare of the trumpets would not disturb the imagery of the final couplet.

He need not have worried. The milling of the aristocracy and the roll of the kettle-drums was sheer seclusion to Shakespeare accustomed to working in repertory. Besides, the sheet at which he was staring was headed:

'Love's Labour Won. Act I. Scene I. A Banqueting Hall. Blare of Trumpets.'

'Gloriana,' said the Earl of Southampton, after a hurried glance to make certain she was nowhere near him, 'is intolerable. It is never safe these days to make a private engagement for fear of State displeasure. I had arranged to sing madrigals with Essex tonight after this bear fight was over,' he finished wistfully.

'You should concentrate on a tenor less high in the Queen's favour,' said Sir Philip Sidney blandly. 'Master Bacon for instance,' he suggested.

'He is a treble,' said the Earl of Southampton stiffly.

The trumpets embarked on a new composition by Master Purcell. One of them had developed a wobble. The flower of England were too finely mannered to notice this, but from the ladies of the Court came a giggle.

The Queen turned and eyed them sharply. The Compton chit, of course!

Her anger vanished. She smiled happily to herself. What a cunning old bitch she was. She had silenced the ugly rumours of jealousy and spite that Viola's absence from Court could not fail to cause by producing her for this great occasion, but she had safeguarded herself by sending Essex out. She cackled. Poor Robert Devereux – how bewildered he had looked! But it would do the Lordling no harm to spend an evening in meditation. No doubt he would pen a sonnet to her.

She warmed to the thought.

'How well the Compton chit looks tonight,' she told Lady Meanwell.

'Her rest in the country has done her good,' said Burghley tactfully.

'It is a pleasure to have her with us again,' said Francis Drake, smoothing his beard.

'Make the most of it,' snapped the Queen. 'The wench leaves tomorrow.' She spat.

'Ah,' said Burghley. He changed the subject. 'Raleigh is very late.'

Raleigh, indeed, was very late. It was a matter of comment throughout the whole hungry room. Some, in fact, were in favour of starting without him.

'Doubtless,' sneered Bacon, 'he is standing in front of a mirror admiring himself in his new cloak.'

Standing in front of a mirror, wrapped in a cloak, trying to subdue his fretfulness and his fuming by the sustaining image of his reflection, stood a commanding figure. It had a beautiful silky wig, a pistol and a prompt copy, but its pantobles did not match.

The backing behind undoubled itself and hopefully offered a Venice goblet.

'Look what I've found,' he said.

Edward Alleyn threw it at him.

'I hear,' said Sir Philip Sidney, 'he bought it from a sailor, and the material is of a shade and texture never before seen in this great kingdom.'

'He can carry his cloak,' admitted the Earl of Southampton, as one wearer of cloaks to another. With a motion of his shoulders he displayed his own gold brocade and looked meaningly at Burghley.

Burghley twitched peevishly at his mildewed emerald velvet. No help for it – he would have to get it relined.

'There is no-one in the land can wear a cloak better than Raleigh,' acknowledged Sidney handsomely. 'I am looking forward to seeing his new one – I admit it.'

'It is no small accomplishment to wear a cloak with an air,' said the Master of the Revels profoundly. 'How many royal princes have there been who could do it? Hal Eight.' He began to count them on his fingers. 'Richard of Bordeaux. Ethelred the Unready.' He babbled himself into silence.

For in the doorway stood Sir Walter Raleigh.

His hat was plumed. His breeches took your breath away. His pantobles matched perfectly. But his cloak – his magnificent cloak – was a pale, drained, shrunken beetroot with the dye in runnels.

Lord Burghley might have come in out of the rain in it.

The flower of England was silent. No-one quite knew what to say as he hastened to the side of Elizabeth to make his apologies.

But Elizabeth of England had no manners. She slapped her knees in unholy glee.

'Your cloak, Walter,' she cackled. 'What's happened to your cloak?'

Raleigh breathed heavily.

'They boiled it,' he said.

To Elizabethan England all was clear. It might have happened to any one of them. Raleigh's tailor had gone down with the plague.

Unlucky!

'Poor Walter,' said Queen Elizabeth. 'Never mind, you shall sit beside me and teach me how to eat the potato.'

Tears came into Sir Walter Raleigh's eyes. His Queen had understood his tragedy. He knelt and kissed her hand.

'It would have been such a lovely cloak,' he murmured sadly.

Sir Walter Raleigh had planned his banquet with an eye for dramatic effect. Naturally it must consist of the two classic great courses – the problem facing him, therefore, was where he could most effectively serve his fascinating new root. After deep deliberation, and much putting in and taking out again, he had decided to serve it, dramatically but quite simply, between the two great courses.

At the moment a regiment of waiting men were bearing in the first course. This ran along the traditional lines of costly viands and in Henslowe's diary would have been entered as follows:

Banquette fore to taste th Poetatoe. per. hedde.
1st Course

					s.	d.
Caviare	..	..	..	..	1	1
Cheate and mancheate		..	..	..	0	8
Bere and ale	..	..	..	..	0	10½
Wine	..	..	..	..	3	6
Mutton boylde	..	..	..	..	1	0
Capon gr. boylde	..	..	..	..	2	0
Chickens boylde	..	..	..	..	1	2
Larks boylde	..	..	..	..	0	9
Partridges boylde	..	..	..	..	1	8
Mutton Pr.	..	..	..	..	0	7
Beafe boylde	..	..	..	..	6	8
Beafe boyld dim surloyne		..	..	1	8
Signett	..	..	..	..	7	0
Capon gr.	..	..	..	..	4	0
Veale	..	..	..	..	5	0
Mutton for allower	..	..	..	1	0
Chines of beafe rost	..	..	..	2	0
Cocks	..	..	..	..	3	6
Chickens	..	..	..	..	2	7½
Plovers	..	..	..	..	3	9

| Veale pies .. | .. | .. | .. | .. | 2 6 |
| Custird .. | .. | .. | .. | .. | 1 4 |

'Personally,' said Burghley, waving aside a boyled signett and a veale pie and helping himself delicately to boyled lark, 'I shall bite my potato most carefully and I advise you, my Lord Leicester, to do the same.'

'Tcha,' said the Earl of Leicester. He reached out and grabbed a connye.

From her position as maid of honour Viola could see Master Will quite clearly. He seemed abstracted but not a bit overawed and he did not snatch or grab at the dishes as they circulated past him. She must tell him that this would never do at Court, where you would never get anything to eat at all if you merely waited for it to arrive. Suddenly she remembered her frock, her position, her duties, her secret. He must not recognize her here. She tried to shrink behind Lady Meanwell. It was like a sparrow hiding behind an angry pigeon.

Shakespeare was looking at her with a deep reflective look. Would the potato taste like an apricok? he was wondering.

Always thinking of his art, thought Viola. She must tell him if you thought about your art at Court you would never get anything to eat.

The Master of the Revels was helping himself largely from a dish of caviare. He was very fond of caviare; he could remember the first time it had been served in England and they had put sugar on it, poor souls.

'Ah,' he said, and swallowed a large spoonful. 'Leicester,' he called, 'pass the cream.'

'What are you eating?' called the Earl of Leicester.

'The roe of the sturgeon,' said the Master of the Revels. 'Delicious.' He poured cream over the plate and stirred vigorously.

The Earl of Leicester looked puzzled.

'Try some,' said the Master of the Revels. He hailed a serving man and handed him the plate he had so carefully prepared.

158

'Caviare,' he said. 'To the General.'

Shakespeare looked up. The Master of the Revels wagged a finger at him.

'Now, now,' he said. 'No quotations.'

Shakespeare blushed. He put away his pencil.

At the head of the table Queen Elizabeth laid down the skeleton of a chicken and slapped her thighs.

'And that reminds me, Raleigh,' she said. 'Are you good at riddles?'

'Well,' said Raleigh cautiously.

'What is it,' asked Elizabeth of England, 'that stands on the roof at midnight and crows like a cock?'

Beads of sweat stood out on Raleigh's brow. If he didn't guess it right it might cost him a monopoly.

He concentrated.

In the tiring room the wobbling behind came up with a suggestion.

'How would it be,' he asked, 'if I went back and brought another pair of pantobles from your wardrobe?'

An idea, by God!

'Post haste,' said Edward Alleyn.

The wobbling behind streaked away.

And now the great moment had come. The remnants of the first course had been carried off, and the clean plates placed carefully before each guest with an implement to match, and the chef had taken up his position in the doorway, staggering under an enormous tray.

He was doomed to stagger for a long time, for before the tray could be triumphantly trundled in the Master of the Revels had to make a speech.

He had promised Raleigh faithfully that, on this occasion, he would try to remember not to remember too much. But somehow or other, after a brisk and confident start, he found himself remembering the new French chef at the marriage feast of Anne of Cleves.

159

'Polonius,' said Elizabeth warningly.

The Master of the Revels pulled himself together.

'Um, ah,' he said guiltily. 'What was it I stood up to tell you? Ah, yes.'

From his pocket he pulled out a sheet of parchment.

'I have here,' he said, 'some verses written by the Earl of Essex.'

Elizabeth of England sighed. She settled herself more comfortably.

The Master of the Revels unrolled his parchment. He studied it. He put his head on one side.

''Tis good,' he said. ''Tis very good.'

'Read it, you fool,' said Elizabeth of England.

The Master of the Revels read.

'Happy were he could furnish forth his fate
In some unhaunted desert, most obscure
From all societies, from love and hate
Of worldly folk; then might he sleep secure;
Then wake again and give God ever praise,
Content with hips and haws and bramble-berry;
In contemplation spending all his days,
And change of holy thought to make him merry,
When, when he dies, his tomb may be a bush
Where harmless robin dwells with gentle thrush.'

Elizabeth of England was weeping. ''Tis piteous,' she said.

She wiped her eyes. 'Bring on the potatoes,' she ordered.

The flower of England was looking at its plates with a mixture of doubt tinged with awe. In front of each one of them lay a soggy island of white mush, shaped rather like a warped egg, only larger.

The potato!

This was it!

'Well, well, well,' said the Master of the Revels, in a resigned voice.

Sir Philip Sidney would not permit his doubts to show on his face. He was making up his mind not to let old Walter down. 'Delicious,' he was going to say, whatever it tasted like.

The Earl of Southampton picked his up and experimented. The potato turned over quite easily, and seemed to be the same on the other side.

In spite of the evidence of his eyes, Burghley showed no relaxation of his vigilance. He had picked up a knife, and was pricking delicately.

'I shall bite it most carefully,' he asserted stubbornly.

But Elizabeth of England showed no such daintiness. Forthright and purposeful she dug her spoon into the potato, collected half of it, and carried it firmly to her mouth.

The flower of England waited.

Sir Walter Raleigh gripped his seat under the table. He had sailed halfway round the world to find his root, he had faced great perils to bring it back, he had withstood the blandishments of the most expert cajolers at Court, and had not even hinted at the secret of its flavour, he had changed his chef six times, and now Elizabeth of England was tasting it.

He looked at her.

Elizabeth of England spat.

'Not enough salt,' she said.

In the tiring room Edward Alleyn was doing a one-footed morris of impatience. If his servant did not return with those pantobles inside one hundred and sixty hops he'd scream the Guildhall down. Already the muscles of his throat were tightening.

The door opened. The wobbling behind trundled in, his hands coyly folded behind him.

'I've got it,' he panted triumphantly.

'Good,' said Edward Alleyn, and held out a foot.

Beaming all over his face the wobbling behind produced a soggy island of white mush shaped rather like a warped egg, only larger.

'The potato,' he said ecstatically. 'I got one for you.'

Edward Alleyn scooped it up and threw it at him.

Outside the Guildhall the rabble was fast becoming festive. The bright lights of candles twinkling out at them through the windows fired their imagination. The snatches of gay music and the glimpses of famous faces as the dance swung them past the casements tempted them to shuffle clumsily themselves. Great barrels of ale, set out by the benevolent Sir Walter, and now empty, had quenched their thirst, and since it was so late already – let it get later.

A hefty fellow had tilted over one of the great barrels, hoping in vain to squeeze out another drop. The crowd gathered round him and shouted encouragement, and some sailors helped him along with a hauling song.

Soon the crowd had picked up the chorus and, when they had tired of this and the hefty fellow had gone thirsty away, they sang snatches to one another till the city rang with their hearty voices and put the lute boys inside the Guildhall out of time.

Till suddenly there was an ill-tempered slam of the Guildhall great door and Sir Walter Raleigh came striding out.

A reveller detached himself from the crowd and came staggering towards him. He doffed his cap and essayed a bow.

'How does it go?' he asked, as one host to another.

Sir Walter Raleigh looked at him.

'Not enough salt,' he said bitterly, and strode into the night.

Chapter Twelve

Through the deserted streets of London a figure staggered happily. It swayed, it waved its arms, and it sang in an unsober baritone.

It was William Shakespeare.

The moon beamed down on him, and Shakespeare beamed back at the moon.

> 'Pastime with good companie
> I love and shall until I die,'

he sang.

'Hal Eight,' he explained solemnly to a gatepost. He leant against it. It wasn't there. Staggering slightly, he continued his song.

> 'Who can say
> But mirth and play
> Is best of all.'

Viola Compton, back in her lad's clothes, and hurrying to her lodgings, saw the singing figure.

Dear God! A drunk!

She steeled herself. Was she not a young lad about to become a great actress and the daughter of her father? And why should a drunk notice a young lad, anyway! Besides, she would walk past him very quickly, without even turning her head.

She took a brave step forward.

'Hunt, sing, and dance,' roared the figure wildly.

Dear God! Why had she let the Master of the Revels go to bed? He had offered to come with her between yawns, but he was so old and so tired, and besides in the candle-lit room she had felt as brave as a lion. It was only the darkness with its strange sounds and shadows and bad smells, and, now, the drunk.

She gathered up her skirts. She discovered she was not wearing them. She legged it.

'Halloo, Master Pyk,' called the figure. 'Hallo-o-o.'

That voice! Viola slowed down. She knew it. She stopped. It was Master Will. But this was even worse.

She came back slowly.

'What do you here, Master Will?' she asked faintly.

'Hallooing your name to the ti-tum-ti hills,' said Shakespeare. He put his hand to his mouth. 'Halloo – there, Master Pyk,' he shouted.

Dear God! He was merry!

'Come home, Master Will,' she said. 'It is late.'

Shakespeare leant affectionately against her shoulder. 'It is very late,' he agreed. 'What do you out so late, Master Pyk?' He tried to wag a finger, gave it up, and dug Viola in the ribs.

Viola twitched away from him.

'No matter,' said Shakespeare grandly. 'Keep your secret. You will never guess where I have been.'

'Never,' said Viola, smiling at her own guile.

'The Potato,' said Shakespeare. 'I've been to it. The only playwright there. Did they ask Beaumont? No! Did they ask Fletcher? Never even thought of it. Did they ask Marlowe? Certainly not. He's dead.' He started to weep.

This would never do. Viola sought to distract him.

'What was the strange root like?' she asked.

'What was it like?' Shakespeare considered. What had it been like? He thought again. From the back of his mind something emerged.

'Not enough salt,' he said triumphantly.

Viola giggled.

'Not enough salt,' repeated Shakespeare, well pleased with the effect. He sang it.

Viola took his arm. 'It is late, Master Will,' she said. 'Let us go and sleep for tomorrow there is much work to be done.'

'Work!' Shakespeare was galvanized. 'I had forgotten. Big production. Seven horses. Not enough salt.' He began to walk very quickly. 'There is so much work to do. So little time to do it in.'

'Master Will,' pleaded Viola. 'Take my arm. You are walking in circles.'

Chapter Thirteen

'But, Father,' said Dick Burbage urgently. 'Be reasonable. Give me a chance to put the theatre on its feet.'

'You have been here three weeks,' said old man Burbage. 'Three very costly weeks. Now I want to see results.'

'Is it not a result that we are still open?' said Burbage.

In actual fact it was a miracle. Every day the plague had been creeping nearer and nearer the Whitefriars Theatre. Indeed, this was the secret why Burbage had been able to acquire the empty theatre so easily. They had lost their ambitious production of Hal Eight, with its robes, thrones, and banners in the fire at the Globe. They had no funds. They were behind with the magnificent production of the play, borrowed by Master Will from the Italians and sponsored by the Court, and though the money for it was promised daily it had not yet arrived. All they could offer the playgoer by way of attraction was a hasty rehash of *Titus Andronicus.* And even if there were some defiant spirits in the house, who liked the play or thought Burbage was impressive as Titus, or Prometheus Melody romantic as Bassanio, they had to run the gauntlet of Philip Henslowe's hired bandits before they could urge their friends not to miss it.

'Excuses,' said old man Burbage, 'sink no galleons with me. If,' he produced from the depths of his experience, 'my bears do not fight it is useless for me to

tell the public that they are tired. If your plays are bad,'
he pronounced, 'make them better.' He leant back well
pleased with himself.

Burbage stifled an oath. After all this was his father
and he was trying to get money out of him.

'It is not,' he explained, 'that the plays are bad.
Master Will has a wonderful touch with a revival. It is
the tiding over.'

'Tiding over!' Old man Burbage threw up his hands
to the English heavens. 'I have been tiding you over
ever since you told me you saw no future in bears. I
wish,' he said, 'I were a scholar like Henslowe. I would
then have an account book to show you how much
your tiding over has cost me.'

Burbage took a deep breath.

'What I have gained for you,' he said, 'cannot be
measured in terms of money. Does it mean nothing to
you,' he asked, 'that your son is the greatest actor in the
world?'

'I am very proud of you, Dick,' said old man
Burbage. 'You are indeed an artist. But I,' he pointed to
his large stomach, 'am a business man. I want to see
results.'

Burbage sighed.

'If my taverns do not pay,' went on his father
doggedly, 'I close them down. If my brothels do not pay
– I close them down. But,' he pointed out with a
chuckle, 'they always do.'

Burbage brightened.

'If you are doing so well with your other interests,'
he said, 'you can afford to give me just a little more
money to,' he caught himself up, 'keep things going.'

Old man Burbage began to shake his head.

'Come,' said his son, taking his arm and levering him
off his stool. 'Do not let us waste the morning in discussion. Come and see my company at work – they are
longing to meet you.'

In spite of himself the old man beamed. So long as
his bears and brothels brought in money, what did he

care if he lost some of it on Art? After all Dick was a figure in his way, no man could wish for a better son. It was a pleasure to keep him happy. But the boy must not feel that money came too easily, that his old father was always there to open his money bags, it was time the boy began to have some money bags of his own. He heaved himself up.

'Come along,' said Dick Burbage, guiding him, 'and you will see that we are all one happy family.'

On the stage the happy family had sorted itself into a series of argumentative attitudes. Theoretically Will Shakespeare's great new masterpiece to be presented to Gloriana was in active preparation, but in fact *Titus Andronicus,* due to be performed tonight, *Two Gentlemen* due tomorrow, and *The Dream* when Will Kempe got back from his morris-dance to Norwich – if he was not too tired – had got themselves onto the stage.

There was also Viola. She was refusing to allow Salathiel Pavey to teach her how to speak her lines.

'But Master Pyk,' said Salathiel, pained. 'You do not seem to see the part. The lad is a young girl disguised as a boy and no girl disguised as a boy could speak the lines as you have just spoken them.'

'She would speak them exactly like that,' said Viola firmly.

Salathiel Pavey sighed. Master Will must be losing his grip. Why else had he given this glorious role in his new play to so piping a boy? Before the Queen, too. He would probably get stage fright and dry up, and even if he didn't he spoke the lines all wrong.

'Here,' he said, 'I'll show you.' He stretched out a hand for Viola's part. Viola held it away from him. He snatched. Viola snatched back. They tugged.

'Ah,' said old man Burbage, arriving just in time to see Viola slap Salathiel hard on the face. 'The happy family.'

'It means nothing,' said Burbage quickly. 'In a

minute it will be forgotten and they will be working together the best of friends.' He glared at Viola. 'Won't you?'

Viola trembled. 'Yes, sir.'

'But, of course,' said Salathiel grandly.

In a corner Titus Andronicus had rounded on Aaron and was beating him up.

'A private brawl,' said Dick Burbage, steering his father past.

The old man nodded. He understood.

'Master Burbage!' Obadiah Croke, as livid with passion as that amiable soul could get, grasped Burbage by the arm. 'Would it please you to tell Master Tarleton that the whitewashing scene Master Will is about to write is my scene and not his.'

'Later, later,' said Burbage.

'He throws the bucket,' said Obadiah whitely. 'I get it in the face.' He lifted his hands to his face and emerged with the ecstatic misery of a clown who has been smothered in whitewash. 'I will have this in my contract.'

Old man Burbage chuckled. 'Very funny,' he said. 'But will it fill your threepennies? Results,' he explained to Obadiah, 'that's what I'm after.'

'Master Burbage!' Pale with fury William Tarleton came hurrying up. 'Have you forgotten your promise? It is he,' he pointed to the glaring Obadiah, 'who throws the whitewash. It is I,' he thumped his chest, 'who gets it in the face.' He put his head in his hands, he tore away large streams of sticky mush from his eyes, and emerged with the melancholy expression of a clown who does not like the taste of whitewash.

'Not funny,' said Obadiah Croke critically.

Tartleton made for him.

Burbage seized his father by the arm and steered him away. He looked for a less turbulent spot to show off his happy family.

In a corner was the Forest of Arden – a peaceful group. Melancholy Jacques was in full spate with a polite Duke waiting for him to finish, surrounded by his outlawed Court reclining on imaginary banks.

Burbage brightened.

'This way, Father,' he said.

But as they approached the Forest exploded. The Burbages were too far away to hear what Melancholy Jacques had been saying to the attentive Duke, but clearly it could not have been in his lines for the whole Forest had sprung to life and the clamour was colossal.

Old man Burbage was not surprised to find himself swivelled round and led in another direction. He'd have done just the same in the boy's place. He chuckled.

'A happy family,' he said, 'is all very well in its way, but what I want is results.'

'Here is where we get our results,' said Burbage abruptly. He pulled aside the curtain to the green room. 'Our playwright,' he said proudly, 'the one and only William Shakespeare.'

'Ah,' said old man Burbage.

They entered.

Stretched out on the tomb of the Capulets, an open note book in front of him, William Shakespeare was snoring gently. He had fallen asleep at his work.

On a bench waiting patiently for him to wake were two resigned figures. They were his printers, Hemynges and Condell.

'What do you here?' asked Burbage sharply.

Hemynges blushed. 'We wait for Master Will to finish his new play.'

'Our presses are waiting,' explained Condell.

'They have been waiting for a week,' said Hemynges.

'Each day he promises us,' said Condell, 'but it is always tomorrow.'

'And now,' said Hemynges with the resignation of one submitting to an act of God, 'he is asleep.'

Burbage made a gesture of impatience.

'Away with you,' he said. 'You should be rehearsing.'

170

Hemynges and Condell rose to their feet. They sighed. They made a gesture of despair at one another. They went.

'Stage-struck,' explained Burbage to his father. 'I let them walk on and they print my programmes for nothing.' An idea struck him. 'Would you like to walk on, father?' he asked.

'No,' said old man Burbage firmly. He waddled over to the sleeping Shakespeare. 'How happy he looks,' he said. 'Seems almost a shame to wake him.'

'A great shame,' agreed Burbage. He shook him.

Shakespeare opened an eye. 'Tomorrow, Hemynges,' he said. 'You shall have it tomorrow.' He closed his eye.

Burbage shook him again. Shakespeare sat up and yawned.

'Will,' said Burbage sharply. 'Wake up. This is my father. You remember I talked to you about my father.' He winked heavily.

'You were enjoying your slumbers,' said old man Burbage. 'I am sorry we have woken you up.'

'Woken,' said Shakespeare coldly. 'I was not asleep. I was thinking. In what manner that I have not already used,' he asked Dick Burbage, 'can I bring a heroine to life who has been most dead?'

Old man Burbage pondered. 'I have it,' he said, 'a magic potion.'

Shakespeare looked at him.

'It is a wonderful idea,' said Dick Burbage quickly. 'Make a note of it, Will.'

'It is a dreadful idea,' said Shakespeare. 'I have used it many times.' He remembered his manners. 'All the same, sir, I thank you for the suggestion.'

But old man Burbage was following a train of thought of his own.

'Why,' he asked, 'should you bother to bring the wench to life? Why not leave her dead? Why not kill the hero also?'

Shakespeare looked at him.

171

'I am a business man,' said old man Burbage. 'What I want is results. So you will pardon me if I speak frankly. The trouble with your plays, Master Will, is that you leave far too many characters alive at the end of them.'

'Oh,' said Shakespeare.

'Now I don't go to the theatre often,' old man Burbage went on happily. 'Too busy,' he explained. 'But there is one play I shall never forget.' He paused.

'Well?' said Shakespeare.

'The *Duchess of Malfi*,' announced old man Burbage triumphantly. 'There's a play for you. All dead,' he gloated.

Dick Burbage placed a restraining hand on Shakespeare's sleeve. Shakespeare shook it off. His burning eyes were fixed on old man Burbage, who, oblivious, was chatting happily on.

'Write a play like that, Master Will,' he finished, 'and my son will have no need to come to me for money.'

Shakespeare rose awfully to his feet. He had forgotten that this was Burbage's father.

'Me!' he said, growing inches with every word. 'Me – write a *Duchess of Malfi*!'

'Come father,' said Dick Burbage quickly. 'We are wanted on the stage.' He trundled the old man off.

Shakespeare threw his hands to the heavens. 'The *Duchess of Malfi*!' he cried. 'What sort of a father is this?'

There was a sudden chill in the atmosphere. Shakespeare felt it through his impassioned soliloquy. He dropped his arms. In the doorway, smiling thinly, stood Sir Francis Bacon.

'Ah, Will,' he said. 'Rehearsing?'

Shakespeare blushed. 'Come in Master Francis,' he said. 'Come in and plague me.'

Bacon advanced, dusted a stool with a lace handkerchief, and disposed himself upon it.

'I have come,' he said, 'to tell you that I am displeased with your Court play, both in its progress and in its content.'

Shakespeare glowered at him. 'I see,' he said. 'Otherwise you like it.'

Bacon's face did not change. 'You are behind with it, Master Will.'

'Behind!' Shakespeare took a deep breath. 'Do you realize, Master Bacon, that I have had my playhouse burnt down, my repertory destroyed, and my poor Dick Burbage driven nigh to drown himself? That we are stranded in a ramshackle playhouse miles from fashion? That I have to work night and day rewriting and refurbishing? That our very existence rests on the whim of an ancient bear-baiter who thinks *The Knight of the Burning Pestle* the last word in art . . .'

'You are behind hand,' repeated Bacon, unmoved.

William Shakespeare rounded on him. 'When have I ever failed to deliver my play?' he demanded. 'When has my company ever failed to give their performance – even though they must con their lines in the wings?'

'Conning in the wings,' said Bacon, 'is no good to the Court. How far have you got with the play? In spite of your protests and promises all you have yet written is a handful of scenes for me to show the Master of the Revels.'

'I know,' said Shakespeare viciously. 'What you want is results.'

The curtains parted. Hemynges and Condell peered timidly in.

'The play, Master Will,' they asked. 'It is tomorrow,' they pointed out.

'Your play!' said Shakespeare. He looked at them. He came to a decision. 'Very well, you shall have your play and then you will annoy me no more.' He turned and rummaged among his papers. 'There,' he said, thrusting a parchment into their hands, 'it is all I have had time to do. Now away with you.'

Outside Hemynges and Condell looked round. The stage was a hum of activity. A rehearsal had actually got under way and old man Burbage had been put on

173

a stool to watch it. Hemynges and Condell, clutch-
ing their manuscript to them, made a delicate detour
to a quiet corner and sat down to examine their
treasure.

'LOV'S LABOR WUNNE'
by Wy. Shikspore

it was entitled.

ACT I. SCENE I. The Battle of Hastynges.
Entr Wyllyam the Conqueror. He falles downe.

There was nothing more.
Hemynges and Condell looked at the manuscript.
They looked at one another. They shook their heads.
'His spelling!' they said.

Back in the green room the argument continued.
'Not even a new play,' Bacon was sneering. 'An old
Italian play. Not even a good old Italian play.'
'Like the *Duchess of Malfi*,' said Shakespeare,
through clenched teeth.
'Elizabeth of England orders a play,' said Bacon, 'and
you hash her up an old one. Girl disguised as boy!' He
shuddered.
An evil glint came into Shakespeare's eye. 'Master
Bacon, you make as much fuss about my girl disguised
as boy as though you had a bed to take her to.'
'You leave my bed alone,' said Bacon, stung. 'You are
far too interested in my bed. The whole of England
is far too interested in my bed.'
Shakespeare chuckled.
'All the same,' said Bacon, livid, 'you may be glad to
hear that I am definitely getting it soon. The Master of
the Revels has promised . . .'
'So,' said Shakespeare, 'my play is the price of your
bed. Interesting,' he mused. 'Very interesting. Tell me,
Master Bacon, is it quantity or quality or cost that will
weigh the balance?'

'It is novelty,' said Bacon. 'Something fresh to divert the Court. I do you the favour of offering you this chance,' he reminded Shakespeare, 'and you reward me with an old plot.' He could have wept.

'Master Bacon,' said Shakespeare. 'Be reasonable. There are no new plots. There is only one plot to please the public. I will tell it to you.' He picked up a quill and began to tap Bacon on the chest with it. 'Lad encounters lass,' he tapped. 'Lad loses lass. Lad gets lass.'

He put down his quill.

'There,' he said, 'you have the whole of Comedy, Tragedy, Pastoral-Comedy, and what you will.'

Bacon blotted himself. 'In that case, Master Will,' he asked, 'why write plays?'

'I will tell you,' said Shakespeare. 'It is for the people in them.' He picked up his quill again. 'It is not the things that you make them do,' he said. 'These do not matter. It is the words that you make them speak.'

'So be ye faithful friend or fearsome foe,' said Edward Alleyn, 'ti-tum-ti, tum-ti, tum-ti, as I go.'

A little figure tore its ruff, jumped onto the stage, and raised protesting arms to the sky.

He was the author.

'These,' he quivered, 'are not my lines.'

Philip Henslowe strode quickly across the stage and laid a soothing hand on the author's shoulder.

'Take it easy,' he urged. 'It is the first time you have rehearsed my son-in-law. He is always all right on the night.'

'But,' said the author, 'the night is this afternoon and all he has said is "ti-tum-ti".' He wept.

'It is not the lines that matter,' said Edward Alleyn. 'It is that you have an Alleyn to speak them.'

'But how can you speak them if you do not know them?' raved the author.

Edward Alleyn waved the objection away. 'I know

the substance. I will give voice to some appropriate sentiment when the time comes.' He beckoned his cast. 'We will continue,' he said grandly.

The author sat down.

'Tomorrow tum-ti, tum-ti, tum-ti tum,' said Edward Alleyn.

The author stared despairingly into space.

In the green room the argument had reached a deadlock. Tempers had risen high. Bacon had been telling Shakespeare how he would like the play altered and Shakespeare had been failing to agree with him.

'So you won't make your heroine a man?' demanded Bacon.

'No, I won't,' said Shakespeare.

'And you won't kill the clown?'

'Certainly not,' said Shakespeare. 'It's Obadiah Croke.'

'And you won't even remove the roisterers?'

Shakespeare shook his fist. 'Over my dead body,' he asserted.

'So, in fine, Master Shakespeare,' said Bacon, 'you won't do anything at all?'

'Exactly Master Bacon,' said Shakespeare. 'I won't.' He mopped his brow and sat down.

Bacon picked up his lace handkerchief and played daintily with it.

'Very well then,' he said. 'There is only one thing for me to do. I will take my suggestions to the Master of the Revels and you will be made to use them.'

Shakespeare sprang to his feet.

'Master Bacon,' he demanded passionately, 'do I write my plays or do you?'

Bacon looked at him. He shrugged.

Outside the theatre a grateful Burbage was seeing his father off. The comforting feel of the bag of gold in his pocket warmed him towards the old man.

'Come again Father,' he invited. 'Drop in as often as

you like. We don't see enough of each other.'

The old man beamed. He remembered himself and wagged a solemn finger.

'Don't forget,' he said. 'What I want is results.'

He waddled happily away.

Chapter Fourteen

'Well,' said Philip Henslowe. 'Do you think you can do it?'

The youth in the opposite chair nodded confidently. 'Master Henslowe,' he said, 'you could not have come to a better man. The Burbages' theatre is as good as burnt.'

Henslowe looked at him. He radiated confidence, resolution and organizing ability. Clearly he had stumbled across a born leader.

'Recapitulate, my young friend,' he said. 'Let us make quite certain you understand your instructions.'

The born leader smiled pityingly at the old man.

'Next week,' he said, 'the Queen goes on her Progress to Greenwich. There will be revelling, bonfires, and a torchlight procession. I,' he said, 'am in charge of the procession. You,' he pointed out, 'are buying the torches.'

Henslowe winced.

'I shall have four hours in which to lead my men around the town to incite them to a mood of destructive revelry, and to arrive with them outside Burbage's theatre at the right moment. It is foolproof, especially as my men will be boisterous with the free ale they have consumed.' He looked pointedly at Henslowe.

Henslowe sighed. 'Very well, I will supply the ale. But look you,' he warned, 'see to it that you yourself stay sober.'

'I never drink,' said the born leader.

He stood up. He clicked his heels. He went.

Henslowe reached for his account book. Ruining the Burbages was proving to be a very expensive business. Ale! Torches! Born leaders! And, of course, the bandits, though they practically paid for themselves.

He turned over the leaves of his diary looking for a blank sheet. His eyes fell on an entry:

Memorandum that J. Robert Shaa haue receaued of mr Phillip Henchlowe the some of forty shellinge vpon a booke Called the fower sones of Aymon wch booke if it be not played by the company of the fortune nor noe other company by my apoynt J doe then bynd my selfe be theis presente to repay the sayd some of forty shillinge vpon the delivery of my booke att Cristmas next.

He shook his head. A bad bargain. *The Four Sons* had not turned out a commercial proposition – Alleyn had refused to play any of them, they would not be to the taste of the market-townsmen and Robert Shaw had spent the forty shillings and now had no money to pay him back. It must be written off and would serve only as a warning against dabbling in options.

Henslowe sighed.

In future, he decided, he must try to find time to read his plays before buying them.

Chapter Fifteen

It was night.

Small velvet waves lapped the sides of the gilded, carven, music-filled Progress Barge on its way back from Greenwich.

Little boats, pottering up and down the Thames, lowered their lights respectfully as Elizabeth of England passed them by. On the banks great bonfires had been lit and the houses of the noblemen by the riverside were flamboyant with torches. The Bankside was black with cheering loyal subjects and the city was threaded with a chain of lights.

It had been a triumphant Progress but exhausting.

On the Royal Barge the flower of England was very tired. It had disposed itself in a large group around Elizabeth of England, lying as comfortably as possible at her feet, drinking ale and watching the lights slide past, while Gloriana herself leant back on her throne and quaffed her ale with the best of them.

Unconventional though this group might seem, a rigid precedence had somehow got itself observed. Nearest to Elizabeth lay her beloved pirates – Drake, Hawkins, Seymour, Frobisher, Howard and Raleigh, with Burghley and Kit Hatton inserted among them. Lesser statesmen elbowed round them and behind these the girls of the Court in charge of Lady Meanwell, conscientiously upright. And so, past diplomats and ambassadors, to Philip Henslowe hovering on the outskirts, there by reason of his newly acquired office of Keeper of the Royal Bears – another injustice to old man Burbage. Behind him was the bear. Behind the bear, at a respectful distance, was Edward Alleyn.

And so torch-lit and radiant, to the sweet tongues of viols and plucked lutes, through the warm autumn air, the Royal Barge slid past the flickering lights of London.

Edward Alleyn flung out an arm that embraced both the barge and the town.

'My public,' he said inspired.

The bear looked at him.

It was a Progress. On shore all London had turned out to see it. The watch was marching in procession and all around them the rabble were regaling themselves with free cakes and ale set out on the tables by the wealthier citizens.

But outside Essex House, no table was laid, no cakes and ale were offered, and no citizens, for the news had spread, were milling around.

Behind the casements curtains were drawn and inside the diamond windows all was whispers.

The Royal Barge was lapping its way up river. The Master of the Revels looked at the bonfires. He remembered something.

'There has not been such a glow on these shores,' he said, 'since the day we sighted the Armada.'

Drake stirred. Elizabeth of England patted his shoulder as one might a shaggy dog.

'There, there, my pirate,' she said. 'It was your Armada.'

'Ah,' said Drake wistfully.

'A man was alive then,' said Howard.

'You are right,' said old man Hawkins. 'Those were the days.'

'Those were not the days,' said Elizabeth sharply. 'Then we were a little country, only part of an island, hopeful, and not knowing what we had to fight against – and not knowing the facts feeling that we were equal to it – whatever it might be. None of you worried – all you wanted was to fight whatever the odds. Only I worried.'

'And I worried,' said Burghley.

'I did not worry about anything except powder and shot,' said Drake. 'You would not give me enough provisions then, you will not victual me now.' He humped.

'My good pirate,' said Elizabeth. 'If I had given you but one half of the powder you asked for you would have had me at war with the whole world before I was ready.'

'And why not?' demanded Drake, truculently.

Elizabeth patted him on the shoulder again. 'They were the good old days for you, my pirate,' she said. 'But these are the good days for England.'

'Haven't had a fight in years,' said Drake sulking.

The Queen was on a Progress and it was a general holiday.

Outside Sir Francis Bacon's establishment a team of horses, dragging a great waggon, clattered to a halt.

'What ho!' shouted the driver. 'A bed for my Lord Bacon.'

Sir Francis Bacon came running out of the house. His bitterness had gone, his fine manners were forgotten, he was an excited little boy.

'My bed,' he gloated, stroking the rough side of the waggon. 'My lovely bed.'

Like a fire running a thatch or water running under London Bridge the news spread. Soon a cheering crowd had collected round the waggon. Master Bacon was no hero to the rabble, but tonight they were prepared to like him – even love him.

'Three cheers for my Lord Bacon,' shouted a ringleader.

'And three cheers for the bed,' shouted another.

Bacon beamed on them. He did not take kindly to rabbles as a rule, but tonight he was prepared to countenance them – even like them.

'Ale,' he ordered recklessly. 'Cakes,' he added, forgetting his debts. 'Viands,' he shouted throwing all caution to the winds.

After all, why shouldn't he be generous? Hadn't he got his bed!

Careless of his fine clothing he clambered onto the waggon and took a peep at it.

The Royal Barge rocked gently on the Thames. The lutes and viols were playing sweetly. The bear was entranced. But the flower of England was not listening. The Armada, once remembered, was not easily dismissed from the tongue and by this time nearly everyone was busy remembering.

But the Master of the Revels was practised. He took himself to Spain and remembered a facet of the Armada on which none of the sea-dogs who had saved England could contradict him.

'Talking of commanders,' he said, 'I shall always remember Medina Sidonia, El Bueno as I used to call him, on the day they brought him the letter from the King of Spain that put him in command of the Armada.'

There was a hush. The sea-dogs were interested.

'I was with him in his orangery at San Lucan,' said the Master of the Revels. He sidetracked himself. 'Lovely oranges he grew. Large, luscious, no seeds – and the flavour!'

Sir Walter Raleigh winced and tried to hide himself in the non-committal cloak he was wearing.

'Keep to the point, Polonius,' said Elizabeth sharply.

'I shall never forget his face,' said the Master of the Revels. 'He handed me the letter without a word.' He shook his head. 'The spelling,' he remembered, 'was appalling.'

Henslowe looked up.

'It was a lovely afternoon,' said the Master of the Revels. 'A lizard crawled out to bask itself in the sun. El Bueno would not even look at it. "I'm not a sailor," he kept on raving.'

'He was not a soldier either,' said Drake severely. 'Why the time I singed the King of Spain's beard he ran away from Cadiz harbour – and he the Director General!' The old sea-dog was really shocked.

'I never saw a soul in such despair,' said the Master of the Revels, coming back firmly to his subject. '"Why," he kept on repeating, "I am seasick on a lake. I shall write to the King and tell him so".'

'He did, too,' said Walsingham. 'I saw the letter – it nearly made me cry. Not that it did Sidonia the slightest good.'

I know,' said the Master of the Revels. 'It was that nun Philip of Spain sent to El Bueno to tell him his cause was blessed. Very convincing she was,' he remembered. 'Why I even had qualms myself.'

'Very convincing,' said Walsingham drily. 'I primed her. It seemed to me that it would make things easier for England if an orange-growing country squire should lead the Spanish Armada.'

'Who wanted it easier?' grumbled Drake.

'Wouldn't eat a single orange,' remembered the Master of the Revels sorrowfully.

In Cheapside the Born Leader, hired by Henslowe, was looking for his gang. According to his orders they should have been assembled outside the Boar's Head ten minutes ago.

He found them inside it.

They were crowding round a big man with a deep voice. He was Richard Burbage. Each one of them was holding a firkin of ale. Further they had not the appearance of men who were holding their first firkin of ale or even their second.

'Come, come,' said the Born Leader scandalized. 'This will never do! Where are your torches?'

Like a scallop of flame the Royal Barge cut through the Thames. The lutes and viols had changed their playing into a lilting dance tune. Edward Alleyn was beating an artistic tempo to the tripping of the younger ladies of the Court. So was the bear. Philip Henslowe gazed steadily at the shore. He was looking for a string of torches that should have been wending its way inexorably towards Burbage's theatre. The prentices were late.

But the flower of England was still talking about the Armada.

'The enemy had a hundred and eighty ships,' Howard was saying. 'Eight thousand seamen, nineteen hundred infantry and gentlemen volunteers, officers, priests, surgeons, and galley-slaves at least three thousand more, and all provisioned for six months.'

'A good thing,' said Sir Philip Sidney, 'that we did not know what we had to face.'

'I knew,' said Elizabeth of England.

'So did I,' said Burghley.

'And poor old El Bueno in charge of all three forces,' said the Master of the Revels. He shook his head. 'All he wanted was to be left in peace to eat his oranges.'

'A fussy anxious little man,' said Raleigh, 'he set himself to enquire into everything, to meddle with things he could not possibly understand and had better have left alone.'

'He should have left that to the heads of the departments,' said Burghley severely.

'But he took it upon himself to look into everything,' said the Master of the Revels. 'He even looked at the stores.'

'And what stores they were,' said Drake. 'Arms, small and great, powder – plenty of it – spars, cordage, canvas and every one of the million of necessities for a ship in action.' He looked meaningly at the Queen.

185

'All these things,' said the Master of the Revels levering himself back into the conversation, 'he took on himself to examine and as he could not understand what he saw and knew not what to look at, nothing was examined at all.'

'Slack,' said old man Hawkins. 'Never happened under my command. Used to know every seaman by his Christian name,' he boasted.

They waved him out of the conversation.

'Is it the truth,' asked Leicester, 'that they had more priests than surgeons?'

'They had a hundred and eighty priests and only eighty-five surgeons for the whole Armada,' said Lord Howard, a natural statistician, promptly.

Walsingham permitted himself a smile.

'Everybody's mind was so much absorbed by the spiritual side that there was no time to attend to vulgar commonplaces. In fact,' said Walsingham drily, 'all pains were taken to make the expedition worthy of its big purpose.'

Elizabeth of England spat.

'No impure thing,' said Sir Philip Sidney, speaking with mock solemnity, 'especially no impure woman, was to approach the yards of the ships.' He lifted a solemn eyebrow at the approving Earl of Southampton. 'Swearing, quarrelling and gambling were prohibited under terrible penalties.'

'Quarrelling!' said Elizabeth shocked.

'The galleons were named after the twelve apostles.'

'They sank no more slowly for that,' said Drake. He swigged his ale.

Sir Philip Sidney looked at him reprovingly.

'At sunrise,' he went on, 'the ship boys sang their Buenos Dias at the foot of the mainmast and their Ave Marias as the sun sank into the ocean.'

'Beautiful voices they had, too,' sighed the Master of the Revels. 'I remember . . .'

They wouldn't let him.

'For three years,' Walsingham took up the story, 'the

stream of prayer had been ascending from Church, Cathedral and Oratory. Every noble family in Spain had sent one or more of their sons to fight.'

'Laudable,' said old man Hawkins. 'But wrong-headed.'

'The King of Spain,' said Walsingham, 'had emptied his treasury.'

'Rash,' said Burghley. He shook his head.

'Hidalgo and tradesman,' said Walsingham, 'all had offered their contributions.'

'And we too,' said Kit Hatton proudly, 'were not without our preparations.'

The sea dogs rolled over and looked at him.

But now the landlubbers began to remember.

Linked arm in arm, in indissoluble friendship forged to last at least a night, Obadiah Croke, Tarleton and Will Kempe had gone out to see the sights. They were jogging together in a morris, prancing about in great good humour, and each declaring that the other was the funniest clown in the world.

'What's that?' asked Will Kempe, curiously.

They had come across a cluster of souls gathered around a concentrating juggler. Every few moments he had to stop concentrating to pick up the balls. It was Dagglebelt.

Three oranges he could manage well enough by now. It was the fourth that was giving him trouble.

'Watch me,' said Will Kempe.

He crept cautiously forward behind the concentrating juggler. He stretched out a foot, he sent him hurtling, and he took his place and he kept the oranges flying without dropping one of them.

'It is easy when you know how,' he told the prostrate figure.

Tarleton grabbed a handful of buns from a stall, jumped on a table, and juggled them in the air – all six of them.

'Swop,' shouted Will Kempe.

Buns and oranges changed places.

A flying orange hit Obadiah Croke. He took the matter personally. Master Tarleton was nearest. He made for him, pulled him off the table, grasped him in a bear-like hug and together they rolled down towards the River Lud.

Behind them, in a confused rain of buns and oranges, none of which he dared drop, pranced Will Kempe.

In the distance, watching them and scratching his head, was the owner of the buns and oranges.

The Royal Barge continued to make sweet Progress up the River Thames. The viols played on, the maidens were still dancing, the bear had gone to sleep. But the landlubbers were now campaigning the Armada.

'We too were not without our preparations,' insisted Burghley. He rummaged in a pocket and pulled out an ancient pamphlet. 'See,' he said, 'I have it all set down.' He began to read.

'The Lords demanded five thousand men and fifteen ships: the Citie craved two days respite for the answer, which was granted; and then entreated their Lordships, in signe of their perfect love and loyaltie to their Prince and Country, humbly to accept tenne thousand menne, and thirtie ships amply furnished: and, even as London, London-like, gave precedent, the whole Kingdome kept true rank and equipage,' he ended smugly.

'And in the meantime,' said Drake, 'you cut down our victuals.'

'That is as it may be,' said Burghley stiffly. 'I have always maintained that sailors have too great an appetite.'

'We had our own land defences to think of,' said Leicester.

'Land!' said old man Hawkins. He turned his back on it.

Burghley went back to his pamphlet.

'About three years before,' he read, 'when the Cittie of London was greatly troubled and charged with continyal musters and trayning of souldiers, certain gallant, active and forward citizens, having had experience both abroad and at home, voluntarily exercised themselves.'

'Yea,' said Leicester, glowing at the memory, 'and what is more they trayned uppe others for the readie use, so as within two years we were almost three hundreth machants.'

'And others of like quality,' said Kit Hatton.

'And others,' agreed Leicester, 'very sufficient and skilful to traine and teach common souldiers, the managing of their peeces, pikes and halberds, to march, countermarch, and ring,' he pointed out with considerable satisfaction.

'It takes two years to make a soldier,' observed Drake, 'but it takes a lifetime to make a mariner.'

'And even then there is only one Drake,' said Sir Philip Sidney gracefully.

'God be thanked,' said Queen Elizabeth. She smiled.

'We had not got two years,' pointed out Leicester. 'We did not know when the invader would be upon us.'

'True,' agreed Burghley. 'But we did our best to prepare.' He referred to his pamphlet. 'The said machants, for their owne perfection in military affayres and discipline,' he read, 'mete every Tuesday in the yeere, practising all usuall poynts of warre.'

'At one time,' said Leicester, 'we thought of calling them the Homme Guardde, but,' he shook his head, 'this was considered too Homme Madde . . .'

Outside the Boar's Head the Born Leader, hired by Philip Henslowe, had got his torch-bearers into order. Now he was walking down the ranks with a taper, lighting the torches.

From his lattice, Dick Burbage was watching the inspection with a grin on his face. After a bit he

189

beckoned and an already inspected torch-bearer came prancing over.

'Catch!' said Burbage and dropped a money bag. There was a pleasant chink as it disappeared into the torchbearer's pocket.

'And mark you,' said Burbage. 'No mistakes. There will be another money-bag to share among you when you get back.'

The torch-bearer nodded confidently. He looked at the back of the born leader and thumbed his nose.

The Royal Barge meandered happily down the Thames. The bear had woken up and was snuffing the deck happily, winding his chain round and round Edward Alleyn. Edward Alleyn held his breath and waited for the bear to change his course. Philip Henslowe, ignoring his son-in-law's silent plea for assistance, was scanning the landscape with the eye of a worried eagle. Was the procession never going to start?

But the Armada fighting group had got itself to sea again. Only before they could settle down to defeating the Spanish Armada all over again it had to sail.

'And then,' Frobisher was saying, 'Philip of Spain sent his last orders to the wretched Sidonia. The Duke was not to seek battle. If he fell in with Drake he was to take no notice of him.'

'Cut him, in fact,' said Sir Philip Sidney.

Like a leashed dog Drake growled. Queen Elizabeth patted his shoulder.

'Sidonia,' said Frobisher with a smile, 'was to sail straight to North Foreland and there communicate with the Duke of Parma.'

Old man Hawkins remembered something.

'The enemy had on their strength many experienced admirals,' he said.

Seymour nodded.

'Martin de Ricalde,' he said. 'Pedro de Valdez. Miguel de Oquendo.'

'Ah, Miguel,' sighed Lady Meanwell. The name seemed to stir something.

They waved her away.

'All these experienced seamen,' said Hawkins, 'great fighters, who had learnt their trade under Santa Cruz – God rest his soul,' he doffed his hat in memory, 'all urged strongly the securing of Plymouth, or at least the Isle of Wight, on the way up the Channel.'

'Plymouth!' said Elizabeth of England, outraged.

'The Isle of Wight,' said Lady Meanwell loyally. 'The impertinence!'

'Mind you,' said the Master of the Revels judiciously, 'that would have been sound strategy. But Philip did not see it that way. And El Bueno agreed with him.'

'All El Bueno wanted,' said Seymour bluntly, 'was to find La Parma, hand over to him, and wash his hands of the whole affair. What a commander!' He threw up his hands.

Elizabeth of England spat. 'You talk,' she said, 'as though you regret that you did not have to face Santa Cruz.'

Drake's face lit up. 'Ah, M'am,' he said. 'That would indeed have been a battle.'

Elizabeth patted him on the shoulder. 'Lie down,' she said. 'Lie down.'

'So the Duke,' Frobisher came back to the story, 'flying the sacred banner on the *San Martin,* dropped down the Tagus on the 14th May, followed by the whole fleet. The *San Martin,*' he reminded them, 'had been double timbered with oak to keep the shot out.'

The sea-dogs chuckled. 'Well, well, well,' they said.

'El Bueno,' said the Master of the Revels sympathetically 'was in a dodder from the start. He had kept on telling himself that his cause was God's cause. God would see that they came to no harm.'

'But he soon found,' said Burghley drily, 'that no cause, however holy, saved men from the consequences of their own blunders.'

191

'The Spaniards,' said Drake, 'were out late. And then they met the north trade wind.'

'Just as Santa Cruz had foretold,' said old man Hawkins.

'They drifted to leeward day by day,' said Frobisher, 'till they dropped down to Cape St Vincent. Then it was that they found their water had been taken in three months before – it was foul and stinking. The salt beef, the salt pork, and the fish were putrid. The bread was full of maggots and cockroaches. Cask was opened after cask but it was the same story everywhere.'

'I was told,' said Burghley, 'that in the whole of the Fleet there was not a morsel of food but biscuit and dried fruit.'

Elizabeth kicked Drake with her pantoble. 'Now complain about your victuals,' she dared him.

Drake opened his mouth. On reflection he closed it again.

'The admirals,' said Frobisher, 'declared they could go no further without fresh water.'

'Miguel,' said Lady Meanwell irrelevantly, 'was very fond of Chianti.'

They waved her away.

'All was dismay and confusion,' said Burghley with much satisfaction.

'The wind,' said Frobisher, 'at last fell south and they made Finisterre.'

'And then it came on to blow again,' said Seymour, 'and they were scattered and the Duke and half his fleet crawled into Corunna with the crews scarce able to man the yards and trying to desert in shoals.'

'The missing ships dropped in one by one,' said Frobisher, 'but a week passed and a third of them were still absent.'

'So,' said Elizabeth maliciously, 'once again it was the wind that saved England.'

Drake rolled over on his elbow and looked at his Queen. Elizabeth of England cursed under her breath. Would she never learn to govern that tongue of hers?

'There, there, Francis,' she said. 'I didn't mean it. I know full well that it is fear of my great ships that even now is keeping Europe at bay.'

Drake relaxed. He rolled back again. He stared straight into the black sky.

'Another despairing letter,' said Walsingham, 'went off from Medina to his master.'

'Poor old El Bueno,' said the Master of the Revels sympathetically. 'He was such a good grower of oranges, too!'

'He was a very eloquent letter writer,' said Walsingham. 'He said that he concluded from their misfortunes that God disapproved of the expedition and that the whole thing had better be abandoned. Besides, he argued, the stores were worthless, the men were sick and out of heart, nothing could be done that season.'

'An eloquent letter,' agreed the Master of the Revels, appreciatively.

'Miguel,' said Lady Meanwell raptly, 'wrote to me.'

They waved her away.

'It was not by flinching at the first sight of a difficulty,' said Drake, 'that the Spaniards had conquered half the world. The old comrades of Santa Cruz saw nothing in what had befallen them beyond a common accident of sea life.'

A murmur of approval ran round the old sea-dogs.

'And quite right too,' said old man Hawkins. 'Ships are not lost because they are out of sight.'

'Philip returned a speedy answer,' said Walsingham. '"A little energy," he encouraged them and all would yet be well. And he told Sidonia not to be afraid of a shadow.' He chuckled and dug Drake in the ribs. 'Not even yours.'

Drake growled.

'Tents were pitched on an island in the busy harbour,' Walsingham resumed, 'with altars and priests and everyone confessed all over again and received the Sacrament.'

The Master of the Revels smiled to himself. 'El Bueno must have enjoyed that,' he said.

'He did,' Walsingham agreed. 'This, he wrote to Philip, is great riches and a precious jewel and all now are well and cheerful.'

'Once again,' said Drake, 'on the twenty-third of July the Armada in full numbers was under way for England.'

Sir Walter Raleigh stirred. 'Sixty galleys and other shipping with purpose to annoy us,' he said.

'Streaming across the Bay of Biscay,' said Burghley, 'with a fair wind for the mouth of the Channel.'

'You frighten me,' said Elizabeth of England.

Outside Master Bacon's mansion the crowd was scattering fast. From an open lattice window bits of bedstead were flying themselves into the garden. They were gilded bits, they formed part of a luxurious whole, and they were followed by bolsters, covers, and a muddle of sheets.

Eager to set up his new bedstead at once Bacon was taking the quickest way of getting rid of the old.

'I frighten you, M'am,' Burghley was saying, 'but when we were so secure we never thought that the King of Spain would have set up his rest for England. Then sent he his navy, termed invincible, and was almost upon the banks of us before we were aware of it.' He pointed an accusing finger. 'Yea, we were so slack in provision that it was too late to make resistance had not God preserved us.'

The Queen sat very still. The old seamen looked at the badly dressed Burghley with awe. He had dared to speak frankly to the Queen. And she had listened.

'And I,' said Drake, an old bitterness welling out of him, 'had to lie in harbour with sails unbent keeping Chatham Church – like a bear tied to a stake.'

The bear looked sympathetic.

'And I,' said Seymour, 'was told that I might cruise

with four or five of the Queen's ships between Plymouth and the Solent.'

'And I,' exploded Howard, 'had to sit in the Thames with the rest.'

The Master of the Revels chuckled.

'I do not know,' he said, 'whether swearing was interdicted in the English Navy as it was in the Spanish, but I will stake my ears that you did not spare your language when the order reached you.'

'Twenty-seven minutes without repeating myself,' said Howard with a touch of pride.

'Our ships,' said Drake. 'Our four finest ships. Still in the shipyards being refitted.'

'The workmen in the yards,' said Kit Hatton, 'were labouring twenty-four hours in the day to get your ships to sea in time.'

'Our four great ships,' mourned Drake. 'On the stocks. Useless. The *Triumph*. The *Victory*. The *Elizabeth Jones*. And the *Bear*.'

The bear stirred.

'And,' said Drake, looking straight at him, 'we had to ask the gentlemen of the coast to meet the Spaniard for us.'

The bear wilted under the stare. He shuffled off.

'And right glad they were to do it,' said Philip Sidney.

'That's not the point,' said Hawkins gruffly.

The sea-dogs had forgotten the Progress, they had forgotten the Queen's Majesty, they were fighting their battle over again.

'I,' said Seymour, 'was left with five ships of the Royal Navy and thirty London adventurers to watch Parma and the narrow straits.' He held up his fingers. 'Five ships!' he repeated.

'And thirty adventurers,' said Lady Meanwell encouragingly.

Drake rounded on the Queen.

'I begged you, M'am, to let me take the *Revenge* and my stout adventurers down to Lisbon, but you would not let me for fear it might offend his most Catholic Majesty, King Philip of Spain.' He spat.

Elizabeth grasped the sides of her chair. Her hands had the strength of claws.

'And you,' said Drake obliviously, 'you charged me with wasting ammunition in practice. In practice!'

'Fools!' rasped Elizabeth.

The seamen came to with a jerk. The Queen was still there. They all tried to look the other way.

But not Burghley.

And not Drake.

'Fools,' repeated the Queen, gathering words to her. 'You dwell only on the battles you have won, you dwell only on your skill, your daring, and resource, you dwell only on results. It never occurs to you that had it not been for the greatest good fortune in the world – all these would have availed you nothing. A little difference in the wind, a more determined commander, an early reverse in battle, and England would have been yet another country under the heel of Spain. And you,' she turned on Drake, 'you talk to me as if I were a criminal because I sought to avoid a conflict.'

Drake looked steadily back at her. 'Avoid a conflict,' he said. 'I do not understand your meaning, M'am.'

'There comes a time,' said Burghley, nodding his head, 'when avoiding a conflict is no longer prudent. It is dangerous.'

'Consider our position,' begged Raleigh. 'In Denmark, the King being young, Spain had corrupted the council and the nobility so as he was very like to spread himself with shipping from thence. In the marine towns of the low countries and in Norway he had laid in a great store of shipping. In his own country there was all possible re-arming.'

'Even at this moment,' warned Burghley, 'it is certain that he hath these last two years builded a great number of ships of war as near as he can to the mould and quality of the English navie.'

196

'Finding by experience,' chuckled Hawkins, 'his monstrous ships unfit for our narrow seas.'

'Ah,' said the Master of the Revels.

They waved him away.

'In France,' resumed Raleigh, 'Spain had the parliament towns at his command. In Brittany Spain had all the best havens. In Scotland Spain had corrupted the nobility. We were surrounded, M'am, by an inimicable foe!'

'And you,' said Elizabeth of England, 'would prefer that I order you to go out and give unequal battle without even seeing what could be achieved by diplomacy.'

'Diplomacy!' said Drake.

He turned his back on it.

The watch was marching. Bonfires were blazing in the streets. The citizens of London sat over their cakes and ale at wayside tables, rocked by snatches of song, ready to cheer everybody and everything that passed their way. Every man's door was shadowed with green birch, long fennel, St John's wort, orpin, white lilies and such like, garnished upon with garlands of beautiful flowers and shone over by lamps of glass with oil burning in them all night. Some had hung out branches of iron, curiously wrought, containing hundreds of lamps at once, which made a goodly show.

The procession of the watch, which started from St Paul's and went down West Cheap and Cornhill to Aldgate and so to Fenchurch Street and back to Cornhill, was furnished with more than a thousand cressets and torches. And from their tables all along the route the crowds cooed at them.

In such good spirits were the rabble that they even cheered a somewhat smaller, a somewhat wilder, a somewhat more wobbly procession that came staggering along, their torches waving, out of one inn and into another, with what could have only been a born leader yapping at them.

London was on a jag.

But in a little room, lit by candles, William Shakespeare was coaching his new boy player.

'Master Pyk,' he was pleading. 'I ask you to remember one thing. You are not Mark Anthony any more.'

'I never was,' flared Viola. 'You said I was a stench in the oration.' She burst into tears.

Shakespeare shrugged his shoulders and sat down on the bed. This was the fourth time Master Pyk had burst into tears that night. He would get over it. These highly strung lads were like girls suffering from green sickness. One minute they wanted to stab you in the guts – a kindly word and they were your slaves again. Maybe he had better say the kindly word. After all he had to think of the play, and Master Pyk was just right for a girl disguised as a boy in love with her Master.

'Come, come,' he said sharply. 'Command yourself, Master Pyk, or you will never make an actor.'

Master Pyk went on sobbing.

Not kind enough, thought Shakespeare. He tried again.

'Cheer up, Pyk,' he said. 'It isn't your fault you have a voice like a sparrow in agony.'

The wretched Pyk sobbed louder.

'I am very fond of sparrows,' said Shakespeare desperately.

The wretched Pyk stopped sobbing. He hiccuped.

Enough of kindness, thought Shakespeare. Now for discipline.

'See here, Master Pyk,' he said. 'I am writing a play for Elizabeth of England.'

'And my Lord Essex,' said Master Pyk a shade impenitently.

Shakespeare waved Essex away. 'It is an important moment in the lives of each one of us. For myself, for Burbage, for my clowns, for everybody right down to the humblest player boy in the company. That's you.' He pointed.

Master Pyk looked surprised.

'You have a natural talent, granted,' said Shakespeare. 'But you are green, you are gawky, and you are much too sensitive.' Master Pyk gulped. 'I am taking a grave risk in entrusting you with a leading part.'

Master Pyk leant forward. 'A leading part,' he breathed.

'The leading part,' said Shakespeare savagely. 'Muck it and we'll all lose our ears.'

Master Pyk turned white. Dear God – to lose the ears of a Shakespeare. What a responsibility.

Shakespeare took pity on him. 'Console yourself,' he said. 'I was joking. At the worst we'll only be tortured a little. No, no,' he said quickly as Master Pyk showed signs of bursting into tears again. 'That was a joke too.'

Master Pyk sat down. 'Oh dear,' he said. 'I do not think you really want me in the company. You are only keeping me here to please Master Polonius.'

Shakespeare inclined his head. 'We did at first, boy,' he agreed. 'But we are all beginning to like you very much. We enjoy your high spirits when you are not crying.' Master Pyk blinked hard. 'And,' said Shakespeare, suddenly serious, 'you can speak a line. By God – you can speak a line.'

Master Pyk leant back and laid his cheek upon his hands.

'Can I?' he asked roguishly.

Shakespeare blinked. What were boys coming to? Still, he must work now. He crossed to the table.

'See,' he said, 'the speech that I have written specially for you.'

He began to declaim.

> 'If I did love you in my master's flame
> With such a suffering, such a deadly life,
> In your denial I would find no sense;
> I would not understand it.'

Master Will was no actor. He spoke his lines badly,

he wrenched the accents out of place, and he kept stopping to peer at his own writing. But Viola sat very still and spoke the words to herself after him.

'Make me a willow cabin at your gate,
 And call upon my soul within the house;
 Write loyal cantons of condemned love,
 And sing them loud even in the dead of night;
 Holla your name to the reverbrate hills,
 And make the babbling gossip of the air
 Cry out, "Olivia!" O, you should not rest
 Between the elements of air and earth,
 But you should pity me!'

Shakespeare stopped. He saw the awed little face looking at him. He beamed.

'A good speech,' he said.

A candle flickered and went out.

'And you wrote these lines for me,' said Lady Viola Compton.

It was a beautiful night. The Royal Barge had run onto a mudbank. Clearly too many admirals had spoilt the broth. Presently the tide would rise and lift the boat off, but in the meantime there was no harm in prodding a bit.

The ladies of the Court were leaning over the side watching the proceedings with interest. But the admirals, after glaring furiously at one another, were making their way back in twos and threes to their monarch. They would wait for the tide to rise, or maybe a wind would blow up, as it always did for Drake, and in the meantime they would remember a bit more about the Armada.

But on their return they found that the landlubbers had taken charge of the conversation and Burghley was reading from his pamphlet.

'It was a pleasant sight,' he read, 'to beholde the souldiers as they marched towards Tylbury, their cheereful countenances, couragious words and gestures.'

'Dauncing and leapin' wheresoever they came,' prompted Elizabeth.

'And in the camp,' said Leicester, 'their most felicitie was hope of fight with the enemie, where oftimes divers rumours ran of their foes approch and that present battell would be given them.'

'Then were they as joyfull at such news,' said the Queen proudly, 'as if lustie giants were to run a race.'

'In this camp were many olde souldiers and right brave Commanders,' boasted Leicester, 'who although in their greatest force did never exceed the number of three thousand horse and fifteen thousand foote, yet there were ready in all places many thousands more to backe and second them; and it was found good policie, not on the sudden to keep too great an army in one place.'

'It was an economical policy,' said Burghley drily.

'Economy,' snarled Seymour. 'It was left to my officers, on their own responsibility, to order wine and arrowroot for the sick out of Plymouth.'

'And to be called to sharp account when all was over,' said Howard.

'We were not much better off on land,' said Leicester, shaking his head. 'One hundred thousand men had given their names and the stations had been arranged where they were to assemble if the enemy attempted a landing. But there were no reserves, no magazines of arms, no stores or tents, no requisites save for the men themselves and what local resource could furnish.'

Drake smiled. 'I am pained to observe, M'am, that you were as short-shrifted with the military as you were with us.'

'Fool,' said Elizabeth. 'I knew for certain that with Parma and Sidonia disposed as they were the invasion could only come at two points. Why should I waste my money elsewhere?'

Seamen and landlubbers looked at one another. They shrugged. These women strategists!

201

But Burghley had been searching the pages of his pamphlet. Now he found the passage he wanted.

'The Queene, upon certayne knowledge of the Spanyardes comming, fortwith settled all her forces in warlike readiness, but ordained no more camps than at Tylbury.'

'And did I not go down to Tylbury in person?' asked Elizabeth of England.

'You did, M'am,' said Sir Philip Sidney, 'and your presence and princely encouragement, infused a second spirit of love, loyaltie, and resolution into every souldier in your armie, who being as it were ravished with their Soverayngnes sight, that as well as Commaunders and common souldiers quite forgate the fickleness of Fortune and the chance of Warre, and prayed heartily that the Spanyards might land quickly.'

'Indeed,' said the Master of the Revels affectionately, 'when later they heard the Spanyarde had fled the men wept. They wept,' he repeated, touched.

'I made a speech, too,' said Elizabeth of England.

She smiled . . .

Outside Master Bacon's house, the crowd, having grabbed unto themselves those bits of the old bed that had fallen into the garden, had gone off to put them into good use.

Inside the best bedroom the new bed had been installed.

Master Bacon, an ecstatic little boy, was bouncing himself up and down on it.

'Springy,' he pronounced rapturously.

'My loving people,' said Elizabeth of England. 'We have been persuaded by some that are careful of their safety, to take heed how we commit ourselves to armed multitudes, for fear of treachery; but I assure you, I do not desire to live to distrust my faithful and loving people.'

She rose to her feet.

'Let tyrants fear,' her voice rang out. 'I have always so behaved myself, that, under God, I have placed my chiefest strength and safeguard in the loyal hearts and goodwill of my subjects. And therefore I am come amongst you at this time, not as for my recreation or sport, but being resolved, in the midst of the heat of battle, to live or die amongst you all; to lay down for my God, and for my kingdom, and for my people, my honour and my blood, even the dust.'

The sea-dogs were silent. Elizabeth took a quick glance at the pamphlet Burghley had thrust into her hand.

'I know,' she claimed, 'I have but the body of a weak and feeble woman; but I have the heart of a King and of a King of England, too.'

'And, by God, she has,' mumbled Drake. The old sea-dogs nodded to each other. Pride in their Prince, at that moment, had banished all bitterness.

Sir Philip Sidney knelt and kissed the Queen's hand. She waved him away.

'Foul scorn that Parma or Spain or any Prince of Europe should dare to invade the borders of my realm – to which rather than any dishonour should grow by me I myself will take up arms.' She towered over them. 'I myself will be your general, judge, and rewarder of every one of your virtues in the field. I know already by your forwardness,' she looked at Drake, her voice took on a tenderer note, 'that you have deserved rewards and I do assure you, on the words of a Prince, they shall be duly paid you.'

The sea-dogs looked sceptical. But Elizabeth was at Tilbury still.

'In the meantime my Lieutenant-General,' she flung out an arm at Leicester, 'shall be in my stead, than whom never Prince commanded a more noble or worthy subject.'

Leicester looked up at her. He glowed.

Elizabeth of England gathered her forces for her climax.

'Not doubting by your obedience to the General, by

your concord in the camp, and by your valour in the field, we shall shortly have a famous victory over the enemies of my God, of my Kingdom and of my people.'

She sat down exhausted and reached for a tankard.

'A great speech,' said Burghley. 'It will ring down history.'

The Master of the Revels tried to look modest.

'All the same, M'am,' said Drake, 'the hope of England at that moment was in her poor patient suffering sailors at Plymouth. Each night we looked out passionately for the Spanish sails.'

Philip Henslowe was looking out passionately to the shore. He could not see very well with all the hauling and pushing going on around him, but it seemed to him that the flicker of torches he could glimpse from time to time did not seem to be anywhere near the Whitefriars Theatre and was stopping a great deal too often.

'Gentlemen,' pleaded the Born Leader to the rollicking procession. 'Can't you march in step?'

The procession stopped. They considered.

'Imposhible,' they told him.

'I shall never forget,' chuckled Howard, 'how Walsingham kept sending us news that the Armada had started for certain.'

Walsingham blushed.

'And you were always ready to believe him,' Seymour taunted Drake. 'Do you remember the time you dashed out as far as Ushant and then turned back lest the Armada should have crept past you in the night and found Plymouth undefended.'

'Undefended!' said old man Hawkins, indignantly. 'I was there, wasn't I?'

'But you had no ship,' they soothed the offended old man. 'You had retired.'

'Makes no difference,' growled Hawkins. 'I could have come out.'

'Do you remember,' asked Frobisher, 'when we got down to half-rations for one week more and powder for two days?'

'I remember,' said Drake, 'that smaller grew the messes and paler the seamen's faces and still no man murmured or gave in.'

'On Friday the twenty-third,' said Walsingham, 'the Armada was sighted a second time. I was right about that,' he pointed out.

'Friday,' said the Master of the Revels disapproving. 'An unlucky day.' He turned to Drake. 'You must remember. You were on the Hoe playing bowls at the time.'

'Aye,' said old man Hawkins. 'And you stopped to finish the game.' He clucked reproachfully.

'Well, how was I to know it wasn't another of Walsingham's false alarms?' said Drake, stung.

Walsingham scowled. 'This time,' he said, 'the Armada had started with numbers undiminished . . .'

'Saturday, Sunday, Monday, they sailed,' took up Frobisher, 'with a smooth sea and soft south winds, and on Monday night the Duke found himself at the Channel mouth with all his pious flock around him.' He chuckled. 'Tuesday morning,' he pointed out, 'the wind shifted to the north, then back to west and blew hard. The sea got up, broke into the stern galleries of the galleons and sent them looking for shelter in French harbours.'

Drake slapped his thighs. 'They had to heave-to for a couple of days till the weather mended.'

The old sea-dogs roared.

'But on Friday,' said Seymour gravely, 'they sighted the Lizard and formed into fighting order.'

'El Bueno,' said the Master of the Revels, 'was in the centre.'

'Alonzo de Leva,' remembered Howard, 'was leading in a vessel of his called the *Rata Coronata*.'

205

'Don Martin de Ricalde was covering,' said Seymour.

'Miguel,' said Lady Meanwell proudly, 'was here, there and everywhere.'

They looked at her.

'The entire line,' said Seymour, 'stretched for about seven miles. I shall never forget the sight.'

Henslowe pushed the bear on one side and peered over a tugging sailor. He could see his line of torchlights quite clearly. They were no longer straight. They seemed to be walking backwards.

The sailor came up suddenly. The bear stepped nimbly aside. Not so Philip Henslowe.

'Father,' said Edward Alleyn severely. 'What do you think you are doing sitting down in front of the Queen?'

But the sacred banner was being run up the masthead of the *San Martin* and the Queen was meeting the Armada with her seamen.

'Each ship in the Armada,' remembered Frobisher, 'saluted with all her guns, and every man, officer, noble, seaman, or slave, knelt on the decks at a given signal to commend himself to Mary and her son.'

The Master of the Revels waggled a finger.

'We shall miss the meaning of this high epic encounter,' he said, 'if we do not realize that both sides had the most profound conviction they were fighting the battle of the Almighty for all time.'

This was a new idea to some of the seamen. They thought it over.

'Two principles were contending for the guidance of mankind,' said Elizabeth of England. 'Freedom and authority.'

'Which side were we on?' asked Lady Meanwell confused.

'At dark that Friday night,' said Sir Philip Sidney, 'the beacons were seen blazing all over the coast and inland of the tops of the hills.'

'I shall not soon forget them,' said the Queen.

'The Armada crept on slowly,' Sir Philip Sidney continued, 'all through Saturday with reduced canvas as though it were feeling its way.'

'Not a sail to be seen,' said Hawkins. 'Not even through my telescope.'

'At midnight,' said Frobisher, 'a pinnace brought in a fishing boat from which Medina learnt that on the sight of the signal fires the English had come out that morning from Plymouth.'

'Presently,' said Sidney, 'when the moon rose Spain saw sails passing between them and the land.'

'With daybreak,' said the Master of the Revels, 'the whole scene became visible and the curtain lifted on the first act of the drama.'

'The Armada,' said Drake, 'was between Rame Head and the Eddystone – or perhaps a little to the west of it. Plymouth Sound was right open to their port. The breeze, which had dropped in the night, was freshening to the south-west and right ahead of them, outside the Mewstone, I had your eleven ships,' he pointed to Howard, 'manoeuvring to recover the wind.'

'Towards the shore,' said Howard, 'lay some forty others of various sizes. The privateers.'

'This,' said Drake, 'formed the whole of the English fleet to challenge the Armada.' He laughed suddenly. 'But we made monkeys out of them that day.'

'We did too,' agreed Howard. 'I shall never forget how amazed the Spaniards were when I sailed cheekily to windward, well out of range, and joined you, Drake, when for them there was hardly enough wind even to rock their bathtubs.'

Drake rubbed his hands. 'Then we got busy,' he remembered. 'The whole of our fleet passed out, close hauled in line behind them, and swept along their rear pouring in broadsides from a safe distance.'

Frobisher roared with laughter. 'Do you remember,' he asked, 'how Ricalde with Alonzo de Leva and Miguel Oquendo, who had hurried to him, tried desperately to close?'

'They couldn't do it,' swanked Drake. 'They were out-sailed, and out-cannoned and out-manoeuvred.'

'Miguel's boat was no good,' said Lady Meanwell in extenuation. 'Too big,' she explained. 'Besides,' she turned on Drake accusingly, 'you never let him get near.'

'Mistress Meanwell,' said Elizabeth, 'you will oblige me and stop babbling.'

Lady Meanwell bit her lips.

'You may tell us about Miguel some other time,' said Elizabeth more kindly. She returned to the group. 'Proceed.'

'Ricalde's division was badly cut up,' said Walsingham, 'and a Spaniard present told me afterwards that certain officers showed cowardice – he must have meant it as a hit at the Duke, who had kept out of fire.'

'Poor old El Bueno facing broadsides,' murmured the Master of the Revels. 'Never had anything harder been thrown at him than an orange – and that by his son-in-law. Missed him,' he said reminiscently. He rubbed his nose.

An orange! Edward Alleyn looked at Philip Henslowe. It was an idea.

'It is an idea,' said Obadiah Croke, 'to pick up a joint and throw it in her face. It is a wonderful idea.' He hugged himself. 'I shall tell him myself.'

'Do,' said Tarleton. 'I am always telling Master Will that there is not enough slapstick in the Shrew.'

'Quite right,' said William Kempe. 'After all,' he asked, 'what does Petruchio throw at Katherine? Practically nothing,' he answered himself.

'If I were playing Petruchio,' said Tarleton, 'I wouldn't stop at the joint. I'd follow it with poultry.'

'And Katherine could catch it in her teeth and start eating.'

'When I play Petruchio,' said Obadiah Croke in a trance, 'I know what I shall throw. It is a wonderful thing to throw,' he told them raptly. 'It is a novel thing to throw, it is an exciting thing to throw – fool that I am – it is the only thing to throw!'

The two clowns waited. But Obadiah Croke was lost in his dream.

'What is it, Obadiah?' they pleaded. 'Tell us.'

A beatific smile lit Obadiah's face. He stretched out his arm to the world like one who offers a new religion.

'A custard pie,' he breathed.

In the meantime both fleets had passed the Sound. Medina, seeing that nothing could be done, had signalled to bear away up channel but the sea-dogs who had followed him were rolling with mirth on the Royal Barge.

'Do you remember,' asked Walsingham, 'how we punished Ricalde's own ship?'

Did they remember? They roared.

'I shall never forget how she leaked,' said Seymour.

'I rubbed my hands when she dropped behind,' said old man Hawkins gleefully. 'Saw it all beautifully from my crow's nest. I knew you had her then.'

'But,' Seymour rolled round and drummed his heels on the deck, 'he was in such a hurry that he fouled the *Santa Catalina* in turning, broke his bowsprit . . .'

'Broke his topmast,' said Drake.

'And became unmanageable,' they crowed together.

The Master of the Revels was getting restless. He could not remember any of this.

'The *Andalusia Capitana*,' he muttered discontentedly, 'was one of the finest ships in the Spanish fleet and Don Pedro was one of the most popular commanders. And rightly so,' said the Master of the Revels, cheering up a little. 'He danced a beautiful Rigadoon.'

'No-one could *hota* like Miguel,' said Lady Meanwell. She bit her lips.

'It was your Miguel,' said Drake, 'who rushed on board the *San Martin* to protest when the flurried

Sidonia signalled the Armada to go on and leave Don Pedro to his fate.'

'And while your Miguel was reasoning with Sidonia,' said Howard delighted, 'a quarrel broke out between the soldiers and seamen in his galleon. Some wretch flung a torch into the powder magazine and jumped overboard. The deck,' he chuckled, 'was blown up.'

'Indeed,' said Lady Meanwell acidly.

'And he lost his argument on top of his ship,' said the unrepentant Seymour. 'Sidonia was firm. He would not risk his whole fleet for the safety of one galleon.'

'It was growing dark,' said Howard. 'The sea and sky looked ugly. The deserted *Catalina* put up a brave defence but she could not save herself and she fell into our hands.'

Queen Elizabeth smiled. 'I remember it perfectly. She had on board a large sum of money and among other treasures a box of jewel-hilted swords, which Philip was sending over to the English Catholic peers. I used them up for Christmas gifts,' said the Queen complacently.

'You gave me one,' remembered the Master of the Revels gratified.

'Monday morning,' said Drake, firmly bringing the conversation back to the Armada, 'broke heavily. The wind was gone but there was still a considerable swell. My men were hulled down behind. The day was spent peacefully in repairing damages and nailing lead over the shot-holes. Sidonia,' he jeered, 'was moved to the front to be out of harm's way.'

'At sunset,' said Howard, 'we were outside Portland – we had come up within a league of them, but it was now dead calm and we drifted apart on the tide.' He shook his head. 'It was very vexing.'

It was very vexing. The watch, which had marched proudly all through London, admired and applauded by all, was being ignored by three common clowns huddled at a table outside a tavern. They had not even looked round.

The watch felt rather hurt and sang a bit louder. The clowns took no notice. They were working out the business for Obadiah's inspiration.

'But why stop at one custard pie?' pleaded Tarleton. 'Why not throw two?'

'Seven,' suggested Will Kempe, 'and you could dance beneath them and juggle.'

'After all,' said Obadiah, 'there is no reason why I should do all the throwing. Why should not the Shrew throw some back at me?' He put his hands in front of him and emerged with the face of a Petruchio who has had a custard pie thrown at him by his newly-wed wife.

'A woman would miss,' said Tarleton judiciously. 'She would hit a manservant who was coming in. Me,' he pointed out with a smirk.

Obadiah Croke trembled. 'This is not in your lines, Master Tarleton,' he said. 'You leave Master Will's play alone and do not start improvising business for it.'

'But couldn't she miss with just one of them?' pleaded Tarleton.

Obadiah Croke considered. 'Very well,' he said. 'Just one but no more. And it must be with your back to the audience.'

'That's very fair,' said Will Kempe. 'And I will think of a funny little step for you to jog off with.'

They thought it over. Then beamed at one another.

'It is a wonderful idea – my custard pie,' gloated Obadiah. 'Let us hurry at once to Master Will and show it to him.'

He staggered to his feet. So did Tarleton.

But Will Kempe came suddenly to his senses.

'One moment, Master Croke,' he said. 'Think you that Dick Burbage will allow you to take Petruchio away from him?'

Croke waved him away. 'Tcha,' he said, 'Burbage

could never be funny with a custard pie. Come – let us hurry.'

But Tarleton had come to his senses too. 'Quiet, Obadiah,' he said, 'there is more than one scene in the Shrew.'

Obadiah Croke stopped dead. 'So there is,' he said depressed. He sat down in a chair. He sagged.

'Ah, well,' he said and reached for his firkin of ale. 'I shall have to be Christopher Sly as usual.'

The bear was bored by the tugging sailors. And his master was taking no notice of him – gazing away at the land and muttering discontentedly to himself. With a shrug the bear shuffled off to the sea-dogs and rubbed his muzzle against Drake's hand. Drake patted him absently.

'The Spaniard,' he was saying, 'couldn't use an opportunity when he had one. Could they now close and grapple with the English ships their superior numbers would have assured them victory. And what did Medina do?' He smiled his contempt. 'He went to sleep.'

'Tired out,' said the Master of the Revels understandingly. 'You get like that when you are old,' he explained.

'Aye,' agreed Burghley.

'Not at all,' snapped old man Hawkins. He stifled a yawn.

'They had to wake him up,' said Drake amused. 'Imagine it – having to wake the leader of a fleet in the middle of a battle! They had to urge him to set his own galliases to work.'

'By the time they got started,' said Howard, 'it was dawn and there was a breeze. Once again we did what we liked with them.'

'The Spaniard,' said Elizabeth of England, 'was outsailed, out-matched, and crushed by the guns that I had given you with a longer range than theirs.'

'Their shot,' said Drake with satisfaction, 'flew high

212

over the English hulls while our every ball found its way through their towering sides. This time,' he pointed out, 'the *San Martin* was in the thick. We ripped and tore her double timbers and cut in two her Holy Standard. The water poured into her through our shot holes.'

'The men lost their nerve,' said Seymour. 'On such ships as had no gentlemen officers on board notable signs were observed of flinching.'

'Bad,' said old man Hawkins. 'Very bad.'

The bear nodded. He settled himself in a more comfortable position.

'And then,' said Drake, 'our powder gave out.' He looked at the Queen. 'Two days' fighting, M'am, and our powder gave out.'

'But by this time,' said Sir Philip Sidney quickly, 'England was awake. Fresh privateers had sailed out of Poole harbour laden with powder, meat, bread, fruit, anything they could bring from the Dorsetshire coast.'

'Wednesday was a breathless calm,' remembered Seymour. 'We were taking in supplies,' he explained. 'They,' he sniggered, 'were repairing damages. Thursday was St Dominic's day . . .'

'St Dominic,' said the Master of the Revels, seizing his opportunity, 'belonged to Sidonia's own family and was El Bueno's patron saint. He had always thought highly of him – up till then.'

'He must have felt pleased with his patron saint at the beginning,' said Drake, 'for the morning broke with a light air that hindered us from moving but which with the help of the galliases would enable him to come to close quarters at last. And Howard here,' he pointed, 'did his best to give him his wish.'

'With scarce wind enough to move,' said Howard, 'I led the *Ark Raleigh* straight down the Spanish centre.' He chuckled. 'Outsailed my consorts,' he said, 'and found myself alone with the galleons all around me.'

'Careless,' said the Master of the Revels severely.

'Just then,' said Howard, 'the wind dropped. The

213

Spanish boarding parties were there – standing at their posts. The tops were manned with musketeers, the grappling irons all prepared to fling into our rigging.' He wiped his brow. 'I tell you it was an awkward moment,' he admitted. 'But then I had an idea.'

The sea-dogs grinned.

'I dropped twelve boats over the *Ark* side,' said Howard, 'and they took me in tow. The breeze rose again and she began to move. My sails filled and she slipped away through the water, leaving the Spaniards as though they were at anchor staring in helpless amazement.'

'Aye,' said Drake. 'With every day that passed we taught the Spaniard some new lesson.'

'We did too,' said Howard. 'And while he was still digesting it,' he laughed, 'the wind that saved me carried you, Drake, and the rest to help me.'

'Once again,' said Seymour, 'we began that terrible cannonade.'

'The Duke had other causes for uneasiness,' said Walsingham, knowingly. 'His magazines had given out under the unexpected demands made upon them. He had expected to fight at the most one battle. He had fought three – and lost the lot.'

'With resolution,' said Hawkins, 'he still might have made his way into St Helen's Roads.'

'In the Solent he would have been comparatively safe,' said Seymour.

'And he could easily have taken the Isle of Wight,' said Lady Meanwell.

They looked at her.

'But when St Dominic too failed him,' said the Master of the Revels, 'poor old El Bueno lost his head.'

'He lost his heart,' said Drake sternly, 'and having lost his heart lost all.'

In Shakespeare's room the candles had burnt low. A very tired Master Will was putting down his fifth mug of ale. A very tired Master Pyk was struggling to finish his third.

They were celebrating.

The coaching had taken a long time, passed through many delicate stages, but had ended in a burst of glory with Master Pyk spouting forth words that both were lost in admiration of.

Now they were worn out, relaxed, and blissful.

'It is a wonderful play,' said Master Pyk sleepily.

'It is a grand play,' nodded Shakespeare.

'It has such gaiety,' said Master Pyk.

'And such poetry,' said Shakespeare.

'Such clowning,' said Master Pyk.

'And such characterization,' said Shakespeare.

They drank.

'One question, Master Will,' said the somnolent Pyk, an idea occurring to him. 'This play – what is the title?'

Shakespeare looked blank. 'Title?' he said. 'Must it have a title?'

'But of course it must have a title,' said Master Pyk severely. 'Have you ever heard of a play without a title?'

Shakespeare considered. His face fell. 'No,' he admitted.

'Then you must find one.'

Shakespeare got up. He yawned.

'It is very late, Master Pyk,' he said. 'I am going to bed. Call it what you will.'

And so Medina Sidonia, bewildered and badly shaken, ran away to France.

'That was on a Friday,' remembered the Master of the Revels.

'We still hung on to him,' said Drake. 'Never let him out of sight.'

'He reckoned,' said old man Hawkins, 'that once he made Calais we would not dare to meddle with him. Thought we'd go home,' he cackled, 'and annoy him no further.'

'I wonder what could have given him that idea,' mused Elizabeth of England.

Howard laughed. 'As he dropped anchor in the dusk outside Calais, he saw to his disgust the *Endemonada Gente* had brought up at the same moment with himself – not half a league astern of him.' He laughed. 'I wonder what he said?' He looked at the Master of the Revels.

'Don't know,' said the Master of the Revels. 'Wasn't there,' he apologized.

The sea-dogs roared and dug him in the ribs.

'Poor old Sidonia,' said the Master of the Revels, drawing the fire away from himself. 'He was less to blame than his master. An office had been thrust upon him for which he had not the slightest qualification.'

'His one anxiety,' said Seymour, 'was to find Parma, lay the weight on his shoulders and have done with it.'

'Philip had provided a splendid fleet,' said Elizabeth of England, 'a splendid army and the finest sailors in the world except,' she looked at her sea-dogs and smiled, 'the English. He failed to realize that the grandest preparations are useless with a fool to command.'

The grandest preparations are useless with a fool to command. Philip Henslowe stood frowning at the shore. There was his procession, with the torches seen as pin lights in the distance, nowhere near any theatre and going round in circles.

He was beginning to question the ability of the born leader.

Round the throne Drake, Frobisher, Howard, Seymour and old man Hawkins were in fateful conference on the *Ark Raleigh.* Though, after a week of disastrous battles, the Armada had sailed itself on to an exposed roadstead, to the English eyes it seemed to outnumber them as much as ever. And Parma was now within reach and Parma had with him an army with which to cross from Dunkirk.

Something had to be done.

Unconsiously the sea-dogs shifted themselves round the Queen till each sat to the other as they had sat in the cabin of the *Ark Raleigh.*

'Which of you,' asked the Master of the Revels admiringly, 'first thought of the fireships?'

'I did,' said Hawkins.

Queen Elizabeth looked at him. 'You weren't there,' she said gently.

'Oh yes he was,' said Drake with affection.

'Came out in a privateer,' said old man Hawkins proudly. 'Knew every man on board by name,' he boasted, 'and the Captain was an old friend of mine. Sailed with me in 'forty-seven. Ferried me across the Channel and pleaded with me to let him come aboard the *Ark Raleigh* as my aide. But I couldn't let him.' He shook his head. 'Too old,' he explained.

'We took eight useless vessels,' said Drake. 'We coated them with pitch. Hulls, spars, and rigging.'

'And while we were doing this,' said Seymour, 'we sent out our frigate to attract their attention.'

'It sailed round them,' remembered Sir Philip Sidney, 'wagged its tail, and sailed right back again.'

'You should have seen the expression on the Spaniards' faces,' chuckled Frobisher, 'as the frigate spread her sails among the Armada, sailed saucily round them, and whisked away again.'

'I was on her,' said Hawkins proudly.

'The night,' said Drake, 'was without a moon. You can imagine Sidonia,' he said, 'pacing his deck, observing our lights moving up and down, and wondering what the English devils would be up to next.'

'He ordered a sharp look-out,' said Howard.

'Wise,' said the Master of the Revels. 'That was very wise of El Bueno. What did he see?' he asked curiously.

'About midnight,' said Seymour, 'when a faint westerly wind was curling the water they made out dimly several ships that seemed to be bearing down upon them.' He chuckled. 'Their experiences since

217

Plymouth had been so strange that anything un-intelligible that the English did was alarming.'

'So when our ships burst into flames,' said Drake, 'and drifted down towards the Spaniards, Sidonia lost his head.'

'He issued a series of muddled orders,' said Walsingham.

'He told the Armada,' said Sidney, 'to weigh anchor and dodge.'

'He ran himself onto a mudbank,' said Seymour lusciously.

'And most important of all,' said Drake, 'he got his great fleet split up so that we could get at them and open our attack.'

'And we got at them,' said old man Hawkins, rubbing his hands. 'How we got at them.'

Elizabeth of England smiled at him. Her gaze wandered to smile at all her sea-dogs.

'You got at them,' she said. 'You hunted, you harried, you pounded, and you drove these would-be world conquerors, who dared to look towards Plymouth Sound, from our shores for ever.'

The sea-dogs smiled up at their Sovereign. How well they understood one another. How they loved one another.

Over in the Clink the prisoners had been put in groves for the night, their wrists and ankles held by rough wooden fetters, so close they could feel each other breathing. They could not even fall into an uneasy sleep, for outside there was a Progress and the shouts and songs of the merry-makers came floating through the chink in the wall and every now and then the dark chamber was lit by the flicker of torches passing outside.

The third prisoner from the left sighed heavily. Habitual optimist though he was, he could find little to comfort him in his present position. Only last week he had been the personal manservant of the temperamental Edward Alleyn, who had kicked him into the streets over a lost pantoble to earn his living holding horses, one of which had not allowed him to do so.

The prisoner sighed. It had been a mistake, he realized now, to stalk that horse and jump on its back when it wasn't looking, and it had been a bigger mistake still to hold on when it had leapt into a gallop. How, after that, could he have hoped to convince the magistrate that it had been making away with him and not he with it.

It wasn't fair. They should have let his pleader produce that horse in court.

A series of very wobbly flames wavered across the walls. Bibulous voices could be heard and among them the voice of what was clearly a born leader entreating his procession to follow him.

'Left!' shouted the born leader entreatingly. 'Over there!' He pointed.

The procession rolled obstinately into an alley on the right. They fetched up opposite Henslowe's theatre.

'A playhouse!' they observed rapturously.

They burnt it down.

Back on the barge Philip Henslowe saw the flames leap up in the City. For the first time that evening he smiled. The theatre was on fire. Excellent. The born leader had done his job after all.

He beckoned his son-in-law.

'Look,' he said, pointing. 'Poor old Burbage.'

Edward Alleyn peered into the darkness.

'Father,' he said, 'are you sure Burbage's theatre is over there?'

'You're mad,' said Henslowe. He took a closer bearing. 'Great God!' he said.

Edward Alleyn thought it over. 'I wonder,' he said, 'if anything has gone wrong.'

*　　*　　*

Up in his bedroom Master Bacon was pulling on his fine yellow cross garters. He must hurry or he would not arrive at Westminster Bridge in time to welcome Elizabeth of England back to Whitehall and thank her for his lovely new bed.

He looked at it lovingly. Here, indeed, was something to hand down to the generations to come.

'Just one more bounce,' he pleaded with himself.

With lights ablaze and lutes playing the Royal Barge cut through the waters to Westminster Bridge. The tide had helped the mariners of England off the mudbank.

The ladies had tired of dancing and had induced Edward Alleyn to recite to them. His father-in-law did not appear to be listening. The bear wondered what could be on his mind.

Round the throne the sea-dogs were disposing of the remnants of the defeated Armada.

'Ricalde,' said Seymour, 'died two days after he landed.'

'God rest his soul,' said old man Hawkins. 'He would have been far happier to have died giving battle.'

'Miguel de Oquendo,' said Walsingham, 'had a wife and two children, but he would not send for them.'

'He just turned his face to the wall and died,' said Lady Meanwell. 'Poor Miguel.' She wept a little.

'Good old El Bueno,' said the Master of the Revels, 'saw no reason why he should die. He returned to his orange groves like the good gardener he was and invited me to visit him. Couldn't make it,' he said regretfully.

'Sidonia did not die,' agreed Raleigh. 'He stayed alive to be chased out by my Lord Essex, just as he was chased out by Drake.'

'Chased out by Essex!' said old man Hawkins unbelievingly. He roared. All the sea-dogs roared.

'Silence,' rasped Queen Elizabeth. 'I will not have you laughing at Devereux. He is a very brave general.'

'Just a little impetuous perhaps,' said Sir Philip Sidney.

'If you insist,' said the Queen. She smiled.

At the pier, their loyal faces lit by leaping torches, a cheering crowd watched the Royal Barge landing its precious cargo. They called coarse jokes to the ladies-in-waiting, they enquired affectionately after Lady Meanwell's lumbago, and they cheered the sea-dogs to the echo and pleaded to sail with them on their next voyage to whatever part of the world they might be going. But they were saving the bottom of their lungs for their Queen.

A little to the fore stood Sir Francis Bacon. He had dusted himself a neat little square and, as the Queen appeared, he rushed forward and knelt on it.

In the light of the torches Elizabeth paused to peer at this dandified petitioner. What could he hope to gain at this time of night? She recognized him and began to cackle.

The crowd cut short its cheering to listen.

'Oh, M'am,' babbled Bacon, the finely constructed speech he had composed flying right out of his head. 'How can I thank you? Your lovely bed! My lovely bed! Our lovely bed!'

Elizabeth of England kicked him.

'Get up, fool,' she said. 'It is Lady Meanwell's bed.'

Chapter Sixteen

At the Whitefriars Theatre a rehearsal was in progress.

There was not a square inch of space on the stage. In one corner the clowns were practising a snatch, in another the principals were snatching a practice. In the centre Edward Alleyn was taking up enough space to have rehearsed a ballet.

'I come ti-tum, ti-tum, ti-tum, ti-tum,' he said.

'Ti-tum, ti-tum, ti-tum, ti-tum, I go,' he announced.

He went.

Straight to his father-in-law sitting by the side of the stage.

'Father,' he said, 'I do not like my words.'

Without looking round Philip Henslowe extended a patient hand and pushed down a bobbing-up author.

'They give me no opportunity,' explained Edward Alleyn petulantly.

'I, on the other hand,' said Philip Henslowe sweetly, 'have given you every opportunity, Edward. Ever since my daughter insisted on marrying you I have been providing you with opportunities. I have given you your theatre. I have given you your companies, I have had plays specially written for you.'

Edward Alleyn glared at his father-in-law. 'You never got me Shakespeare,' he said stiffly.

'No,' admitted Henslowe. 'But I have outbid Burbage for you. And a pretty penny it cost me. See.' He opened his account book and pointed to an entry.

It read:

To Ruinying Dick Burbij:

Jtem.	To burninge dn Plaihse	22s.
Jtem.	To planning burninge down Whitfrs.	22s.
Jtem.	To mscarrge of planne and sayvinge of my worldlie goodes	53s.
Jtem.	For outbyddynge Burbaj for lease of Whitefrier Theatre	17s. 10d. each week

'Good heavens,' said Edward Alleyn. 'Are you paying as much as all that!'

Philip Henslowe nodded gloomily.

'Then,' said Edward Alleyn, ' I will get it all back for you. I must work.'

He rushed back onto the stage.

'Ti-tum, ti-tum, ti-tum, ti-tum, I return,' he announced.

Outside two disconsolate figures were trudging past the Whitefriars Theatre. They paused to look at one another as a spate of Edward Alleyn's ti-tums came cascading over the wall.

'What a rotten play it must be,' said Dick Burbage comfortingly.

'What an impossible ranter Alleyn is,' said Shakespeare.

Both of them were thinking: 'It should have been us rehearsing in there.'

'To the tavern,' said Burbage abruptly. 'I've got to drink ale.'

'So have I,' said Shakespeare desperately.

'All the same,' said Burbage, as they left the Whitefriars behind. 'I can't help thinking that this calamity has been my fault.'

'It is a theft,' said Shakespeare. 'And it is my fault. I

ought not to have spent so much time thinking about my play for the Queen. And,' he added viciously, 'I ought to have knocked Henslowe down.'

'No, no,' said Burbage, 'it is my fault. No use shutting my eyes to it. I ought to have read that lease before I signed it.'

'You are not a man of business,' said Shakespeare. 'What could options and renewals mean to you? You are an artist.' There was no regret in his voice.

'Then I should have sent my father,' said Burbage. 'He always reads a contract from top to bottom before signing it.'

'How dull,' said Shakespeare.

Arm-in-arm they made for the tavern.

Inside the Boar's Head all was depression. This was because it was occupied entirely by Mr Burbage's evicted players. It had been a miserable December, even before they had been evicted, bitterly cold, and with their houses growing sparser every day. But they had buoyed themselves up with the glittering promise of the Royal Performance and they had hung grimly on. And then, a professionally charming thunderbolt, Philip Henslowe, had descended on them on Christmas Eve, and taken possession of bricks, mortar, and props.

The dispossession had been accompanied by the prettiest compliments on both sides. Henslowe was full of hopes that Burbage would build a new playhouse; Burbage confidently prophesied enormous successes for Edward Alleyn. Neither side mentioned the fire. Indeed a party was held at the Mermaid to drink to each other's success, and not a single one of the drinks was poisoned.

But when the fumes had cleared away the result was all too plain. Henslowe was installed at the Whitefriars Theatre and Burbage was out on his ear. He had no theatre in which to play to the Queen, the Earl of Essex, or indeed to anybody.

In a corner of the room, the farthest away from the

224

fire, the boy-players were huddled together. They had with them the parts they had been rehearsing – were they not players – and though Burbage had no plans for the future beyond the vague one of speaking to his father when he got back from Birmingham, a pretence of rehearsal had been kept up.

'Just as I learnt to manage my skirt,' said a carroty urchin miserably, 'they take it away from me.'

'You have no need to worry,' said a raven urchin with envy. 'Your colouring is like the Queen's, it is the great fashion both for damsels in disguise and damsels drinking potions. You could go over to Henslowe this minute.'

This was the final insult. The carroty urchin swung his fist.

Viola looked at them in some dismay. A great tragedy had befallen a great playwright, the Queen was not going to see the greatest play ever nearly written with possibly the greatest girl-boy player in it, and here they were taken up with their own petty squabbles.

She moved towards another group.

'The first time I have ever been word perfect,' lamented Prometheus Melody over by the fire, 'and the company gets kicked out.'

'Why worry?' said Salathiel Pavey. 'Surely all London is crying out to hear your falsetto! Have you forgotten that the Blackfriars nearly closed down because you left and has been playing to packed houses ever since? Why,' he asked, 'don't you go to Henslowe?'

Prometheus Melody swung his fist. He missed. He burst into tears.

Selfish oaf, thought Viola contemptuously. She passed on.

At a table covered with empty mugs the clowns were in conference. As usual, when plans have fallen through, everybody was full of bright ideas. As Viola approached the clowns were working out a new gag from its first stages.

'I have it,' said Obadiah Croke, 'I insult you.'

'Excellent,' said Tarleton. 'I show fight.'

'Exactly,' said Obadiah. 'You and Master Kempe set on me.'

'Oh,' said Tarleton.

'On me,' said Obadiah firmly. 'I roll on the ground and you screen me from the audience. And when I get up,' he bent himself double, 'I have lost my trousers.'

Tarleton jumped to his feet. 'What's this – I thought I was going to lose my trousers.'

They glared at one another.

Imbeciles, thought Viola, thinking only of their own work at a time like this. She left them.

Burbage and Shakespeare had come in and were hard at it lowering tankards of ale in the corner. Viola warmed to them. Here were two great men, not concerned with their own glory, thinking only of the good of the company. And even if they drank a little while they were doing it – who could blame them?

She edged a little closer.

'Burnt me out,' Burbage was saying. 'There was I, dressed as Hal Eight, ready to give the performance of my life. I was going to be terrific!' he assured Shakespeare.

'I was going to be pretty terrific myself,' said Shakespeare, 'as the Bishop of St Asaph,' he remembered.

'The grandest costume I have ever worn,' mourned Burbage. 'The finest entrance I have ever devised.'

'The longest lines you have ever let me speak.' said Shakespeare.

Burbage looked at him. 'Maybe the fire prevented something after all,' he said.

Shakespeare swung his fist. Viola darted in and caught his hand.

'Stop,' she said. 'I am ashamed of you.' She stamped her foot. 'Both of you.'

They looked at her.

226

'Master Pyk,' said Burbage wonderingly. 'Have you drunk too much ale?'

'You should not drink if you cannot carry it,' said Shakespeare severely. 'It will spoil your voice.' He picked up his mug. He drank largely.

Burbage picked up his mug. He drank largely.

'Stop it,' said Viola. 'You are like children, worse – you are like fops at Court.'

'And what do you know of fops at Court, Master Pyk?' said Shakespeare, wagging a finger.

'They are like peacocks flirting their tails to catch the eye,' said Viola passionately. 'They are like fawning spaniels. They are like performing bears pleading for favours.'

The door opened. Old man Burbage came lumbering in. Behind him lumbered seven bears.

'Bad houses in Birmingham,' he said abruptly.

At London Bridge a frigate was making fast to the pier. Hurrying towards it was Sir Walter Raleigh. He had come here post-haste on a rumour.

He buttonholed the Captain. 'I hear,' he whispered urgently, 'that you have great treasure on board.'

The Captain beamed. 'The Queen will be pleased with me. I have brought doubloons, jewels, pearls the size of ostrich eggs, and . . .'

Sir Walter Raleigh waved them away.

'The material,' he urged. 'I hear you have some material of a richness . . .'

'It is the finest weave ever seen in the whole breadth of this mighty island,' said the Captain. 'It was made in Flanders to the order of Phillipe of Spain to wear to greet the victorious return of the Armada.'

'Ah,' said Raleigh.

'It was by the greatest good fortune that I heard of it,' said the Captain. 'But see for yourself.' He pulled out a small piece the size of a pocket handkerchief.

Raleigh examined it. He held it to the light.

'It is exquisite,' he said. 'I will buy all you have.'

'This is all,' said the Captain. 'It is all I have brought with me.'

Raleigh stared.

'The price,' said the Captain, 'was too high. I could not be certain of a profit.'

'Fool,' said Raleigh. He eyed the Captain. 'You will return to Flanders tomorrow,' he commanded.

'But—' said the Captain.

'Tomorrow,' said Raleigh sternly, 'and if you don't I will commandeer your ship and sail her myself.'

He strode blackly away.

The sea-dog went muttering down to his cabin. He shut himself in. He opened his locker and pulled out a bale of rich brocade. He glared at it.

That is what came of holding out for a better price.

'So we're sunk,' said Shakespeare. 'Scuppered. No playhouse, no props, and a father who subsidizes bears with his money-bags. More beer!' He drank.

'He is an old man,' said Burbage apologetically, 'and Birmingham always puts him in a bad temper.'

'Of his bones be coral made!' said Shakespeare. He drank.

'More beer,' said Burbage. He drank.

'Pommage,' said Viola. She drank.

It had been a grueling half-hour. They had worked on old man Burbage in pairs, together, and separately, but it had been no good. Old man Burbage had a simple mind. If bears failed to attract, he kept on repeating, how could the players?

He also added tartly that if Richard had spent a little more time reading his leases instead of burning down his opponent's theatres, he would not now be pestering a worried father who had other things to think about. Finally he had stumped away, his bears lumbering after him, and his money-bags safe around his person.

'More pommage,' said Viola. She drank. 'Tell you what,' she announced, emerging from the bubbles, 'I've been thinking.'

228

'Yes, yes, Master Pyk,' said Shakespeare, patting her. 'Now go home and have a nice sleep. Master Dick here and I are going back to have a nice sleep – aren't we?' He winked.

'Wassat?' asked Burbage.

Viola looked at them owlishly. 'You want a theatre,' she said. 'I will shget it for you.' She staggered to her feet. 'Come, Master Will. We are going to the Queen. She has lotsh of playhoushesh.'

'Millionsh,' said Burbage approvingly. 'But,' as an idea struck him, 'will she give ush one?'

'I'll show you,' said Viola. She put her hands in her pockets and strutted. 'I'll tell you jusht what I'm going to shay to the Queen. I will shpeak to her firmly. I shall shstand no nonshensh.'

'Shright,' said Burbage. 'Give her hell.' He drank.

'M'am, I shall shay, you have the greatesht play-wright in the land.'

'The univershe,' corrected Shakespeare.

'And the greatesht actor on the globe,' prompted Burbage.

Viola turned on them peevishly. 'I shay,' she said. 'Whosh making thish speech?'

'I'll write it for you,' said Shakespeare. 'Wheresh my pencil?'

The door opened. Old man Burbage lurched in.

'A bear short,' he said testily. 'Losht it,' he explained.

He wandered round the inn, he looked under tables, he glanced behind the bar, he peered up the chimney, he shook his head, and he glared accusingly at Master Will.

Master Will looked up absently from his parchment. He saw old man Burbage glaring at him. He decided to consult him.

'How shall I shpell Shakeshpeare?' he enquired.

Chapter Seventeen

It was New Year's Day. All over England people were waking up with headaches.

In his bedroom Philip Henslowe awoke to find his pillow hard and pressing into his head. He moved it. It turned out to be his account book.

In his lodgings Edward Alleyn came unhappily to life. His head was splitting, and he could not remember any of the lines he was due to speak that evening.

'Ti-tum, ti-tum, ti-tum,' he muttered uneasily; 'tum,' he finished, not altogether satisfied.

At the Palace of Whitehall Lady Meanwell awoke with a migraine. She feared it would be much worse by the time she had attended the Queen while she assessed the New Year's gifts the nobles of England, or anyone else hoping to benefit by her favour, were expected to pour on her.

In his room the Master of the Revels awoke to find Dagglebelt the jester bending over him and extending a pack of cards.

'Take a card,' he was urging. 'Any card.'

The Master of the Revels put his head under the bed-clothes.

In the counting house Burghley, who had been checking over the official list of the Queen's gifts, put his head in his hands. But it was not last night's excesses that had given him the headache.

By the Lady Marques of Northampton, a gurdill of golde with buckells and pendants of golde, garneshed with sparks of rubyes and diamonds, and also 10 perles settled in collets of golde.

By the Countes of Warwyk, a cap of black vallat with 13 buttons of golde, in every one of them eyther a ruby or a diamond; and a know of small perle, with a garter and byrde upon the same; and a perle pendant.

By the erle of Ormonde, a very fayre juell of golde wherein are three large emeraldes sett in roses white and redd, one bigger than the other twoo; all the rest of the same juell garnished with roses and flowers enamuled, furnished with very smalle dyamonds and rubyes; about the edge very smale perles; and in the bottome is parte of a flower-de-luce garbished with smale diamondes, rubyes, and one spaherm with three meane perles pendaunte two of them smale; the backsyde a flower-de-luce enamuled greene.

He looked at another entry. He frowned.

By the Lady Baroness Burghley, 35 buttons of golde, one broken.

Had his wife been insufficiently lavish, he wondered?

Up Cheapside two horses were jogging towards the palace. They had started out at a smart gallop but the nearer they got to the palace the slower the pace. Presently they would be walking.

'Oh, dear,' said Viola Compton, 'I'm frightened.'

'Pull yourself together, Master Pyk,' said Shakespeare. His head was splitting and this was the fifth time Master Pyk had made this observation.

'Look at me!' He straightened his back, he puffed out his chest, he thrust his pointed beard into the air. His headache was pierced by a sharper pang. He slumped.

'Do you think the Queen will be very cross?' asked Viola.

'She will have you de-eared, de-toed, beheaded, and flung to the bears,' said Shakespeare, exasperated. 'Come along.' He struck her horse a sharp blow on the flanks.

'Whoa,' cried Viola, tugging at the reins. 'Slow down!' The horse looked puzzled. He compromised himself into a sidle.

'I do hope,' said Viola, 'that the Queen won't be too cross.'

'Come, come,' said Shakespeare. 'What has become of your yesterday's courage? Do you remember how you planned exactly what you would say to the Queen?'

'That was the pommage,' said Viola, explaining all.

'Yesterday,' said Shakespeare, 'you had the heart of a leader. Today it is the affair of the cobbler. Tug it up, Master Pyk!' He brandished his arm. His head gave a twinge. He dropped his arm.

A leader! To rescue the players from their plight! To save the hour for Master Will, to score a great triumph as his leading boy-player.

'Have no fear, Master Will,' she cried. 'I will face the Queen as I have sworn.'

'That's better,' said Shakespeare. He sagged.

'Only,' said Viola in a small voice, 'I hope she won't be too cross.'

Shakespeare glared at her. 'We are nearing the palace,' he said. 'You will know soon enough.'

They jogged on in silence. As they entered the gates a figure came mincing out.

'Good morning, Master Bacon,' called Shakespeare. 'How goes it?'

Bacon looked at them with lack-lustre eyes. 'I have a

headache,' he observed. 'Everybody at Court has a headache.'

'Has the Queen by chance a headache?' asked Viola apprehensively.

Bacon looked at the lad with distaste. Effeminate, he decided. He nodded.

'The Queen has a headache,' he said, and walked away.

The Queen had a headache. Her doctor was in attendance. He was a sallow-faced man with beautiful manners and sad eyes, but he had saved the life of the King of Spain. His name was Lopez, and the anxious Burghley, the succession not yet secure, kept him in England in case. Besides the Queen liked him. She would call him her pet spy and jokingly send him jeering messages for transmission to his royal master.

But at the moment she had a headache.

The well-mannered Dr Lopez was wondering anxiously how he could convey the fact that this was due to gourmandizing the night before without giving offence. He stroked his beard pensively.

'Um,' he said.

The light from the window shone on the great ruby that he always wore on his third finger. Elizabeth eyed it avidly.

'A lovely jewel,' she said. 'Was it Phillipe who gave it you, sawbones?'

Dr Lopez bowed.

'A lovely jewel,' repeated the Queen. 'As lovely as any that I possess – nay, lovelier.'

Her covetous eyes fixed on it.

'You should value that jewel, sawbones, as you value your life.'

A cold finger touched the Spaniard's spine. It was all he could do to stop his hands from guarding his neck.

But his head was still on his shoulders – at the moment.

Outside the palace Shakespeare was pacing up and

233

down. He had had to cajole, plead, and practically push Master Pyk into the palace; he had handed him over to the Master of the Revels who had seemed unaccountably pleased to see him, and now he had to await the issue. He wondered how the lad was getting on.

'Take a card,' said Dagglebelt the jester. 'Any card,' he added spaciously.

Viola, back in the Court dress the Master of the Revels had insisted on her wearing, stretched out a preoccupied hand. There were other things on her mind. But Burghley was all eagerness.

'A magician,' he said, pleased. 'Take one, my child,' he urged. 'It will help pass the time while you are waiting for audience with the Queen.'

'Any card,' said Dagglebelt encouragingly.

Viola took one.

'Now put it back,' said Dagglebelt. 'Shuffle,' he ordered.

Viola made a few vague passes.

'Here,' said Burghley. 'Let me.' He did it with his usual thoroughness.

'Now,' said Dagglebelt.

The door opened. Lady Meanwell came bustling through with an armful of dresses.

'Wouldn't wear one of them,' she complained.

Viola paled.

'Now!' said Dagglebelt. He took the pack, flicked it across the table, and held the knave of spades triumphantly in the air.

'Your card,' he said, and bowed.

Viola looked at it. She shook her head. 'But it isn't,' she said, hoping this wasn't an omen.

'A bad magician,' said Burghley, disappointed. 'Go away and practise.'

Lady Meanwell came bustling back.

'The Queen is waiting,' she said; 'hurry.'

'Good luck,' said the Master of the Revels.

'Don't annoy her, child,' said Burghley. 'She has yet to approve the list of gifts.'

Outside, Will Shakespeare had got tired of pacing up and down, wondering how Master Pyk was faring. He was a busy man. There was so much to do – so little time to do it in. He might as well do some of it now.

In the farthest corner of the passage was a chair. Master Will made for it, sat down, and pulled out a piece of parchment and pencil. Soon he was immersed.

'If there is one thing I deplore more than another,' said Elizabeth of England, 'it is inattention to detail.' She put her wig straight. 'And right from the beginning of this affair, my child, no-one seems to have attended to any details. Gross carelessness all round.' She spat.

Viola's eyes began to fill with tears.

'You tell me,' said the Queen, 'that Master Henslowe burnt down the Globe Theatre. That was reprehensible but it was also slovenly. For he failed first to put an end to Burbage's source of supply. His father,' she explained. 'He should have poisoned him.'

'But he is a nice old man,' said Viola.

'That, child,' said the Queen, 'has nothing to do with the question. Henslowe showed an insufficient grasp of the art of plotting. If one is to bring off a successful plot one must neglect no detail.' She smiled suddenly. 'Mind you,' she said, 'it is as well for me that most plotters are amateurs else I would surely not be here today.'

Viola cheered up a little.

'It was unforgivable of Burbage not to read his lease,' said Elizabeth. 'As a play for me was involved it could almost be said to be treason,' she brooded.

Viola blanched.

'I myself,' said Elizabeth, 'never sign anything without reading it several times and then as often as not I recall the messenger.'

She cackled suddenly. 'Did I ever tell you about the time I recalled Drake? He was livid.'

Viola essaycd a smile. The Queen frowned.

'As for your suggestion,' she said, 'that I should save Burbage's fortune by imprisoning Henslowe for some convenient offence – that is impractical. The Tower is crowded out.'

Viola burst into tears. The Queen took off her pantoble and threw it.

'Stop bawling, child,' she said. 'Have I not occupied myself with your welfare always? Now I will see about your precious Burbage. Besides,' she added frankly, 'I am anxious to see Master Will's new play. They tell me there is a most unflattering portrait of Master Bacon in it, and it tempts me.'

'Malvolio, M'am,' said Viola. She giggled.

'It tempts me,' said the Queen again. 'I must see it. What can we do?'

'What can we do?' Viola bit her nails.

'There is a feast at the Temple on Twelfth Night,' said Elizabeth. 'How would it be if we had Master Will's play performed there?'

Viola tasted the idea. 'Oh, M'am,' she said, 'it would be wonderful.'

'It isn't bad,' said the Queen complacently. 'Quite neat.' She cackled.

Viola cackled.

'What's the matter now, child?' asked the Queen, noting that the cackle rang a little false.

'The props,' said Viola. 'The costumes. How shall the players eat while they wait?'

'Tcha,' said the Queen. 'Details. Don't bother me with them.'

'But . . .' said Viola.

'Vision,' said the Queen. 'Sweep of design, not details. These will be looked after. I offer you the Temple and you prate to me about food. Now be off with you.'

'Then,' said Viola, hardly daring to breathe. 'Can I

tell Master Will that we have a subsidy and a Court performance?'

Elizabeth of England rose to her full height. 'Have you taken leave of your senses, chit?' she demanded. 'The plan has only just occurred to me. It has to be weighed, moulded, discarded, brought to light again, and finally accepted, or,' she paused, 'rejected. Come back in a month.'

'But,' said Viola, 'Twelfth Night will be over by then and we shall be starved.' She looked at the Queen beseechingly. 'Please, M'am, couldn't you make up your mind a little more quickly – just this once?'

Elizabeth considered. She smiled. What a ninny the chit was.

'Run along, child,' she said. 'You shall have your play-acting, and I shall speak to the Master of the Revels about the subsidy.'

Viola beamed. She bobbed the quickest curtsy in the world and rushed away before the Queen could change her mind.

Outside the door she collided with the coming in Master of the Revels. She threw her arms around him.

'The Temple,' she cried. 'We got the Temple.'

In the passage she bumped into Lady Meanwell. Three dresses fell on the floor.

'We are saved,' she crowed. 'The day is saved.'

Hearing the commotion, Burghley poked his head out of a door. Viola waved an arm at him.

'The subsidy,' she babbled. 'We got the subsidy.'

At the bottom of the passage Master Will was huddled over his parchment. Viola flung her arms round him.

'It's wonderful,' she cried. 'The whole world is wonderful.'

Master Will looked. A pretty girl was kissing him. Excellent. He kissed her back.

But it was a pretty girl he had seen before. No matter. He kissed her again.

'The Temple,' gasped the pretty girl. 'The subsidy. I

am going to be the greatest girl-boy player in the world.'

The pretty girl must be mad. Shakespeare backed. Good heavens – it was not a pretty girl. It was Master Pyk.

Viola drew back. She had remembered her skirts.

'Oh, dear,' she said.

Lady Meanwell came thundering down the passage. In her arms was one of the fallen dresses.

'Look what you've done with your romping, Lady Compton,' she said, pointing sternly to a ripped ruffle.

Viola looked at Lady Meanwell. She looked at the staring Shakespeare.

'Dear God,' she said. 'That's torn it.'

'I knew all along you were a girl,' said Shakespeare. 'Never fooled me for a minute.'

Viola twinkled. 'You're a liar,' she giggled. 'Do you remember the night you boxed my ears?'

Shakespeare blushed.

'And the night I found you merry and had to escort you to that very bed and leave you snoring on it?'

'Nonsense,' said Shakespeare. 'I wasn't a bit the worse.'

'And the night you made me cry in this very room rehearsing the willow-cabin speech.'

Shakespeare got up. 'That,' he said, 'was merely to make you fond of me.'

He grabbed.

Viola pushed him away. 'Oh, Master Will,' she said. 'You shouldn't be doing that.'

Master Will grinned fiendishly. 'Quiet, Master Pyk,' he said. 'It's quite all right if it's Shakespeare.'

Chapter Eighteen

The Attorney-General looked out of the window of his chambers by the Fleet. He rubbed his eyes.

Coming towards him was a peculiar procession. While it could not be called a progress neither could it be called a rabble. A band of happy lunatics, doubtless escaped from Bedlam, were jogging uproariously towards the Temple. Some were playing drums, others waving flags. One lunatic was juggling with custard pies, while another was balancing seventeen plates upon his head and pleading with a third lunatic to climb up and stand on top of them. Leading them was an energetic little man doing the merriest morris in the world. Indefatigable he seemed.

A little ahead of the procession, like a king leading his troops, rode Hal Eight, his costume only slightly singed, while alongside, his arm round a stripling lad, strode the Bishop of St Asaph roaring a song unfitted to the Cathedral.

The Attorney-General turned to his buxom housekeeper.

'What is this exhibition?' he asked.

The housekeeper smiled indulgently.

'These,' she said, 'are Master Burbage's evicted players coming to hold rehearsal at the Temple Hall for the new play to be given on Twelfth Night to the Queen and my Lord Essex.'

'Essex,' said the Attorney-General. He smiled.

'Essex,' said Elizabeth of England. She frowned.

Sir Francis Bacon drummed his fingers against his sword hilt.

'You misunderstand me, M'am,' he said.

'I understand perfectly,' snapped Elizabeth. 'Robert Devereux has sent you here to plead for him for his sweet wines, just as you used to send him to plague me to make you Attorney-General.'

Bacon's lips were very thin. 'Robert Devereux,' he said, 'is my friend. I have noted his deep concern that you have not yet arrived at a decision to renew his monopoly of sweet wines. It is a matter,' said Bacon, 'that affects not only his fortune but his honour in the eyes of all England.'

'I know that,' said Elizabeth drily. 'Proceed.'

'I am not here at Robert Devereux's injunction,' said Bacon, pulling out a lace handkerchief and playing with it. 'I have come as his friend, hoping for news to reassure him.'

Elizabeth laughed in his face.

'What a liar you are, Master Bacon,' she said. 'Not even a good one. You, who have never done a disinterested action in your life, ask me to believe that of your own impulse you would brave my displeasure to help a friend. Deny that he nagged you for weeks and threatened you into the bargain.'

Bacon stood his ground. 'If you slight him thus publicly, M'am,' he said, 'I cannot answer for the effect it will have on him – on his love for you.'

Elizabeth of England laughed grimly. 'Robert Devereux,' she said, 'has written me many dutiful letters but it seems that what I took for an abundance of heart is only a suit for the farm of sweet wines.' She looked at Bacon. 'And what a suitor!'

Bacon, stiff, dandified, cross-gartered, tried to smile.

The Queen spat.

'Go,' she rasped. 'Tell Devereux that if he wishes to beg a favour of my hands he must come and cringe for

240

it himself. Go quickly,' she flung at him, 'before I remember that I despise you both.'

Bacon bowed. His lips were almost invisible. Without more ado he went.

Alone the Queen crossed to the window. The snow-covered boughs did nothing to cool her resentment. She crossed to the fire-place and stared into the flames. But the heat from the logs did nothing to warm her spirit. On an impulse she snatched a letter from her gown and read it.

It had never failed to move her yet.

> 'Haste paper to that happy presence, whence only unhappy I am banished; kiss that fair correcting hand which lays new plasters to my lighter hurts, but to my greatest wounds applieth nothing. Say thou comest from pining, languishing, despairing Essex.'

Unruly boy! As always the Queen was moved by his youth, his despair. Moved but no longer swayed.

She sent for Burghley.

'The profits from the sale of sweet wines,' she ordered, 'will in future be reserved to the Crown.'

Chapter Nineteen

'What-ho, I say – Peace in this prison,' said the Clown.

Sir Toby Belch smiled encouragingly at the Clown he had bribed to ape a parson and goad his niece's steward into madness. From his pen Malvolio, looking exactly like Master Bacon, glared whitely out.

'I am not mad, Sir Topaz,' he pleaded. 'I say to you this house is dark.'

'Madman,' said the Clown. 'Thou errest. They say there is no darkness but in ignorance.'

'Stop!' said William Shakespeare.

The little group, caught in the ray of sunshine that filtered through the high windows of the Temple as limelight catches the players in any stage Illyria, turned round.

'Obadiah,' said Shakespeare, torn. 'Is this scene funny?'

Obadiah Croke stuck his chin in the air. 'Sidesplitting,' he pronounced and turned to resume his baiting.

But the dress rehearsal had stripped Shakespeare of his certainty. Today he was just like any author before his first night.

'Dick,' he pleaded. 'This is no time to think of my feelings. Tell me truly – is it funny to drive a man mad?'

'Very funny,' said Burbage soothingly. 'They'll eat it up. You see if they don't. Now could we,' he pleaded, go on to the next scene?'

'One moment, Dick,' said Shakespeare. 'Just one more run through. I want to make quite certain the scene is funny.'

'The twenty-fourth repetition of any scene,' said Burbage, bitterly, 'can never be funny. It can only be tedious, mechanical, uninspired, badly spoken and flat. For God's sake, Will, let me do my wedding scene.'

'The wedding scene,' said Shakespeare. He sighed. 'I don't know how you'll get enough pace into it to take the mind of the audience off the cobbling of the plot. I wonder,' he said thoughtfully, 'if the wedding scene is funny.'

'Tcha,' exploded Burbage. He strode away.

'Never mind, Will,' said Viola, appearing pat at his elbow. 'Master Dick does not understand you.'

'Go away,' said Shakespeare.

Viola stood her ground. 'An artist like you,' she began . . .

'Go away,' said Shakespeare. 'For God's sake go away. And,' he added savagely, as Viola moved rapidly off, 'if you value your life don't call me an artist.'

He sat down and glared at the waiting company.

'What's the matter with everyone,' he snapped. 'Why aren't you running through something. Must you wait for me for every word.'

'You make such a fuss if we don't,' muttered Will Kempe.

'Silence,' said Shakespeare. 'I will have no rebellion in my theatre.'

'And if you shout at me again,' said Will Kempe wildly, 'you will have no ballet either.'

They glared at one another. They were on edge.

All the players were on edge. Dick Burbage had taken to fussing about with the candles. The clowns were mistiming their business, the boy-players trebles had all started breaking at once, the carpenter had developed doubts whether his trellis would stand Sir Toby Belch's shakings, and even the cook in the Temple kitchens had started asking himself whether

243

his custard pies were of the right consistency.

Master Melody, called away from a tearful soliloquy with himself in which he was both tendering his resignation and alternatively saving the day, forgot his words.

'This is the air,' he began. 'This is the something sun. Ti-tum, ti-tum, ti-tum, ti-tum, ti-tum . . .'

Shakespeare rose dangerously from his seat.

'Master Prometheus,' he said into the silence, 'who do you imagine you might be? Edward Alleyn?'

There was a tug at his coat-sleeve. Shakespeare turned. It was Viola carrying a beaker of milk and some bread.

'Your lunch,' she pleaded. 'You haven't eaten anything since this morning.'

Shakespeare looked at her. His fists clenched. He was doing his best not to throw it at her.

Viola shrank. Dear God – didn't he love her any more!

'Great God,' said Burbage. 'What's that?'

The noise in the Temple, which had been considerable, was swallowed up by the noise outside it. It sounded as though the whole of London had gathered in the street outside – and in fighting mood at that.

The company looked at one another. They rushed out.

Approaching the theatre was a straggle of men, their gait exhausted, their voices hoarse, their faces desperate. Leading them was the most desperate figure of all, pale, dishevelled, with the energy of one who refuses to believe his cause is lost.

It was the Earl of Essex.

He was raising a rebellion against the Queen. Trusting to the spur of the moment, goaded at last into action, and too late to save his cause. As he marched he called out desperate incoherencies. 'Saw! Saw! Saw! Trey! Trey! Trey!' Anything that would attract the mob and bring followers to him.

244

'Dear God,' thought Viola, watching that working face. 'Can this be Robert Devereux?'

Burbage turned to Bacon. 'What goes on here?' he asked. 'What will be the end of this?'

Bacon shrugged. 'He will be tried for treason,' he said. 'I shall appear for the Crown.'

The players looked at Robert Devereux's straggle of followers dwindling down the street. They looked at Robert Devereux's protégé.

'You will appear for the Crown,' said Will Kempe. He spat.

Shakespeare was looking at Bacon.

He turned to his players. 'Benefits forgot,' he said.

'Back to work, gentlemen,' ordered Burbage. 'We give a performance tomorrow.'

Chapter Twenty

By the bright light of seven candles Fabian was making up, striving to get some strangeness into his clear and well-known countenance. He was trembling.

'Obadiah,' he called, 'what can I do about my forehead?'

The Clown, past-master in every sort of make-up, inspected it.

'Difficult,' he said.

Fabian fidgeted. 'My ruff, Obadiah,' he said. 'It is too tight.'

The clown adjusted it.

'My lines,' said Fabian. 'I never will remember those awful lines.'

Obadiah twinkled. 'You should complain to the playwright about them.'

But Fabian had picked up a candle and was peering into the mirror.

'It's no use, Obadiah,' he said. 'I still look like William Shakespeare.'

In the next room Master Pyk was trembling. He was attired as a girl. He looked unbelievably lovely. He could manage his skirts. He knew his lines backwards. He had the sweet treble pipe of Viola Compton.

But he was trembling.

*　　*　　*

Up in his room Sir Walter Raleigh rose to his feet.

'You have come,' he said, and pulled his tailor into the room.

'Show me,' he said. He was trembling.

With a proud professional flourish the tailor whisked the brocade off his arm and spread it like a back-to-front peacock before Raleigh.

'No lovelier cloak has ever come to these shores,' he boasted. 'It has colour. Substance, it will wear for ever. And it is cut on the cross.'

Raleigh swallowed and turned his shoulders. Reverently the tailor put the cloak around his client and hurriedly wheeled up a mirror to stop Raleigh from twisting his head right off.

Raleigh let out a sigh of content.

'Ah,' he said.

The tailor took five professional paces back and dodged himself into various angles.

'The rubies,' he observed, 'are very tasteful.'

Lady Meanwell came out of the Queen's room. She was trembling.

'I dressed her in silence,' she said. 'She never spoke a word of blame. Not even when I pulled her stomacher.'

Burghley looked at her. He twitched at his bit of sable.

'The poor child,' he said. 'What can we do?'

'She dressed with care,' said Lady Meanwell. 'She was insistent on her make-up.'

'She is a Prince,' said Burghley.

'She is a Prince,' agreed Lady Meanwell. 'She never spoke his name.'

Outside the Temple gates the Master of the Revels stepped absently into a puddle. He was remembering the first Court performance he had had to organize. How nervous he had been then. He stepped out of the puddle smiling indulgently and wandered towards the hall.

He knew just what he would find. Nerves, tempera-ments, hysteria, and, of course, there would be something not arrived. But he would soon get things running smoothly. All it needed was tact, just a little firmness, and a breezy confidence.

A man came hurrying by. The Master of the Revels thought he had seen him about the place before. Switching on his breezy confidence he hailed him.

'Hallo,' he cried as one good fellow to another. 'Everything all right?'

'Fine,' said the Lord Chief Justice of England cordi-ally. 'Hanged six this morning.'

He strode on.

The Master of the Revels blinked and went hastily into the Temple. So much to do. So little time to do it in.

He peered into a curtained-off tiring-room. What a pretty boy player! Wouldn't know it wasn't a girl. Did he know him?

He stepped in. The boy player got up and flung his arms round his neck. 'Oh, Master Polonius, I'm so frightened.'

'Take it in your stride,' said the Master of the Revels. He peered. 'Great heavens – it's you!'

'It's me,' said Viola. She looked at him accusingly. 'Why did you make me go on the stage?'

The Master of the Revels patted her shoulder.

'There, there,' he said. 'You wanted to.'

'I shall forget,' said Viola. 'I know I shall forget. I can-not even remember the lines of my first speech. They go – how do they go?'

'There, there,' said the Master of the Revels. 'When you need them they will come back to you.'

Viola looked at him suspiciously. 'You promise?'

'I promise,' said the Master of the Revels solemnly. 'You will not forget. Look at me,' he encouraged. 'I never forget.'

'Before the Queen,' said Viola. 'Supposing I spoil his play before the Queen.'

'The Queen,' said the Master of the Revels gently, 'has other things to trouble her tonight.'

He kissed her absently on the forehead and wandered away.

'So you've arrived,' said Dick Burbage. 'How do I look?' he asked.

'Magnificent,' said the Master of the Revels vaguely. 'You'll be quite all right.'

Burbage looked at him.

'As good as Edward Alleyn,' said the Master of the Revels breezily.

Burbage took a step forward. A custard pie, out of control, flew through the air and caught him neatly on the ear. After it came Obadiah Croke.

Burbage cursed. Obadiah rushed up and inspected him anxiously. He pulled some of the custard through his fingers.

'Not thick enough,' he said dissatisfied.

High on her palanquin, borne through the streets of the London that she loved so well, Elizabeth of England was going alone to the Court performance of *Twelfth Night* that she had ordered as a diversion for the traitor Essex.

Tomorrow she would go to Nonsuch. Or Hampton Court. Or Greenwich.

And not even Burghley should go with her.

Crowds lining the streets cheered her. The cheers had a quality of sympathy that pricked and stung. Gravely Elizabeth of England acknowledged their loyalty.

The palanquin was lowered to the ground. So the procession had arrived at the Temple.

Elizabeth of England extended a hand and allowed Sir Francis Drake to help her to alight.

Before her lay a puddle.

Consternation! The train-bearers shivered. A puddle! What a place to disembark a Prince!

Elizabeth of England looked keenly around her. A

puddle before a Prince! Someone would have to pay for this gross mismanagement.

Her gaze fell on Sir Walter Raleigh. She noted the gleam and sheen around his shoulders. The new cloak! A glint came into her eyes.

She beckoned.

The consort of recorders, which had been sounding so sweetly in Mr Byrd's cadences, modulated into 'Greensleeves'.

Orsino looked up.

'If music be the food of love,' he said, 'play on.'

Twelfth Night had begun.

In the wings Viola clutched hard at Master Will's hand. It was one thing to play-act before the Court with a cautious eye on the door, where the worst that could befall you was that the Queen should come through it – it was quite another to know that your every movement was watched by dyed-in-the-wool professionals, who had been acting before you had been born. The Court was nothing. The clowns were everything. It was rash of Master Will to give her so big a part so soon.

'Quiet, child,' said Shakespeare. 'Stop trembling. Look at Burbage.'

Viola looked. Orsino was speaking:

'Oh, when mine eye did see Olivia first
Methought she purged the air of pestilence.'

Dear God, what assurance Master Dick had. He seemed not to be aware of the reserve of the faces spread out before him. What timing! What smoothness with difficult consonants. With what authority he spoke his lines.

'I wrote that,' said Shakespeare, pleased.

Dear God, her lines! They had gone again. Wildly she raked the hall for inspiration. The shadows all the darker for the flicker of candlelight, the sheens of stuff and the flash of jewels. The dark faces of the sea-dogs strained with attention, entranced, the polite fidgetings of the courtiers, the set face of Elizabeth of England. And above them all the great rafters of the Temple Hall.

'Oh, Will,' she said, 'what is my first line?'

'On with you, Master Pyk,' said Shakespeare roughly. He pushed her onto the stage.

For one frantic moment Master Pyk looked like legging it. The Captain, standing in the centre of the stage, swore softly. Master Pyk was going to lose his empty head. He fixed him with a stern glare. Master Pyk swung wildly round. From the wings Shakespeare glared at him. From the back Salathiel Pavey tittered.

It was enough. Master Pyk gathered his skirts, flung back his head, and like any Lady of the Court addressing a group of ignorant sailors, spoke.

'What country, friends, is this?'

'It is Illyria, lady.'

'And what should I do in Illyria?' asked Viola, bewildered. 'My brother is in Elysium.'

In the wings Will Shakespeare sat down and mopped his brow. Orsino came over with a mug of ale.

'Drink this, Will,' he said. 'You'll need it.'

It was a difficult audience. The flower of England lacked the simplicity of the sea-dogs, who loved to see a story unfold. And tonight there were other matters to engage their attention. How was the Essex episode going to affect them? Would his disgrace result in their discredit? It was difficult to keep one's mind on the players with Elizabeth of England playing her role in their midst. They were fatally drawn to look at that unmoved countenance, those beady eyes, those hands, heavily jewelled, that clenched a motionless fan.

Burghley was hardly aware of what was happening on the stage. Where in this sorry situation could be found one crumb of comfort to offer his suffering child – Elizabeth of England?

Sir Philip Sidney, unable to bear the pain he could feel behind the stillness of the Queen, tried to concentrate on the candle-lit antics of the clown.

Bacon, sitting alone and thin-lipped, was no longer weighing the arguments with which he would mollify his own conscience and justify himself in the eyes of the world for his indictment of his friend, and was concentrating his hatred on William Shakespeare, that bibulous oaf, who had dared to ridicule him in a play. He glared at the unfortunate Malvolio, who at that moment might have been speaking Essex's epitaph.

'I marvel your ladyship takes delight in such a barren rascal.'

No escaping Will's deliberate taunts at him. Malvolio stood with his stance, spoke with his voice, and played with a handkerchief exactly like he did himself. Crude, overdrawn, a vile caricature – but so unkind. Bacon nearly burst into tears. No matter, he promised himself, he would get even with Master Will for this. He would devise some dark revenge, something deep and literary to obscure Will's name to all posterity. Bacon should deface the name of Shakespeare! But how?

He concentrated.

The rest of the Court was on tactical tenterhooks. They could not disown Essex quickly enough, all were busy bent on explaining away the occasions they had been seen with him. None could wait for the interval to launch their defence before they were attacked.

Only the Master of the Revels was enjoying himself. He was sorry for the Queen but, bless her heart, she would get over it – just as her father had done. It came natural to a Tudor. And really this was a very fine play Master Will had filched from the Italian. Pretty. How nice his little Viola looked. And she was not acting too badly either. So far she had only had to be prompted twice.

The Master of the Revels glowed. He nudged Burghley.

'To think,' he said, 'she once acted Mary Stuart for us on the terrace.'

'That will make something else for you to remember,' said Burghley.

The play went on. Gradually Master Will's words took a hold on the audience. Illyria was the perfect escape from the problems of Elizabethan England. Even the Queen was seen to smile as Obadiah Croke stumbled from Olivia's cellar his face streaming with custard pie. The love scenes succeeded the clowning. Viola piped her lines most boyishly. The audience was very quiet. The actors relaxed. Master Pyk was doing well enough.

But in the wings playwright and actor-manager did not relax. They were listening to each line with attention, noting the reactions of the audience, timing their players, noting the business of the clowns, noting the position of the candle-lights, deciding what could be altered and improved and where the play could be tightened.

Viola, bewildered by the turn of events, caught in the complex weavings of the trick her disguise had played upon her love, was speaking:

'My state is desperate for my master's love . . .
Oh, Time, thou must untangle this, not I;
It is too hard a knot for me t'untie.'

Her voice broke.

'Good God,' said Shakespeare. 'What have I done?'

'Tcha,' said Burbage with a shrug. 'The lad is in love with you.'

Chapter Twenty-one

Five o'clock of a fine winter's morning. Time the city
was astir.

Already housekeepers all over London were carrying
beer mugs to the breakfast table.

Past St Paul's and by the Temple gates strode the
night-watchman, gulping greedily at the fresh air and
singing lustily.

'Five o'clock,' he chanted. 'Five o'clock and all's
well.'

Only last week he had been a prisoner in the Clink,
facing impalement or at least de-earment and now here
he was as free as any man in the country.

The night-watchman swung his lantern jauntily.
What was there to stop him ending up as Lord Mayor
of London?

'Five o'clock,' he chanted. 'Five o'clock and all's
well.'

In his lodgings Shakespeare was already seated at
his desk writing. There was a tap at the door. Viola
poked her head in.

'Will,' she said. 'How did I do?'

Shakespeare looked up. 'Well enough, Master Pyk,'
he said. 'Well enough.' He went back to his work.

On the verge of coming in, Viola stopped dead.

'Will,' she said. ' It's me.'

Shakespeare laid down his pen and pushed his work
carefully on one side.

'Come in,' he said. 'I want to talk to you.'

Viola fidgeted. 'Will,' she said, 'I'm sorry I dried at the beginning. But that was only the beginning,' she pleaded. 'The Queen applauded. Truly she did.'

'You did well enough,' said Shakespeare again. 'There is no-one in England could have played it as well. Listen, child,' he said. 'I am going to write a play for you.'

Viola's spirits soared. *'Love's Labour Won?'* she enquired.

'No, no,' said Shakespeare quickly. 'Some other play – a play that needs a woman and cannot be acted by some prancing boy.'

Viola tasted the idea. 'Will it be sad?'

'It will be tragical,' said Shakespeare. 'It will be about the most fascinating woman who ever lived. It will be about Cleopatra.'

Viola went dim. 'Why not Helen of Troy?' she asked mutinously. 'I can see myself as Helen of Troy.'

'You can see yourself as everybody,' said Shakespeare. 'But first, Master Pyk, you have to learn your trade.' He stared straight at the table in front of him. 'I am sending you to Philip Henslowe.'

Viola jumped up. 'Henslowe!'

'You will be apprenticed to Edward Alleyn,' said Shakespeare. 'He will teach you well. You are to be obedient and do us all honour.'

'You are sending me away!' Viola spread her hands. 'But why, Will? I do not understand. What have I done?'

'He will teach you well,' said Shakespeare again. 'And what have we to offer you? We have no theatre and we must go into the country towns and we must do one-night stands in rough places, like gaming cocks or bears. It is no life for a girl.'

'But, Will,' said Viola, 'I would be with you.'

'You have been with me too much,' said Shakespeare. 'A change of company will be good for you.'

'You are tired of me, Will,' said Viola. She stamped her foot. 'You have never loved me,' she said.

Shakespeare looked out of the window. 'You will be very happy with Alleyn,' he said. 'Study him. He has great qualities in spite of his ranting.'

'You want to be rid of me,' said Viola. 'You have always wanted to be rid of me,' she accused. 'Why, you have never so much as written a single sonnet to me.'

Shakespeare sighed. 'You must go now, child,' he said. 'Dick Burbage wants to speak to you and I have much to do.'

Viola went slowly to the door. Suddenly she turned.

'Will,' she said pleadingly, 'was it my Willow Cabin speech?'

But Shakespeare had already turned to his desk and appeared to be working.

Viola's hands dropped. She went out of the room.

'Half-past five of a fine winter's morning.' The night-watchman's voice came floating through the lattice.

Shakespeare laid aside the sheet he had picked up. It read:

LOVE'S LABOUR WUNNE
Act I. Scene I. The Garden of Eden.
Enter a serpent

He reached for another sheet. He thought. Soon he was writing again.

'Shall I compare thee to a summer's day . . .'

THE END

About the Authors

Under the pen names, respectively, of CARYL BRAHMS and S. J. SIMON, Doris Caroline Abrahams (1901-82) and Seca Jascha Skidelsky (1904-48) began writing together in 1937. Their bestselling first book, *A Bullet in the Ballet* (1937), inaugurated their popular series of comic ballet thrillers; other titles in the series are *Casino for Sale* (1938) and *Six Curtains for Stroganova* (1945). In addition to *No Bed for Bacon* (1941), their other novels include *Don't Mr. Disraeli!* (1940), *No Nightingales* (1944), and *You Were There* (1950). A volume of memoirs by Caryl Brahms, *Too Dirty for the Windmill*, was published posthumously in 1986.

Common Reader Editions

As booksellers since 1986, we have been stocking the pages of our monthly catalogue, A COMMON READER, with "Books for Readers with Imagination." Now as publishers, the same motto guides our work. Simply put, the titles we issue as COMMON READER EDITIONS are volumes of uncommon merit which we have enjoyed, and which we think other imaginative readers will enjoy as well. While our selections are as personal as the act of reading itself, what's common to our enterprise is the sense of shared experience a good book brings to solitary readers. We invite you to sample the wide range of COMMON READER EDITIONS, and welcome your comments.

commonreader.com